Jersey Law

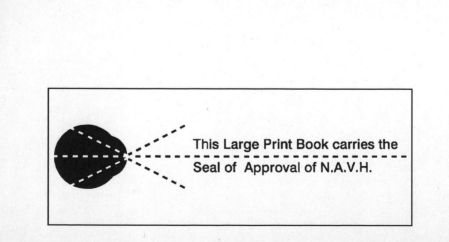

JERSEY LAW

RON LIEBMAN

THORNDIKE PRESS
A part of Gale, Cengage Learning

Detroit • New York • San Francisco • New Haven, Conn • Waterville, Maine • London

GALE
CENGAGE Learning™

LIBRARY OF CONGRESS CATALOGING-IN-PUBLICATION DATA

Liebman, Ronald S.
  Jersey law / by Ron Liebman. — Large print ed.
    p. cm. — (Thorndike Press large print thriller)
  ISBN-13: 978-1-4104-4134-8 (hardcover)
  ISBN-10: 1-4104-4134-2 (hardcover)
  1. Legal stories. 2. Attorney and client—Fiction. 3. Camden (N.J.)—Fiction. 4. Large type books. I. Title.
PS3612.I33526J47 2011
813'.6—dc22   2011030156

Published in 2011 by arrangement with Simon & Schuster, Inc.

Printed in the United States of America
1 2 3 4 5 6 7 15 14 13 12 11

As always, for Simma

CHAPTER 1
LOCATION, LOCATION, LOCATION

Reginald Shawan Dupree, inmate number 65392, Camden County Jail, is definitely not liking the situation he has found himself in.

He shrugs as best he can, given that Slippery Williams's two beefy fellow inmates have effectively strapped him in place, each man firmly grasping Reginald's muscled arms, just about lifting his feet off the ground. He's like a suicide-to-be up in his attic, precariously balancing tiptoe on the wobbling chair under the noose he's secured to the rafters. Even though they are in an opened-door cell — this being tier community time — they are enjoying relative privacy. Ensured no doubt by some of Slippery's other crew out on the tier, forcefully keeping any curious inmates at bay.

Reginald is called Reginald only by his grandmother. To the rest of the world — which for him consists of a narrow slice of southern New Jersey — he's known by his street name: Chink.

Chink's never had the pleasure of actually meeting his biological father. His mother, dead now maybe three years, was eventually discovered in the abandoned and condemned building that was her home away from home, with the overdosing needle still stuck in her rigor mortised, track-marked arm. She earned her livelihood by sucking and fucking anyone having the price of admission.

Chink is an exceedingly good-looking guy. The penis-wielding side of his DNA design was clearly Asian, most likely Chinese. So, there's the street name. Chink. Political correctness not being a feature of the thug life.

Chink is milk-coffee complected, well built, thanks to years of in-and-out incarceration providing near-unfettered use of the prisoners' weight room. One of the few perks of doing serious time. He sports the requisite gang tattoos. Wears his African hair in tight, short braids. But it's his mix of Oriental features with what was once his mother's striking beauty that makes Chink a standout. Asian wedged green eyes, high forehead, thinnish nose.

"Ain't no thing," Chink repeats to Slippery Williams, like maybe he didn't get it the first time he said it when they came in here. Soon as they grabbed him. Showing Slippery he's cool with whatever.

These men do not speak in sentences; their well-worn street phrases have all the meaning needed to convey their intent.

Slippery Williams has heard Chink. Knows exactly what he's saying.

Let's forget about the whole thing. My mistake. That's what Chink is saying.

The Camden County Jail is overcrowded. Seems like it's been that way since forever. And like all jails, the place reeks of stale urine, male sweat, excessive testosterone. Day and night an asylumlike rumbling and shrieking bounces from cement wall to cement wall; diminished in volume for only an hour or two sometime near dawn.

Other inmates can be heard from where Chink is being uncomfortably detained.

"Motherfucker, motherfucker, motherfucker," someone is rapid-fire shouting. Without question, the most frequently used word in the prisoners' lexicon.

"Fuck you, you pussy-assed bitch," someone else can be heard shouting above the ever-present din, no one giving any thought to how that makes no sense at all.

Hard metal gates clank. The occasional guard can be heard ordering some inmate to "stand down, stand down."

But right now, in this open, lonely cell, Chink is doing his best to alleviate what he has no trouble seeing as a bad situation.

It was a coincidence, a real fortuity, Chink at first decided, when he was transferred here from the also pitifully overcrowded neighboring Atlantic County Justice Facility.

Camden County claims ownership to the worn-down city of Camden, but Atlantic County has the rejuvenated jewel of Atlantic City in its tattered crown. And Chink is, and has been, the drug kingpin of Atlantic City.

On paper, Chink looks to be more successful, and better positioned, than Slippery Williams, who has quietly held the reigns of power over Camden's flourishing drug markets longer than any of his predecessors, each and every one of whom is either doing life with no parole or is dead with bullet holes in his rotting corpse.

But appearances can be deceiving. Chink has to answer to Atlantic City's organized crime syndicate. Guys mostly from New York and Vegas. Law enforcement may have weakened its hold over the years, but a mere street thug like Chink is no match for them. He's an indentured servant who has been allowed to plow the land. The land in this instance being the street corners of his town and the boardwalk hotels when a guest has made inquiry of the bellman where he/she might score a little something to make their stay a bit more exciting.

So while Chink's gross revenues may be higher than Slippery's, his take-home pay is considerably smaller. And that's why he at first found his transfer to the Camden County Jail so fortuitous.

It gave him an opening to seek a liaison with Slippery. A high-level parley of two street-corner CEOs. His stated intention: to explore some sort of fee-sharing partnership arrangement. A combination of crews and drug distributions. A pursuit of the economies of scale.

Naturally, Chink saw no need to mention how big a slice the uptown boys have been helping themselves to of his operation. Nor how, if he could only get inside Slippery's network, with a minimum of time, he would be able to "dispense" with Slippery altogether. Chink naively fancying himself the Donald Trump of the New Jersey drug trade. Where "You're fired!" is communicated in lead.

So they met. Over dinner, so to speak.

Because of woeful overcrowding most

inmates were forced to eat their meals in their cells, on paper plates and with plastic utensils carefully collected and inventoried after each meal. In an apparent random selection, due to diminished mess hall seating space, only a portion of the inmates got to eat at tables.

The tables in question are several rows of six-seaters, the stools on either side bolted to the cement floor.

For all intents and purposes Slippery Williams owns the Camden County Jail. His crew is dominant over any other incarcerated grouping: black, white, or Latino. Doesn't matter. Not all the guards are on his payroll. Just enough to ensure his creature comforts, such as they are. So, Slippery eats in the mess hall.

Eventually he and Chink had their meet, each seated opposite the other at Slippery's regular table. Each had been allotted three gang members — one seated on either side at the table, and the third on his feet behind. They had spoken as they ate, like all proficient businessmen and -women do.

"So, like I'm sayin'," Chink had said, carefully chewing the stringy mystery meat he had fished out of the oily liquid in his bowl. "They no stopping us, we combinin' like I'm sayin'. Know what I'm sayin'?"

Slippery Williams is a man of few words. He's doing what's called wait-and-see time. His first criminal trial ended with a hung jury. The judge called a mistrial. The Camden DA can't decide whether or not to risk a retrial and a possible acquittal. That would be bad for his long-term elective office ambitions. So Slippery continues to reside in the Camden County Jail, marking time.

Chink, on the other hand, is actually doing time. Though not all that much. He cut a deal on his latest case, since the evidence of felony conspiracy drug distribution was painfully thin. So he copped to yet another simple possession. With his priors he got a year and a day. Then came the nonsensical transfer from one overcrowded jail to another.

Slippery sips from the tepid, watered-down coffee, replaces the cup on his mess hall tray. He simply nods at Chink seated across from him, knowing there's no stopping this boy from motormouthing his way through his proposal. As Chink resumes his pitch, Slippery simply nods what could reasonably be taken for assent.

To an outsider, Slippery is just another thirty-something ghetto rat. He's thin, medium dark, standard facial features. Not one outstanding characteristic. An inner-

13

city African-American Everyman. But his intellect is aflame. Given different circumstances of birth, the world could have been his oyster.

"Yeah," Chink had said, gently thrusting his close-fisted arm across the table for a consent bump from Slippery. Slippery complied, but remained otherwise mum.

"All right, then," Chink had said, motioning to the two guys flanking him that this powwow was at an end. A tacit agreement in principle had been reached. He had lifted himself off the bolted stool, nodded at Slippery, told him, "Later, my brother," and walked off toward his tier. Chink silently assuring himself it won't take six months and he'll have Slippery dead.

Slippery watched him go, his plan already formulated.

Chink knows there is no real point in struggling with the two giants who have him pinned in this cell. Still he wrenches one arm this way, the other that way. The only result is that the grip on his arms is tightened. He tries looking past the cell bars. His crew should be out there. Why aren't they here? Chink listens for the sounds of bodies bumping bodies, threats shouted as the two crews confront each other out there. But all Chink can hear is the ever-present

14

jailhouse drone.

Several days ago, Slippery had privately cornered Chink's main lieutenant. He wasn't hard to single out. Seated in another quiet cell, on side-by-side bottom bunks, he and Slippery had a heart-to-heart. Explaining the facts of life. Succinctly conveying how Chink was in a really bad place. A place he'd unfortunately put himself in.

Slippery gave the lieutenant a choice. Not much of a choice, really. But the guy didn't need long to see where things were headed. He accepted Slippery's gracious offer (the other choice being a premature death), making the lieutenant the presumptive new crown prince of Atlantic City drug trafficking.

So, after Chink was first isolated and brought to the cell he now so unfortunately finds himself in, this guy and some of Chink's other crew stood as near the open cell as Slippery's men would permit. Chink's other crew members waiting for the lieutenant to make his move. Their muscles already tensed in anticipation of the impending clash. Instead, they watched as the lieutenant simply turned and walked away. Those remaining at the line of scrimmage exchanged looks.

Then they got it and they too took off.

So, Chink's posse-to-the-rescue evaporated. He returns his attention to Slippery.

"Slip?" Chink says, the pleading in his voice clear as a bell.

Slippery stays eye to eye with him, until Chink can't hold it any longer and looks away.

"Got to be," Slippery finally says as Chink's eyes shoot back to him.

"No, no," Chink says. "Slip, lemme axe you . . ."

Chink never gets to finish his thought. Slippery brandishes the shank he's been deftly holding behind his back. It's a razor-sharp sliver from one of the mess hall trays that had worn and cracked to the point of having to be discarded. The guard who sold the shard had asked if any binding was needed for the handle. Slippery's guy had said no, they had that covered.

Chink's eyes saucer for the second or two he sees the shank materialize, his brain trying to catch up to the image his eyes have recorded. But Slippery is too fast as he surgically thrusts the shank directly into Chink's windpipe.

Almost immediately, the two guys release Chink from their grasp. They and Slippery watch as Chink's hands instinctively shoot to his neck. But he's already in shock and so can't get a hold of the shank, his hands violently tremoring. Chink's head rolls back, he's gurgling, now shoving himself from side to side as a pinkish flow of blood and saliva precedes the gushing of his blood down the front of his clothing. His eyes roll back in his head as he falls to the cell floor, still writhing, still gurgling.

It only takes a bit more time before Chink's body gives out. Slippery waits until Chink has exhausted two or three violent body jerks and is then still before he exits the cell. His two men wait just a little while longer, simply to ensure no further cleanup action is warranted, and then they remove the shank and walk out.

Seeing the three file out from the cell, those few still standing nearby all make an orderly exit back to their own cells.

Lockdown is coming. Seconds from now the guards — including the shank seller — will make the discovery. Whistles will be blown, a siren sounded, and then will come the lockdown.

Slippery is already in his cell, on his bunk, reading his iPad. Devices such as these are definitely not permitted to inmates. On the occasions when cells are searched, Slippery hands the device off to a guard who will hold it until the all clear.

Years earlier, Slippery had trouble reading, having to sound out the words. But by now he's become pretty proficient at it. Understanding the concepts, descriptions, and thoughts of the writers was far less difficult — almost second nature, once he acquired proficiency with the written word.

His iPad has e-mail capacity. But Slippery never uses it. Nothing he does is ever committed to writing. Today, he returns to Machiavelli's *The Prince*. Days before, he read up on the book, using the Internet to take him to explanatory sites.

So the whistles are blaring, the siren has been sounded, and Slippery lies on his bunk reading.

Okay, so, here's the thing: Slippery Williams is my client.

Mine and my law partner's. Michael Mezzonatti. To just about everyone he's Mickie. I'm Salvatore "Junne" Salerno. Junne morphed from Junior, my Camden neighborhood name.

Anyway, Slippery is, and has been, our client. You could say he's our best and longest-standing client. (Okay, I just did.)

And me and Mickie actually like Slippery. Well, that's an overstatement. It's more a real-world kind of respect.

We understand Slippery. Can see his

unrealized innate talents, how the circumstances of his birth have put him where he is. He's unquestionably made a success of the hand he was dealt. And Slippery has always played it straight with us. He pays on time. Almost never asks us to do something we as lawyers shouldn't do.

There is one little wrinkle involving a past client named Rodrigo González, who's dead. Me and Mickie are alive thanks to Slippery. But that's another story.

Anyway, guys like Slippery are our stock-in-trade. It's what we do. Mickie and me. And maybe except for Dumpy Brown, our biggest Camden legal competitor (a guy whose business card says "Black On Black Get You Back"), we are the street's go-to lawyers.

What can I say?

But the problem now with Slippery isn't Chink. Chink's gone. History. Another unsolved jailhouse murder. Mickie and me will hear about what happened with Chink later, but it's of no professional concern to us.

No, the problem is Slippery's wait-and-see time.

That's why tomorrow the jailers will escort him to the Camden County Courthouse.

Me and Mickie need to do something. That's what he pays us for.

CHAPTER 2
INNOCENT UNTIL

Mickie and me walk up the steps to the Camden County Courthouse. It feels like we've done this a million times.

Like I said, it's what we do. We're a couple of ex-cop, night law school criminal lawyers. Diamonds in the rough. Some say.

Don't be looking for eloquent legal briefs from us. What briefs we do file in our cases have mostly been "borrowed" from what other lawyers have filed with the clerk of court in their own cases. Yeah, one of our bigger business expenses is our Xcrox bill.

There are no doubt more qualified lawyers around here. Most probably across the river from Camden, New Jersey, in Philadelphia. But know what? Me and Mickie have got them scratching their heads. They're thinking, How come those two guys keep winning their cases?

These Philly lawyers are certainly better educated than us. Their offices are better looking than ours. But better than us in court? With our clients? New Jersey's worst of the worst?

Honestly?

I don't think so.

It's a bright, sunny day. Nine-thirty A.M. Real nice morning, but chilly. Summer is over. Gone are those hot and sticky days — and nights — you see in this part of the state. The few scraggly trees dotting the inner-city streets still have their leaves, such as they are. But the air has noticeably changed.

Once inside the courthouse we joke with the security guards we've known forever as we empty our pockets, put our briefcases on the X-ray conveyer belt, and walk through the metal detector. Then we head for the elevators.

The heat's been turned on in the building. The hallway smells like the grade school me and Mickie went to. A kind of stew of woolen clothing, steam heat, and that disinfectant they use when they wet-mop the floors of the boys' and girls' bathrooms. And voices bounce off the walls here like they did there, though not nearly as bad as in the Camden County Jail.

We get off the elevator and walk to the courtroom where Slippery Williams's case will be heard. We check the docket sheet taped to the door. Good, his case is the first one on today.

We enter the courtroom. In the visitors' gallery we greet the few other lawyers already in here, sitting, reading the newspaper, and whatnot, waiting for their own cases to be called.

There's a smattering of folks — mostly black — relatives, friends, and "business associates" of the defendants who will be brought in here from the holding pen to face charges throughout the day. The judge is not yet on the bench.

As me and Mickie head for defense counsel table, one of the jailers sees us.

"Counsel," he mutters. "How you doin'?"

We know this guy. He's a big fat sausage stuffed into a Department of Corrections uniform. He's cordial with the lawyers. But he's got a reputation for brutality in the courthouse lockup when no one's looking. With Slippery Williams there's no worry. This guy wouldn't dare lay a hand on Slip.

"Lou. How you doin'?" we say to him. Then the jailer motions to his cohort to go into the lockup and get our client.

A few minutes later out comes Slippery. We wait while the guards unshackle him, then we offer him a seat at the far end of the table.

Slippery is orange-jumpsuited, "DOC" (Department of Corrections) in thick black letters printed on the back.

He's entitled to wear street clothes in the courtroom and the jailers would have let him change in the holding cell before coming out here. But there is no jury today. This isn't a trial. Only a hearing. The judge knows full well that Slippery's being held without bail. So, Slippery has decided to dispense with the pretense of civilian duds.

Like I said, Slippery's first trial for drug conspiracy and murder ended without the jury agreeing on a verdict. That was three months ago. The witnesses against him were shitty, including Slippery's nephew, the main prosecution witness. In protective custody, otherwise he'd be dead by now. But the kid was pitifully stupid on the stand.

So the jury hung and the judge granted a mistrial. The DA's in a quandary. Can't decide what to do. He does have the option of biting the bullet and dismissing the charges. Then waiting for Slippery's inevitably resumed illegal business activities to generate a new prosecution. Hopefully with a stronger case next time around.

To me and Mickie, that would be the smarter move.

Slippery's in the game. (In Camden he *is* the game.) He gets sprung, he's back to business. The fact is he never left the business. Running his drug enterprise from the Camden County Jail — really nothing more than a branch office for the city's habitual criminals.

There's a loud rap on the door leading from the judge's chambers into the courtroom. Everyone stands as the door opens.

First one out is the bailiff. He's a big bear of a black man, crisp-suited, drill sergeant's demeanor — and voice.

As he speaks to the assembled, the judge and his law clerk follow him out.

"All rise," orders the bailiff to the already risen.

"This honorable court's in session. The Honorable Thurgood Rufus Brown presidin'. All persons [comes out "All poisons"] having business draw nigh and give your attention."

No one bats an eye at "draw nigh." To those standing as the judge mounts the bench and takes his seat it means keep standing, shut up, and wait.

We all stand, shut up, and wait.

This judge is a big guy too. Got to weigh in near 230. He's flat-nosed, dark-chocolate complected. Never changed out of that big, bushy Afro from the eighties. Though these days it's showing some serious flecks of gray.

He's been around awhile. A Camden guy, like Slippery. Probably from the same general neighborhood. But he came up different.

He had a mother took an interest in him. Named him Thurgood after the first black Supreme Court Justice. Made sure her boy got himself educated. And here he is, former activist lawyer, community organizer, Camden City Council member. And now on the bench.

Judge Brown nods to his bailiff.

"Be seated," the bailiff commands like we're his troops on the parade ground.

"Call the first case," the judge tells the bailiff as he reaches over on the bench to where his law clerk has stacked the files he will need for today's cases. Me and Mickie see Judge Brown open what must be Slippery's file and start reading as the bailiff calls our case.

"Your Honor. First [foist] case on the docket is *State of New Jersey versus* [voices] *Avon Williams,* aka Slippery Williams. To be heard is defendant's motion for release on bail pending retrial."

With that the bailiff takes his seat. He's got the morning paper spread out in front of him flat on his little desk. Starts reading the sports pages. Tunes out.

Judge Brown looks up from the file.

He's got that look.

The one that's telling me and Mickie: You gotta be kidding. You're asking this court to release this thug? This drug-dealing, murdering scumbag on bail? Give me a fucking break, that look is telling us. Clear as if he was actually saying it.

But of course he doesn't say it. Every word uttered in here is recorded. The judge's stenographer, a milquetoast white guy with an Errol Flynn mustache in a rumpled sport coat and mismatched slacks sitting just below the bench. His little machine on a tripod between his legs. Tapping at the keys. Then whenever there's a lull in the proceedings pulling his Black-Berry from out of his pocket, furtively checking for messages. Slipping it back the minute the judge starts up again.

It's true. Me and Mickie did file a motion for the release of Slippery Williams on bail pending retrial. Is it a loser? Probably. But, listen, the DA can't keep this guy — or anyone — in prison indefinitely while he diddles with the question of retrial.

It's simply not right. Slippery is what he is. But one of the things he is not — at least not yet — is convicted of anything in this case. Sure, he's got a record. One or two juvenile convictions, an adult rap sheet of simple possessions and assaults and batteries. One gun charge thrown out for lack of evidence. On the murders, nothing. Like I said, Slippery is smart. And careful.

Judge Brown takes his eyes from us.

"Good morning, counsel," Judge Brown then says to us and to the DA and his two assistants, who entered the courtroom just as the judge took the bench and are now sitting across the aisle at their own table.

"Good morning, Your Honor," we all say in unison, like we're a bunch of eighth graders in front of the teacher.

"It's your motion, Counsel," Judge Brown says to me and Mickie. "Which one of you gonna speak to it?" (In the "which one of you" part of his question I mentally hear the word "bozos" after the "you.")

Like I said, the DA himself is in the courtroom today. Even though his assistants will try the case, if there is a retrial. The DA wants to make the point with the judge that this is important. The DA wants Slippery to remain behind bars until he makes up his mind what he wants to do with him.

The DA and Judge Brown are oil and water. Judge Brown doesn't like the prosecutor's office. Thinks they racially profile too many of their cases.

I'm not sure that's true. Camden's demographics are what they are. More poor white folks still living here? Then there'd be more white defendants than the judge is seeing day in, day out. But, hey, Judge Brown's got a hard-on for the DA's office? Fine with me and Mickie.

With all that, Judge Brown's still a smart and careful judge.

The DA sees himself as Camden's Lancelot. His name is Robert Cahill. Around here? In our world? You're likely to be African-American, Hispanic, Italian, Jewish, Irish. In that order. Me and Mickie filling the Italian spot, both of us first generation, our parents still very much living their old-country lives inside their Camden homes, no matter how the neighborhood has changed since me and Mickie were kids. The White Anglo-Saxon Protestants are here too. But, trust me, in this rough-and-tumble part of Camden they are in the decided minority.

Cahill sees himself as Camden's Irish savior. The city's avenging angel. Thin as a rail. Sallow. Mid-fifties. Dandruffed, colorless hair that was probably pale red as a kid. Big drinker. Threadbare conservative Brooks

Brothers suits.

There are no gray areas for Cahill. Everything to him is simple. You're guilty if his office charges you. It's your job to prove you're innocent.

Yeah, I know. He's got that backward.

The big character flaw of some prosecutors, Cahill among them, is fear of losing. But you know, you can't be a really good trial lawyer unless you're willing to step up to the plate and take a hard swing at the ball. Even if it's not a perfect pitch.

Mickie rises from counsel table and takes the lectern between our two tables.

Mickie: (*Pausing a moment to arrange his papers, looks up to Judge Brown.*) Good morning, Your Honor. Michael Mezzonatti, (*then pointing to me*) together with my law partner, Salvatore Salerno, for the defendant, Avon Williams. (*There's no need in pointing to Slippery; he's the only guy at the table in an orange jumpsuit.*)

(The judge interrupts Mickie before he can get the first substantive word out.)

Judge Brown: You want me to release your client on bail? How can you possibly justify that, Counsel? This guy's facing a major drug conspiracy–murder retrial. You want me to cut him loose? What? Get his word he'll both stick around and not murder the witnesses against him? That your point here?

(Like I said, Judge Brown's a bull of a man. I can almost see steam coming from his ears. This one's looking like a loser. Yeah, but never underestimate the power of your opponent's stupidity.)

Cahill: (*Rising to his feet, prematurely injecting himself into the fray.*) That's exactly right, Your Honor. This man. (*Pointing an accusing finger at Slippery, who turns his head toward Cahill. Their eyes meet. Cahill quickly looks away.*) This man's a menace to society.

(There are two well-worn rules to the practice of criminal law. Rule number one: get your fee in advance. Rule number two: you're winning, keep your mouth shut. Stay seated. Robert Cahill just violated rule number two.)

(*Judge Brown waves Mickie back down in his seat. Turns his attention to Cahill.*)

Judge Brown: (*To Cahill.*) So, the DA's office has finally made a decision on retrial?

Cahill: (*Hesitates. Clears his throat.*) Yes, well, Your Honor, the state is carefully considering the issue of retrial.

(Carefully considering? Give me a fucking break. It's been three months since the jury hung. Mickie's thigh gives me a little push under the table. I pass it on to Slippery. Cahill starts to retake his seat. Judge Brown fingers him back up.)

Judge Brown: Okay, Mr. Cahill. When will we have your decision?

Cahill: (*Quick glance down to his two assistants. No help there. They're busy studying the tabletop for imperfections.*) When?

Judge Brown: That's what I'm asking.

(Mickie's not about to break rule number two. He stays seated. Keeps his mouth shut.)

Cahill: (*Now feigning annoyance with the court.*) Your Honor. The state will make its decision on retrial at the appropriate time. With all due respect, that decision — and its timing — is the prosecution's to make. And not the court's. (*With that Cahill retakes his seat. Letting Judge Brown know* *he's got nothing more to say. A really brilliant move. Snubbing the judge.)*

(I get another thigh slap from Mickie. And this time, on my opposite thigh, one from Slippery.)

Judge Brown: The defendant will rise. (*Mickie and me stand alongside Slippery. The jailers behind us also get to their feet. They do that in case a prisoner gets ideas. With Slippery it's simply a courtroom formality.*) This court will set bail at $100,000. It is also the order of this court that the defendant is to be confined to home detention, fitted with an electronic ankle bracelet that will transmit his whereabouts to the court. (*The DA starts to rise in protest. Judge Brown signals him back down. To Slippery.*) Mr. Williams, do you understand what I have just ordered?
Slippery: Yes, Your Honor.
Judge Brown: That's it, then. (*Starts to leave the bench. The bailiff picks his head up from out of the morning paper, stands, near shouts, "All rise." All do.*)
Cahill: (*On his feet.*) Your Honor, may the state be heard?
Judge Brown: You've been heard, Mr. Cahill. This matter is adjourned until

33

further notice.

Cahill: (*Not knowing when to quit.*) Your Honor.

(*Judge Brown ignores Cahill and starts to leave the bench.*)

Cahill: (*Under his breath, though not under enough.*) Asshole.

(*Judge Brown stops. He's heard that. Mickie hip-bumps me.*)

Judge Brown: (*Still on his feet, but now facing Cahill.*) What was that, Counsel?

Cahill: Nothing, Your Honor. (*Judge Brown gives him an unmistakable look. Then leaves the courtroom.*)

Cahill is so furious he storms from the courtroom, forgoing the ritual handshake with the opposition. His two assistants clear his papers away. The jailers take custody of Slippery.

Making a $100,000 bond's a piece of cake for Slippery. He signals he'll see us soon. Me and Mickie start to leave the courtroom.

And there's Dumpy Brown. He's apparently been in the courtroom, on one of the back benches, since the proceedings began. Dumpy and Mickie don't like each other. More like, they hate each other's guts. Dumpy watches us as we approach on our way out of Judge Brown's courtroom. (Judge Brown, by the way, is Dumpy's second cousin.)

Dumpy's looking like his usual self. Over-dressed in a purple suit, powder-blue-silk pocket hanky, matching tie under a two-tone high-collar shirt. His paunch pressing at the closed two buttons of his four-button jacket. Dumpy wears a comb-over, with wiggly strands of his hair pomaded over his scalp.

"It's the White Shadow," he says to Mickie, extending his pinky-ringed hand. Dumpy gives me only a nod. I return it.

Mickie shakes with Dumpy. "Whose case you fucking up today, Dump?" he says, grinning to Dumpy, like he's joking. Only he isn't.

Mickie's wrong about Dumpy. Wrong about his lawyering abilities, anyway.

Like us, Dumpy was a cop before law school and the bar. (He got the moniker "Dumpy" because he had a reputation for "dumping" contraband on any suspects he arrested that came up clean. Also, for the occasional brick from the trunk of his squad

35

car he'd "dump" over top the head of any of his informants who had a memory lapse when he needed to know something.)

Dumpy's an effective trial lawyer. The ghetto's his bailiwick. With the right defendant — the right jury — Dumpy's as good as they come.

Dumpy smiles, sucks air through his teeth like he does. Purposely keeps hold of Mickie's hand.

"Slippery be happy with you now, huh?" he says to Mickie.

That's another thing about Dumpy. His strategic use of street talk. He's doing it here to get under Mickie's skin.

Mickie won't pull his hand away. Won't give Dumpy the satisfaction.

Dumpy has tried to steal Slippery from us. Multiple times. Hasn't worked. At least not yet.

Mocking Dumpy, Mickie says, "Yeah, Dump. Slippery be happy with us."

I walk out of the courtroom. I'll wait out in the hall for these two bulls to unlock their horns.

CHAPTER 3
FATS DOMINO HAD IT RIGHT

So Slippery makes bail. Is home ankle-braceleted over the weekend.

Monday morning, he sits in his living room. Business hours. He's got his boys coming over. The same boys who visited him at the Camden County Jail when distribution and supply issues required some direction from him.

Slippery's worried the DA's got his place bugged, so he's trying to get them to speak in code. Problem is they are simply not capable of turning their street language into any kind of indirect communication. (Me and Mickie chuckle about this when Slippery later describes what happened. Leaving out all of the details, of course.)

One of his boys is over the house, talking. Slippery's frantically waving at the guy to shut up like he's flapping a blanket at a raging fire.

The boy's saying, "Yeah, Slip. We done

got the, you know, packages and shit of that, you know . . . shit. Know what I'm sayin'? Three kilos, uh. I mean, uh . . . uh."

Slippery's exasperated, finally telling the guy, "Nigger, shut your stupid-ass mouth." Leaving the room and then returning with a legal pad and a pen, motioning for the boy to write what he's trying to say without saying.

That's worse. The guy dropped out of school in the fourth grade. But he gives it a valiant try. Sitting there in his oversized sports labeled, brightly colored duds, his flat-billed baseball cap on sideways, spotless, unlaced size-fifteen Nikes. Laboring over the pad, silently dry-mouthing words, his tongue licking his lips, his eyes all screwed up like he's trying to parse the archaic language of some ancient biblical text.

He hands the pad back to Slippery, who tries to decipher his childish gobbledygook.

"Damn. What you meanin' here?" Slippery says, tossing his arms up in the air. He's so agitated. Saying to the guy, "Nigger, please!" Then realizes the man is really giving it his best shot. So he calms down. Tells him, "Okay, okay. We straight."

Next visitor to the house is Dumpy Brown.

You see, Dumpy was the lawyer for the other guys who were taken down with Slippery. Part of his crew. When me and Mickie managed to spring Slippery in front of Judge Brown. Well, Dumpy jumped on that bandwagon and filed his own motion with second cousin Judge Brown for release on bail on behalf of those of his clients still in lockup. That's really why he was in the back of the courtroom during the proceedings.

Dumpy's not as finicky about the rules we lawyers play by. He's okay with carrying messages and the like that lawyers can only do if they don't mind entering into their client's criminal enterprise and becoming coconspirators. Since Mickie and me won't do that, Slippery uses Dumpy. He knows full well Dumpy would like to replace us as his main counsel.

Slippery will use Dumpy. But he's got his number. Keeps Dumpy in his place. So, the next visitor to the house is Dumpy. He at least knows how to speak in code.

That's Slippery's Monday.

Mine is just another blue Monday. Just like that old Fats Domino song. I'm sitting at my desk. Bad coffee in front of me. I've got a sentencing in Camden County court for some doper had no case whatsoever and so I had to plead him to possession with intent to distribute. But that's not until two P.M.

So, here I sit in the Law Offices of Mezzonatti and Salerno.

We sublet this space. From a guy got this cash-and-carry ambulance-chasing practice. Calling himself these days Law Offices of Bernstein, Smulkin & Blumenthal. And there is a Smulkin. And a Blumenthal. And some other ambulance chasers as well. But all of them working for Arty Bernstein. All but one of them Jewish guys. What he's got looks like a real law firm. But it's not. It's Arty's sole domain. In reality a bucket shop for lawyers.

Arty's under criminal investigation. The Feds have his number. They're collecting evidence that Arty's been bribing insurance adjusters for quick and easy cash settlements for his bullshit cases. Word on the street's Arty's also got a judge or two in his pocket.

And me and Mickie are Arty's lawyers. He cut this deal with us. Free rent for free legal representation. Tell you the truth? Arty's a royal pain in the ass. He's like one of those carnival bumper cars, bouncing from one too-clever scheme to the next.

I hear Mickie go into his office next to

40

mine. Our common wall's thin. Mickie's clearing his throat. Probably a little hungover. No doubt popping the Rolaids I've been seeing him eating like candy the past few weeks. Then I hear him go out in the hall. To the kitchen for some of that awful coffee Arty provides for his staff.

For the coffee, Arty makes us pay. A buck twenty a cup. And for Xeroxing, by the page. Mickie saying to Arty soon after we cut our deal with him, For fuck sake. You said free lawyering for free rent. Arty raising his forefinger, telling Mickie, Ah, but not for out-of-pocket expenses. We didn't talk about that. Mickie staring at Arty, shaking his head, saying, You cheap son of a bitch. Arty still smiling. Signaling to Mickie, hey, you shoulda asked. Not my fault, yours, as Mickie walks away shaking his head.

Yeah, so, me and Mickie go way back. Been friends since the sixth grade. Did junior and high school together, like I said earlier, became cops. But on different forces. Mickie with vice in Philly. Me with homicide here in Camden. Finally we went to college, then did law school together. Mickie's idea. At night. Mickie's been married twice. No kids. Me? Once, very, very briefly. Now? No women in my life. Won't be. I'll explain later.

41

I hear Mickie reenter his office. I rap once on the common wall like we do. Mickie raps once back. He's still clearing his throat. Sipping that awful shit Arty's calling coffee. Mickie's Monday morning is about to get under way.

I'm thinking Mickie's feeling a little rough because of the weekend. His weekends are busy when he's got a new woman. Like he does now. Her name's Carla. She's a nurse at Our Lady of Lourdes Medical Center, over on Haddon, a stone's throw from our old neighborhood. Carla's not Italian. That doesn't matter to Mickie. Carla's got the look Mickie goes for. Leggy, nice curves. Most of his women, like Carla, you'd call "pretty enough." They're not great lookers. Then, neither is Mickie. But the girls do like him. So, when he's got a new woman, I don't see him much over the weekend, like I normally do. Mostly just Sunday-night football over at his house on the oversized flat screen in his living room. I get it. Am okay with it.

I open the file for the two P.M. sentencing; start to remind myself about the case. I hear someone knock on Mickie's closed door, then enter. It's Arty. Can tell his raspy voice. He starts talking with Mickie. I go back to reviewing the file.

In no time at all I hear Mickie shout to Arty, "No fucking way, Arty. Forget it. No fucking way."

Arty's keeping his voice low. I can't really hear what he's telling Mickie, but I'm guessing whatever it is, Mickie's not gonna buy it.

For a while their voices remain more or less low. Then I again hear Mickie tell Arty, "No. What're you deaf? No."

Arty's now shouting through the wall, "It's the only way, Mickie. Trust me on this. The only way."

That's when I get the two raps in quick succession. That means, get in here, Junne. I need you.

So I go.

CHAPTER 4
ARTY BERNSTEIN'S
BIG NEW IDEA

When I open the door to Mickie's office, Arty turns. Sees it's me, so keeps talking. He's repeat-telling Mickie, "You gotta trust me on this. It's the only way."

Then he points Mickie to me, says, "Tell Junne. He'll see it. Right, Junne?"

Of course, I don't have a clue what kind of malarkey Arty's trying to sell here. But when Arty's got one of his bright ideas? Grab your helmet and dive for cover.

He's standing in that small space on the other side of Mickie's desk, where the two visitor chairs are, quickstepping, back and forth, back and forth, like some country-western line dancer.

I'm telling you, Arty gets like this. He's fucking uncontrollable. Barrel-chested in his custom-made, monogrammed dress shirts, his Windsor-knotted ties, and the braces with the scales of justice on them, should instead be skull and crossbones.

Arty's got these little, beady eyes. A beak nose belongs on a parrot. His Larry King hairdo. Arty's arms waving up a storm with every bullshit point he's making. Like one of those NFL linebackers trying to get the home team all juiced up for the next play. I can see he's got Mickie on the brink.

Arty's not linebacker big. Nor is Mickie, though like Arty, he's a sturdy guy. Mickie's former-high-school-athlete sturdy, but he's been softening up some through the years. He's still got that boyish twinkle in his eyes, his acne scars diminished with age. Me? I'm smaller, and for some reason (though not from regular exercise) more in-shape looking, dark curly headed and olive-skinned like from the old country.

I see Mickie pop a Rolaids.

"You're not listening," Arty's telling Mickie. "Tell Junne," he says to him. "Tell him. Tell him."

Mickie just looks at Arty, rolls his eyes. Arty says, "Okay. Okay. If you won't, I'll do it."

"So, listen, Junne," Arty says. And then I get this long-winded explanation of Arty's surefire, no-can-lose, it's-the-only-way, I-swear-to-Christ, Junne-you'll-see-I'm right-even-if-Mickie-can't plan.

In a nutshell?

Arty's decided that one or more of the Bernstein, Smulkin lawyers working for him are secretly cooperating with the prosecutor's office. Ratting him out, not only behind his back, but under his very nose here in his own law offices. And he's come up with a plan. His big new "idea."

What Arty wants is for me and Mickie to bless his plan. As his criminal defense lawyers. This gives him cover.

Anything goes wrong? Then me and Mickie are his insurance policy. He says to the U.S. Attorney's Office, Hey, don't look at me. I ran it by my lawyers. They said it was kosher. So, it ain't on me. Talk to them you're not happy with what went down.

What Arty wants to do is hire some private investigator to tap the phones of the lawyers working for him. Wants to see who the squealers are.

Problem is, for Arty or us, it's illegal. The DA can do it. With a court order. But a private citizen? No way, José.

So, Arty's watching his ass. I think Arty truly believes that me and Mickie are just a couple of dumb dago lawyers he can browbeat into green-lighting him.

When Arty finishes I just stare at him. Unbefuckinglievable. I'm about to say so, but Mickie's back behind the wheel.

"That's it," Mickie says to Arty. "Enough."

"Okay, okay. At least think about it. You'll give it some time, right?" Arty says, adjusting his tie, running his hands airlessly over top his hairdo.

That slimy bastard. He's trying to leave things up in the air. Ambiguous. You know, like maybe he can walk out of here without a final "no means no." Thinking no doubt that gives him the argument later to say, Hey, my lawyers never said no. I relied on them, what can I tell you? Not perfect protection, but at least he'll walk out of here with something he can use (against us) if the shit hits the fan.

"Come on, Arty," Mickie says. "You do it, you're on your own, pal."

Arty looks at me. I nod my confirmation to what Mickie's just told him.

Then, just like that, Arty drops it. Pastes this big fat smile on his face. Shrugs his shoulders like he's just heard some absolutely charming story about this great guy named Mickie Mezzonatti. Still looking at me. Pointing to Mickie. That guy, he's signaling. You just gotta love him.

"Okay, okay," Arty says, finally allowing his arms to float back down to his sides. "You guys are the lawyers in this. What do I know?" (Meaning he knows better than we

47

do, or probably anyone else ever went to law school.)

With that, still smiling up a storm, Arty leaves Mickie's office. Letting us know, no harm, no foul. Worth a try, that's all.

The door closes. Mickie gives me a look.

Says, "This shit ain't worth it, Junnie. Free rent or no free rent."

CHAPTER 5
THE CHEAPEST GUY IN TOWN

We have a new potential client. This would be a big case for us.

If you live around here you've seen the awful TV commercials for Sami's Electronics. They're on day and night. No actors telling you about all the washer-dryer combos, big-ass fridges, and flat-screen TVs just waiting in their showrooms with your name on them. Nope. Sami Khan himself is always the star of the show, hurriedly urging you to go to one of his many stores, like the Indian version of a carnival sideshow barker grasping the tent flap to the unbelievable things you'll see inside once you pony up the dough.

Pudgy Sami with his singsong Indian accent, that really bad wig, never seemingly on right, listing to one side or the other like a ship caught in a sea storm. Sami reminding you he's the cheapest guy in town. No one's gonna beat his prices. He guarantees it.

Well, turns out Sami's Electronics is in a shitload of trouble. The Feds raided their corporate offices. Looks like they're about to be charged with massive fraud, tax evasion, false reporting. You name it.

And while it seems they already have hired defense counsel, some big-name law firm across the river in Philly, there may be a role for me and Mickie. The investigation is being run out of the Camden branch of the New Jersey U.S. Attorney's Office. We have been recommended to Sami as New Jersey local counsel.

And get this. The recommendation came to Sami by one of his old friends from back in the day.

Who, you're wondering?

Slippery Williams, that's who.

Get outta here, you're thinking. Right?

Well, get this.

Long before Sami's Electronics outlets took over most of New Jersey, with stores across the state, this young guy makes his way from India.

Sami grew up in one of those impoverished places. Delhi. New Delhi. Something like that. (What do I know about India?) From a down-and-out family. Poor as poor can be.

And I'll bet poor over there is worse than any down-and-out slum neighborhood in inner-city Camden.

Somehow young Sami gets himself to the U.S. By hook or crook. Makes his way to Camden. He's got some distant cousin who immigrated here. By the time of Sami's arrival the cousin's got himself a small ghetto grocery/convenience store.

The cousin gives Sami a job. Behind the counter of the store.

The black folks in the neighborhood at that time had little or no access to supermarkets. The Acmes and so on of the world not about to set foot in the Camden ghetto. So those stuck there buy what they need with what little money they can muster from the grocery/convenience. And from the liquor store next door, which has enough bulletproof Plexiglas to fend off an army.

Sami's a smart guy. He sizes up the situation quickly. Makes some connections. Starts selling small appliances and assorted electronics. Clock radios, toasters, etc. Stuff "fell off" the boat at the docks, or maybe comes out the back of a car trunk.

Starts selling it under the nose of the cousin. Who is definitely not liking this. Worried the police are going to shut him down. Or maybe worse. And there's Sami. This

51

skinny little brown-skinned Indian kid, prematurely balding, an illegal alien, working in the place. The cousin's shitting bricks, picturing the police raid that never comes.

But Sami makes sure to give the cousin a cut. So he grimaces when Sami's handing over the toaster or whatever, furtively pocketing the under-the-counter cash. Most going into Sami's pocket, the rest to the cousin. So he complains to Sami when it's just the two of them alone in there. But he does nothing.

All the while, out on the street, there's this open-air drug bazaar. The usual operation, with the corner boys, taking the cash, handing it off, another one then handing over the plastic vials with the dope.

One of the new corner boys turns out to be Slippery Williams. Just a kid back then, no more than thirteen, fourteen at the most. (That's not his street name at the time. That comes later.) He's a lot younger than Sami. Learning the dope ropes. Then noticing the unusual activity going on inside Singh Groceries and Confections. None of the other corner boys paying it any mind.

They're telling Slippery, Yo, what you care what go on in there, man? What them half niggers in there doin' ain't no affair a yours. Do you feel me?

But Slippery's catching the action. When he's in there at the counter paying for a soda from the cooler, or the sea-salt-and-vinegar chips he likes. Watching Sami handing over the appliance to some mope from the nearby projects, taking in the cash. No register ring-up. Not one electronic item or whatever displayed for sale on any of the Singh Groceries' shelves.

Slippery at first lets it go. Concentrating on his "apprenticeship" on the streets. Learning how to run his corner to its maximum profit potential. But then he gets an idea. Finds his own fence. Then approaches Sami in the store.

"Hey, yo, you maybe interested in a new supplier?" he asks Sami — the cousin listening behind the counter, making clucking sounds showing his disapproval, but otherwise staying out of it. "Give you a better price than you be gettin' now from whoever. Know what I'm sayin'?"

Sami looking over the counter at this kid. Smiling, saying in his lilting Indian-accented English, "I do not know what you are speaking of, young man."

Slippery nodding, okay. Not saying more.

Then a few days later he's back with some samples of what he can provide. Gives Sami his pricing scheme.

Telling Sami, "So. Big man. You still stickin' with what you got? Lettin' your low profit margins keep you poor? Or you be wantin' to deal with someone know how to treat you right?"

Then he and Sami are in business. Slippery's supplementing his dope income with what he's making supplying Sami with stolen electronics merchandise. Slippery's getting his cut at the end of each week. Still just a kid. Not letting the other corner boys in on his new action. They're imploring him, now they're seeing he's making good money on the side. They're saying to Slippery, "Yo, my brother. Give me some a that action."

Slippery's telling them, "Nigger. You don't get shit from me. And listen up good. You be sharin' any a this with the bosses come by here? They in they real fine wheels sittin' at the curb. Collecting the take. They big, tattooed arms leaning out the car window. Asking, everything cool here, little man? Know what I'm sayin'? You rat me out, motherfucker? Then next morning you wakin' up dead." Pointedly, adding, "Do you feel me?"

Slippery is now carrying a big Glock nine. The other corner boys see it hanging from his skinny hip, black rubber handgrip out, the rest of the weapon bulging his already baggy jeans. So they bitch and gripe, but they give Slippery space. Keep their mouths shut.

And that goes on for a couple of years. But neither Sami nor Slippery is satisfied with small-time ghetto operations. Sami by then married, his son on the way. Now with enough money to open his first legit retail store. Leaving the cousin behind. (Later employing him as a floor salesman when the corner grocery goes under and he's forced to sell for a song to the Koreans.)

And Slippery by then has worked his way up from corner boy to street captain. And when the thug he's ultimately working for gets shot in the back of the head one night when he's stumbling out of some club (wonder how that could have happened?), Slippery assumes control of the guy's territory.

It takes Slippery a few more years, but by the time he's finished, all the best spots in Camden are his. There's not another drug operation in the tristate area that enjoys his profit margins. And no one can get the supply lines Slippery has managed to establish. His dope's purer and more plentiful than any of his predecessors'.

The years go by. Sami becomes an electronics mogul.

Slippery has become Slippery.

When Sami gets raided by the Feds, he contacts Slippery.

Slippery's telling Sami, "Yeah, sure. You good. Use that big-time lawyer from Philly you tellin' me 'bout. But, I was you? I'd — whatchacall it? Supplement my legal team. Know what I'm sayin'? Lawyer up some more. Hire me some Camden local boys. Ones who know the ropes here. Know the judges. Hear? And I got just the boys for you."

It seems Slippery's throwing us a bone. (On account of what Slippery did for us with Rodrigo Gonzáles, our representation of him in his current case is on the house. It's the least we could do, so I guess he's making up for it.)

He's got another thing on his mind too.

But me and Mickie don't learn that until later.

CHAPTER 6
BARRACUDA EYES

Sami and his son are standing three steps into the Bernstein, Smulkin & Blumenthal conference room. (Arty lets us use it for meetings. He charges us fifty bucks an hour. In cash.)

Mickie's closing the door, making the introductions. And as he's doing this, I see Sami give me a quick glance, but then lays his attention square on the room. He's taking in the shabby surroundings, his look saying, What in hell?

This conference room is as far from what you see in the big uptown law firms as a housing project is from a Wall Street mogul's penthouse. None of the usual law firm trappings are here. No nice art on the walls. In fact, there's no nothing on the walls. Not even a decent paint job. The table's marred and scratched. The chairs around it mismatched.

Arty runs his firm tight as a fat man's belt.

57

Not one penny for amenities. His practice is all about maximizing profits from his ample contingent fee recoveries.

When Mickie once said to Arty, Why don't you fix up the place? Your clients in here, seeing their lawyers. Giving depositions in the conference room. Check out how this place looks, Arty. Mickie waving his arm around for Arty to see as he's saying this.

Arty tells Mickie. What? For these schwartzes coming in here? Mick, they don't know no better. They get their settlement money after my fee cut comes out. That's all they care about. How much easy cash I'm putting in their pockets. Arty chuckling at Mickie's naivete.

Mickie's now saying to Sami, "Mr. Khan, this is my law partner, Salvatore Salerno. Please have a seat. Want coffee or something?"

I get up from the table and walk around so I can shake Sami's hand.

His hand's in mine, Sami's grip not even squeezing a little, completely slack. No kind of handshake at all. And he's still ignoring me, his eyes roaming the room.

Sami seems about ten years older than us. Maybe more. He looks less pudgy than he does on the TV. Today he's wearing an open-necked white dress shirt. Dark slacks.

I can see tufts of graying hair at his throat. And how can a guy that rich wear such a bad rug? It doesn't even look like hair. Looks more like a collection of tightly woven nylon strands, dyed artificial black. And like on the TV it's not sitting quite right over his forehead.

His hands are ringless. He's wearing a gold Rolex watch. There are graying patches of thickish hair over the backs of his hands, covering his knuckles too.

He may look clownish. But those eyes belong on a barracuda. They're set deep, real deep. And dark. Nothing escapes those eyes. His nose, thick mouth, five o'clock shadow, all swallowed up by those eyes. They're telling me this guy is way beyond sharp. He's ruthless. Maybe that's why him and young Slippery hit it off all those years ago.

Sami's hand slips away from mine. He now looks to Mickie, waiting to be told which of the mismatched chairs to take. As he's doing that, I reach toward the son. He at least has a handshake.

"Junne," I say to him.

"Rafat," he says, watching his old man with what I can clearly see is a worried look. Here they are, in yet another criminal lawyer's office. Their world no doubt turned

59

on its head. And papa's distracted by the interior decoration (or lack thereof). Rafat's not liking this at all.

Rafat must take after his mother. I can't see much of a resemblance between him and his old man. He's nice looking. Early twenties. Wearing a wedding band.

I'm already stereotyping Rafat. Thinking. Arranged marriage between Indian immigrant families. (Not fair.) Like Dad, he's chestnut brown, not like some Indians you see, way African dark. (Is that another stereotype?) Rafat is dressed in a Polo plaid button-down shirt, olive gray slacks. Also with a gold Rolex on his wrist. He looks more like the rich guy, casually dressed, than does his old man. Second-generation money. (There I go again.)

So, with some shuffling we get ourselves seated around the table. Two and two. Me and Mickie facing Sami and Rafat. Coffee has been offered and declined. Water too.

Sami's got a thin manila folder he brought with him now lying flat on the table between his guarding arms. In it is the search warrant and the "inventory" the FBI gave him of seized items.

The FBI's "inventories" are notoriously bullshit. No help whatsoever in actually identifying what has been seized and carted off to the federal building. An example: "Misc. computers and documents from desk drawers."

Sami's no longer eyeballing the room. He's now eyeballing us. And he's got that same look plastered on his face. Thinking, no doubt: This is what Slippery Williams sends me to?

I see it. Mickie sees it.

Mickie and me are dressed for the occasion. Wearing our go-to-court suits.

Mickie's suits don't really fit right. They're discount store, off the rack. His shirts and ties JCPenney specials. As always, he needs a haircut, floppy strands hanging over his ears.

Ah, but Mickie's shoes.

No one's seeing them under the table. But the money Mickie saves on decent clothes he blows on shoes. Always top of the line Ferragamos, Bruno Maglis. You name it.

Curious, though. Mickie should know. People doing business with you? They look at your clothes, the watch you're wearing. (Like Sami and Rafat's gold Rolexes.) Rarely down at your feet. Mickie's Italian kicks are top of the line. Under the table. But top of the line.

Me? I too have to admit, I buy my stuff on year-end sale. Or at the outlets out on the highway near Atlantic City. But I guess I'm easier to fit. My shoulders aren't bigger than the rest of me like Mickie. Okay, maybe my ties are too colorful, flashy even. And I got that pocket hankie thing going. Like Dumpy wears. But I look like a lawyer. At least I think I do.

Does Sami think so? Nope, not one bit, I'm thinking, as I watch Sami's eyes wander back and forth between me and Mickie.

So the four of us are sitting here. Clocking one another. Consumed momentarily.

But now it's time to get down to business.

CHAPTER 7
I DIDN'T DO NOTHIN'

As Mickie starts the meeting I pull one of the half-used legal pads from the center of the table.

We don't write too much stuff on the first meeting. Really not too much ever. Our notes will most likely never see the light of day. Stories change. Clients will do that. Still, there's no point in memorializing changing (conflicting?) versions of what happened that brings them to a criminal lawyer's office.

"Let's begin," Mickie says. Waiting. Will Sami start talking?

He doesn't, his barracuda eyes fixed on Mickie.

Mickie points to the folder in front of Sami. "Is that the warrant and inventory?" he asks.

Sami silently slides the folder across to Mickie. Mickie opens the folder, extracts the search warrant and accompanying

63

inventory. Glances at it, then slides it to me. Like I said, there's nothing helpful there.

Mickie takes a different tack.

"So, you guys already retained counsel. In Philly. Right?"

Sami's still staring at us. Rafat looks nervously at his dad.

Most people, other than habitual criminals (our usual client staple) are really ill at ease sitting across from a criminal lawyer they're needing to open up to. Confide in.

"Yes, that is correct, Mr. Mezzonti," Sami finally says. Mangling Mickie's name. Prompting Mickie to tell Sami, Call me Mickie. Sami nods, but doesn't.

More silence. Sonny speaks up. Out of turn.

"You see . . . ," is all he gets out before Sami places his hand on top of his boy's. Gives him a look that says, No you don't. I will handle this. Then turns to us.

"Yes, we have retained this Mr. Gerald Rubino of the Buckmaster, Thomas law firm in Philadelphia. That is the very well-respected law firm our company uses for its various business needs. Mr. Rubino is a criminal specialist."

And me and Mickie are what? Chopped liver? We know who Jerry Rubino is. He's a topflight, big-firm criminal lawyer. No doubt about that.

Sami's corporate offices were raided, the Feds descending on the place, barging in with a show of force. Armed to the teeth, needlessly wearing Teflon vests, "FBI" and "IRS" stenciled front and back. Screaming, "Raid." "Nobody move." Things like that. Scaring the living shit out of all the clerks and bookkeepers working there. One hysterical overweight lady throwing her hands in the air yelling, "Oh my God, Oh my God." While all this is going on, with one finger in his ear so he can hear, Sami's on the phone to the law firm he uses for his corporate needs. Within seconds, he has Gerald Rubino on the phone, saying to Sami, "Put the agent in charge on the phone. I'll take care of this." Sami did. The agents calmed down.

"You see, Mr. Mezzonatti [comes out "Missing Lady"], we have a very substantial business. Perhaps you have seen us on the TV?"

Both me and Mickie nod. Both unhelpfully shooting a quick glance at Sami's lopsided hairline.

"We have so many sales transactions," Sami continues. "We cannot be expected to be aware of each and every one. How the sales are reported."

Ah, now I get it. My guess, Mickie does too, as Sami prattles on about how they have such a volume of day-to-day sales in their many stores. How can they be sure they have reported each and every one for sales tax purposes. Yaddita-yaddita-yaddita.

While Sami's doing his version of Ricky Ricardo's "Lucy, let me splain you somethin'," I'm thinking I already got what this case is about.

Maybe the numbers are bigger on account of the statewide stores, but I'll bet this case is nothing more than another tax evasion case. (Turns out I'm right. And I'm wrong. But we don't learn this until later.)

The stores don't report all of their sales. There's no doubt two computer entry codes for cash sales. One gets reported by the front office, since stores like this would be expected to take in some amount of cash. The other doesn't.

And I'm betting that the various store managers have been instructed to place some small portion of credit card sales into a separate data entry code. Told some bullshit, like this is for spot-checking inventory, or some other nonsense like that. Each manager given a monthly quota they're needing to fill. End of each month the front office "disappears" that electronic file for sales tax reporting purposes.

And if Sami and son are underreporting sales tax, then they're no doubt doing the same on their own tax returns for the actual income they're taking from the business. And their doing that drops them waist deep into some serious income tax evasion.

Most of our clients we see in here are street crime defendants. Not "suite" crime defendants like Sami and son. Our regular type of clientele come here accused of drug dealing, murder, armed robbery. Stuff like that.

Our usual type clients, sitting in here, me and Mickie waiting for them to tell us what went down. Well, they give us a slightly different version of this long-winded spiel Sami's in the middle of.

Yeah, our regulars, dressed in the latest hip-hop street styles, the ever-present spotless canvas lace-ups under the table across from Mickie's glossy slip ons. The more successful ones sporting gold Rolexes. (See?)

And what do they say? Almost always starts the same way. "I didn't do nothin'," they tell us, nervously moving around in their chairs, their legs under the table swinging open closed, open closed.

Sami's just doing the uptown version of that. Me and Mickie listening politely to all the verbiage, how could Sami be expected to be a policeman for each and every one of their many stores.

In the middle of all this, there's a loud knock on the door. Without waiting it opens to reveal Arty Bernstein's poking head. Looking for us. Again.

Sami turns as the door opens, stops mid-sentence. Like I said, Arty's got his head in the doorway. Sees our clients, exchanges glances first with Sami, then with us.

"When you're finished," is all Arty says to me and Mickie, then slowly closes the door. He seemed to recognize Sami too. The power of TV is not to be underestimated, I guess.

So Sami's winding down. All the while, Rafat's listening to Daddy, looking like he's got the stomach flu. Me and Mickie wait patiently. (I haven't taken a single note.)

"So," Sami says. "You gentlemen will call Mr. Rubino. Make an appointment to see him. He will tell you how you can be of assistance to him."

Both me and Mickie pick up the "be of assistance to *him*" — not to my son and me — part of what Sami's saying. But we let it slide. This case is likely to generate a nice fee. Probably for doing very little. Sami wants Jerry Rubino to be ship's captain and us deckhands. Fine by us. (At least that's what we're thinking now.)

Sami pulls his checkbook from his pants pocket. He looks at us. Doesn't say a word. Just waits.

Mickie tells Sami, "Fifty thousand for the initial retainer."

Whoa, I'm thinking. That's way more than we usually ask. I guess Mickie's making Sami pay for relegating us to the backseat of his legal team's bus.

Well, what the hell. Money's money.

Right?

CHAPTER 8
TAMARA REENTERS OUR LIVES

I was the one who caught Tamara's call. She asked the Bernstein, Smulkin receptionist who's supposed to screen our calls (another twenty-five a month in cash to Arty), "Is Mickie there?"

The girl's saying to her, "Please hold."

Arty has instructed the receptionist always to take his firm's calls before ours. Even if a call for us comes in first.

"You got that?" Arty saying to the receptionist. "Ours first, then those two schmendricks."

"Yeah, yeah, okay, Arty," she tells him since he's given her these instructions about a thousand times already.

And who is this Tamara, you're thinking?

She's Tamara from the Courthouse Café. Dark chocolate, tall, and shapely. Tamara was our waitress at the café that's catty-corner from the courthouse.

The place is the Little Switzerland of the

lunchtime crowd. Everyone on the same break eating there. A temporary suspension of hostilities. The judges, the lawyers. Even the perps. All nodding how you doin' over their sandwiches and coffees and sodas before we all go traipsing back to the courtroom for a continuation of the legal warfare we all live by — and some for.

Me and Mickie really liked Tamara. Always innocently flirting with us. Most all the customers really. Saying things like, "I know you looking at my taillights when I'm takin' your orders back to the kitchen. You likin' that, huh?"

Making me and Mickie chuckle. All the while she's handling the whole café single-handed. Not dropping a beat. Rarely screwing up an order. Tamara being nice and friendly no matter who's at the table. A judge. A perp. Never mattered to her. Calling them all "sweetie."

Yeah, Tamara. Ebony dark, high rear end. And cleavage. Trust me, Tamara could do cleavage in those pink rayon waitress uniforms, top two buttons undone. Her name amateur-tattooed in script high up over her left breast. (Tamara came up hard too.)

Tamara's got so-so features. By most accounts you'd say she was below average in the looks department. Her nose is too flat

71

for her long face, her eyes too small and close together, lips too full. Hair too frizzy.

But you know, as with most people you like, who've got something to them? You get to know them? Like me and Mickie with her? If they're nice inside, somehow that gets outside and they're looking pretty good to you. That's the real kind of good-looking, as far as I'm concerned. Like with Tamara.

So, one day, a couple of months ago, me and Mickie walk into the Courthouse Café. Like I said, just about the entire courthouse population (at least those not in the lockup) emptying in there for a quick lunch. And there's no Tamara. Some new girl's waitressing, the place in pandemonium, everybody and their uncle calling out to her, where's their goddamned order, court's gonna start and they can't be sitting here much longer without what they ordered.

We see the Greek guy owns the place. Never comes out from the kitchen. But today he's on the outside of the swinging doors, his hairy arms folded over his belly, glumly watching his lunch trade business turn to shit. Me and Mickie ask him, Gus, where's Tamara at? Quit, is all he says, as he blows the toothpick he's been sucking on to the floor and goes back into the kitchen.

I do remember Tamara telling Mickie and

me that she had no intention of spending the rest of her life serving tunas on rye, wet-mopping floors, and refilling Heinz ketchup bottles.

The receptionist finally does get back on the line with Tamara. Just about the time that Tamara's thinking maybe she's been disconnected, this has taken so long. About to hang up and try again.

The girl's saying, "Who you calling for?"

"Mickie," Tamara repeats, thinking, Damn, this girl can't remember one simple-ass name, that's her job. Tamara can hear another line ringing on the girl's switch-board.

"Hold please," she tells Tamara again as the line goes dead.

Then after another few minutes the girl's back on, saying to Tamara, "Law Offices of Mezzonatti and Salerno, how can I direct your call?"

Before Tamara can get a word out, she hears, "Hold please."

Tamara's about to hang up when the girl pops back on.

"Not here," she tells Tamara. Adding, "In court."

Tamara asks for me.

The phone at my desk buzzes.

"Hello?"

73

"Call for you," is all the receptionist says. Since she didn't screen the call, didn't ask who's calling. Like she's supposed to for the twenty-five bucks Arty's taking from us for "screening" calls, for fuck sake.

Then I've got this female voice on the line, saying, "Junne, wha's up wich you, sweetie?"

I know that voice. And she's got a proposition for us.

So, now Mickie's back in the office from court. We talk it over. He doesn't have much time. A prosecution witness he is cross-examining is still on the stand and Mickie has hurriedly returned during the lunch recess to pick up some additional papers he now needs for his remaining cross.

"Got a minute?" I'm telling him as I stand out in the carpeted hallway in front of his office. "Tamara called."

Mickie's stuffing papers into his briefcase, checking his watch. He's got to hoof it back to court he wants to get there in time. Asks can I give him a ride.

So, I tell him in the car. Tamara called looking for a job. As our secretary, or whatever.

He says, "Well, we don't need one. But what the hell. Why not."

Tamara was up front with me, saying, "Junne, sweetie, now you needin' to know. I

74

don't know jack-shit about no law office. But, baby, I can learn. Don't wanna be goin' back to no job I'm asking, Take your order? Ain't gonna have no more Gus's pawing me in no overheated kitchen I'm in there for pickups."

So, "Okay by me," I tell Mickie in the car, he's again checking his watch, seeing does he actually have time to eat.

"Drop me at the café," he says.

With that new girl still messing up orders at the Courthouse Café, lunch today for Mickie's a dubious proposition. If he wants a decent shot at making it back into the courtroom in time. I'm about to tell him that.

Then, "Fuck it," he says. "Drop me at the courthouse." He pats his tummy and grins. "Wouldn't kill me to miss a meal," he says.

"Yeah," I say, as I pull up to the courthouse entrance. "Make you mean and lean."

We both grin. Then he's out of the car and trotting up the wide steps.

Me and Mickie have never had help before. But, hey. We just banked the 50K Sami laid on us for the retainer. That's more than we will need to pay Tamara. We'll let Tamara learn on the job. Or better yet, we'll maybe send her to some office training course, let her learn the basics. We'll spring for the fee.

I'm back in the office later that afternoon. Phone at my desk rings. It's the reception-ist.

"Someone here for you," she says.

"Yeah," I tell her. "Like who?"

I can hear another line ringing. She snaps me on hold.

I wait. But I'm seething.

I know who's out there. I'd just like her to do her fucking job for once and reception like she's supposed to reception.

Then she's back on, saying to me, "Law Offices of Bernstein, Smulkin, and Blumen-thal, how may I direct your call?"

I hang up on her and go out to the recep-tion area to get Tamara.

The Bernstein, Smulkin reception space most days looks like the emergency waiting room at Our Lady of Lourdes. Scattered on the worn-out chairs (Arty buys them used from some wholesaler who takes them when doctors refurnish their offices) is an assort-ment of accident clients. Most all are decked out with crutches, arm slings, neck braces.

Most are nothing more than props. Arty's telling his clients to wear them at all times. Telling them, Don't tell me you don't need it. Just fucking wear it 'til I tell you not to. Adding, You want the money or no, bro?

I'm at the receptionist's desk. Tamara sees me across the room and gets up from her seat. I hear the receptionist on the phone, now with what must be her girlfriend.

The receptionist is this fat white girl sports African braided hair with beaded ends. Her dimpled hands got too-long fake nails with some kind of moon crescent Day-Glo polish. And trust me, this girl should not be wearing sleeveless dresses.

As Tamara smiles at me, gives me a little wave, I can hear the receptionist saying into the phone (the other lines ringing, but Arty or no Arty, this girl's gonna give priority to her own personal calls), she's saying, "Well, you ask me, the guy's a dick. Treating you like that? Fuck his skinny ass, is what I say." She listens, then adds, giggling, "Yeah. That's right."

She looks up and sees me watching her. Mistakenly thinking I don't know which of the people waiting out here is Tamara. The phone still cradled in the hollow of her fleshy neck, keeping up her patter on the phone, she points me to where Tamara's standing.

I roll my eyes at her, shake my head. She doesn't notice. Off in conversation-land with her girlfriend.

I walk over to Tamara. I can see that some

77

of the younger men seated here waiting for Arty or one of his other lawyers are appreciatively clocking her. I see an older black woman, heavyset, kind of with a church lady look. She's also eyeballing Tamara, but this woman's got a clear look of disapproval on her face.

"Hey, Tamara," I say.

"Hey, how you doin', sweetie?" she says.

We awkwardly shake hands. Then she reaches over and gives me a quick peck on the cheek.

I would say that Tamara is sort of dressed like a legal secretary. Or maybe more like a lawyer. Whichever it is, it's the Victoria's Secret version.

She's wearing a matching navy blue pinstriped skirt and jacket, both seemingly sized for someone less tall and less . . . endowed. Her hair is frizzed up as usual, but piled on top of her head. She's got on a white blouse and a man's dark blue polka-dot tie. And some serious high heel pumps.

She's a female James Cagney. How she managed to actually sit in the reception room chair in that fabric wedge of a skirt is beyond me.

And then I notice the briefcase. Tamara's holding a briefcase. Strangely, this touches me. I'm certain it's completely empty. But its very presence is telling me how serious, in her own way, Tamara is about "making it" in this new world she's so eager to enter.

"Come on," I tell her. "Let me take you back to where your office is at."

Immediately, Tamara lights up. She gets this big grin on her face. Like some little girl's Christmas fantasy just came true. An office. Tamara's obviously thinking, Junne and Mickie gonna give me a office. And she is absolutely delighted.

And so am I.

Tamara follows me past the receptionist, who is still jabbering away to her girlfriend.

Missing the smiles on both our faces.

CHAPTER 9
JUVIE COURT

Mickie's in trial. It's likely to take a few more days. This one is a court appointed case. Me and Mickie don't as a rule take court appointed cases. We are privately retained, strictly cash-and-carry. True, but every now and then lawyers like us get selected by the court to take on a criminal client.

Both court systems here in Camden, the state court one (where the DA is puzzling over what to do with Slippery's prosecution) and the federal one (Arty's grand jury investigation — and Sami's) have their own public defender offices. But conflicts occur. When that happens, the judges reach out to lawyers like us. You really can't say no. Yeah, sure, you can try and wiggle out of it. Tell the judge you got a scheduling conflict with some other case. Or you got a vacation coming up. Maybe the judge lets you out. Maybe he doesn't. But if he or she does?

Next time you're in front of that judge? You're gonna pay. The judge will see to it. Guaranteed.

You can't annoy the judges with stuff like that. If you do, sooner or later it will come back to bite you in the ass. The courtroom's our bread and butter. And the judge is the spreading knife.

So, Mickie drew this case. Two defendants. Mickie's got one (name of James Earl Wilson) and the state public defender's office got the other (name's Tommy Lee something or other). These are some serious bad apples. Full-time, highly professional armed robbers. They never do homes. Retail businesses only. They've been around for a while. Moving throughout the state. Makes them harder to apprehend.

Both white guys, both have done some heavy time in the past. Big guys. James is prison-tattooed, long pony tail, Fu Manchu mustache. A man of few words. He and his partner, Tommy Lee, took down the nicest and oldest jewelry store in Camden. (I know that's not saying all that much. But still.)

These guys are among the best in the business. No hair triggers, no panicked, hopheaded, nervous, crazy shouting. They're in the store. They know just how to do what they do. In and out. Cool as cucumbers.

But this time, their luck turned bad. The old Lebanese-American couple owns the store were there, but so was the daughter-in-law. Everything's going to plan, the old lady opening the display cases, telling the robbers, Just take it. And then the daughter-in-law, also behind the counter, her hands shaking up a storm, she's totally and utterly panicked. She takes the pistol from under the cash drawer. Mickie's guy tells her, Don't do that, don't do that. Her in-laws now screaming to her, Put it down, Rachael, for God's sake put it down.

But she's hysterical, can't hear any of them. She's pointing that shaking pistol directly at Tommy Lee. The two robbers exchange quick glances. No choice. They open up on the daughter-in-law, both old folks, and the one customer unlucky enough to be in the store at the time.

All four are shot dead. Before they leave, they take care to ensure the security camera chip is destroyed. They know to fully abort and not take a single piece of jewelry. And of course, no fingerprints are left.

So the DA's office has got a weak case. James and Tommy Lee have a real good shot at walking. Totally clean. Out the door. Free as birds.

That's justice, huh? It is what it is.

So, Mickie's in the courthouse in trial and today I'm walking up the steps myself.

I'm on my way to what's called chancery court — family division.

I am heading for juvenile delinquent's court, no matter what soft name it gets around here. A family court judge presides. In Camden, "juvie" court is the feeder court for tomorrow's adult offender thugs.

If you're under eighteen and you commit a crime, this is where you go. The state can seek a waiver for any kid commits a crime so bad he/she deserves adult court justice. But the DA's office rarely asks for waivers and only does so when there's a murder involved that is so heinous and bloody they will be skewered by the local media for not treating the little punk who did it as an adult.

In juvie court the public is barred from the courtroom. The doors are locked. Only parents and de facto guardians like grandmothers are allowed in, sitting on the benches alongside the social workers and intake counselors. The whole bunch so out of touch with these little tykes being brought into the courtroom in chains just like their adult counterparts, they might as well have stayed out in the hallway in front of the locked courtroom doors.

Me and Mickie don't do juvie law. Not as a rule. But I told Mickie I would do this. Being as it's for Tamara. Neither of us were bothered by her coming to us so soon after we took her on. (Which, by the way, is working out fine. Tamara has signed herself up for two six-week adult evening courses on business administration at a local junior college. One for bookkeeping. The other for general office whatever. All the while putting in full days for us.)

She came to us. Asked if we could recommend a lawyer does juvenile law. Saying she didn't have all that much money saved up, but thought she could pay for the lawyer if he didn't charge too much.

"For what?" Mickie asked her, both Tamara and me sitting in Mickie's office, the door closed. (I really do believe Tamara had no intention of asking us to personally handle this matter.)

Turns out Tamara's got this crackhead older sister. Tamara's mother washed her hands of this girl years ago. The sister's lost somewhere out on the street. Another woman turning tricks for dope. The sister's got this kid. Gregory. He's fifteen. Young as he is, the boy's already had a taste of the gangster life. More than a taste really.

Chapter 10
Gregory

The kid's in a wheelchair. Last year he caught one in the back meant for the sixteen-year-old standing next to him. A corner boy, brazen and stupid enough to dip into the G-Pac he was working on the street.

For those of you who don't frequent the inner-city open-air drug bazaars, a "G-Pac" is a "re-up." Meaning it's the re-supply of drugs (usually plastic vials of single-dose heroin) given the corner drug boys to sell. It's a thousand dollars' worth (the "G") and it's in a package (the "Pac").

So, this stupid sixteen-year-old, who was unfortunately standing next to Gregory at the time, shooting the shit with him. Well, he stole some of the vials out of his G-Pac, wholesaled them to a rival gang, then told his street boss (an eighteen-year-old) that the package was light when he got it. Then the dummy goes out and buys a bunch of new hoodies, new Michael Jordan lace-ups. And sports them all on the job.

The shooter in the drive-by got confused. Shot the wrong boy. (They killed the other kid later. One to the head at close range after they dragged him out of his aunt's house, the old lady screaming for someone — anyone — to help. The neighbors leaving it be, lest a similar fate befall them.)

Gregory's now a paraplegic. But that's apparently not stopping him from doing his utmost to stay in the gangster life.

So, I'm in the first row of the visitors' gallery. The bailiff rises and calls the case. Then the jailers lead in this motley array of four or five underaged knuckleheads. The judge waits patiently while they're de-shackled and led to the row of chairs just behind defense counsel's table.

Looks like I'm the only retained lawyer here today.

The assistant DA is sitting at counsel table trying to speed-read the file, no doubt for the first time through. That's not unusual. These young lawyers can't keep up with the relentless traffic flow of those accused of crimes, both in adult criminal court and here too.

The judge waits patiently until the ADA has at least read enough to generally understand the charges. She looks up from her file and scans the row of now seated kids, all wearing prison orange. And of course, one of them is Gregory. In a wheelchair at the end of the row of seats. Prison orange jumpsuited like his pals.

The ADA is a slight mousey-looking white woman. Early thirties, I'd say. She's wearing a JoS. A. Bank knockoff version of a Brooks Brothers skirted business suit. Her hair needs a wash. From where I'm sitting in the first row I can smell the cigarette she quickly finished before coming in here. Her reading glasses keep slipping down her nose, forcing her to balance the file on her knee with one hand while readjusting her glasses with the other.

The judge is also white. Middle-aged. He's been on the family bench for a while. A soft, porky-looking guy. Never broke a sweat exercising a day in his life. His premature snow-white hair is seriously recessed on his pink, rounded scalp.

He looks at his watch. He's a kind man, but he too needs to ensure that this polluted stream of young offenders keeps flowing through the drainpipe of the court system. Else it gets backed up and clogs.

The judge clears his throat. Both the ADA and the assistant public defender rise.

"Counsel," the judge says. "Time's a-wasting. Can we begin?"

Before either lawyer can get a word out, bedlam breaks loose in the seats behind them.

"You punk-ass bitch," one of the kids shouts to another kid two seats away from him, then he lunges for the kid. Both of them now tumbling to the carpeted floor. Fists flying. Invectives growled.

The judge doesn't rap his gavel. This seems a common occurrence in here. He waits patiently for the jailers to separate the two boys. Both kids violently resisting, their legs kicking out in front of them. Both still shouting threats.

"Motherfucker."

"I'm gonna get you, bitch."

And so on.

The jailers cuff each kid's hands behind his back, then shove both in their seats. Each kid still deadeyeing the other.

When these two are older, they will learn how to kill their opponents more efficiently, with less drama. That is *if* they get older. The odds are unfortunately not in their favor. And, believe it or not, they too know this.

The other kids — including Gregory in his wheelchair at the end of the line of chairs — are snickering like they do when they're cutting up in class in junior high. Which they attend only sporadically.

Things settle down.

The assistant public defender remains standing at defense counsel's table. His body is turned so he can watch these boys, his clients, disgrace themselves. This guy's white too. Another baby lawyer. As bad suited as the ADA. He's a twenty-something, dandruffed, skinny guy; you can just about see his shoulder blades through his flaking suit jacket. I notice his sleeves are way too long. Is that really his suit?

So today there's a trifecta of whites for these black kids. Nothing sinister here, just the luck of the draw. I'm wondering though, will the grandmothers sitting behind me, the real line of parenting in most of Camden's down-and-out sections, see it that way too?

"Okay, let's go," the judge finally says. "What do we have here?" he asks the ADA.

We all listen to the charges as she addresses the court.

It seems that young master Gregory and his playmates would hang near the bus stop where the kids from the one charter school that has survived in inner-city Camden go at the end of the school day so they can transit back to their various neighborhoods.

This charter school has apparently been a noble experiment. Inner-city parents teaming up with the usual array of white folk dogooders wouldn't set foot on the streets where these kids and their parents live for love or money. But this charter school's working. The kids are actually learning. Liking it. Staying full term. Getting into colleges based as much on their grades and achievements as skin color and place of abode.

So Gregory and his mates wait at the bus stop. Then they rob these kids. Take whatever they've got. Gregory in his wheelchair is the one they shove the uncooperative boy or girl to. So he can hold them, their heads clenched in his lap while the others beat up on him or her, go through their knapsacks, their pockets. Threatening them. Telling them, You tell on us, this what you get. Pointing them again to Gregory who's showing the pistol he's got wedged in the side of the chair by his hip. It's only a starter pistol, but it does the trick.

The ADA finishes. Remains standing for the judge.

I can hear one of the grandmothers behind me, no doubt shaking her head. Clucking under her breath, murmuring, "Uhm, uhm,

uhm." Vocalizing her disappointment while at the same time trying to adhere to the courtroom's decorum.

"How many of these young gentlemen been here before?" the judge asks the ADA.

She scans the file, then looks back at the kids. Seems to me she actually recognizes one or two of them.

Back to the judge.

"All of them, Your Honor," she says.

"Okay," the judge says. "So there are no virgins here."

We all wait for the judge who's eyeballing the kids.

Then some woman in one of the back rows of the courtroom stands.

"He a good boy," the woman shouts to the judge.

Everyone in the courtroom turns to see who's said this.

"Don't you be hurtin' my baby none," the woman says.

She's all disheveled looking. Dope, speed coursing through her veins. High as a kite. Her unkempt Afro all over the place. She's a pretty woman, light skinned, thin. Nice features. But stoned to the gills. Weaving. Her focus going in out, in out.

Like I said, this judge is a kind man. He's been here, seen all this time and time again.

91

He lets the woman rant for a while. Doesn't stop her. Doesn't gavel and call for order. Everyone in the courtroom waits. The grandmother's stage-whispering her disapproval again.

It doesn't take long before the woman's finished. She retakes her seat. Slurring, "He a good boy's all I'm sayin'."

"All right," the judge says. Then to the assistant public defender, "Your office counsel to all these young gentlemen?"

I rise from the front row bench just behind the rail that separates the permitted public from the lawyers.

"Afternoon, Your Honor," I say.

The judge looks over at me.

"Why, Mr. Salerno," he says, smiling my way. "To what do we owe this unexpected honor? Don't see esteemed members of the private criminal defense bar round these parts too often."

Both the ADA and public defender swing around toward me. I give them a friendly nod.

"Has one of these young gentlemen before me come into an inherited fortune? Able to retain your expert professional services?" the judge asks.

Now, this sounds like a benign inquiry, but trust me, it's a dangerous question this judge has just asked me.

He wants to see if one of these kids has sufficient funds to retain an experienced criminal lawyer. One like me who is often in this courthouse on behalf of gangsters who have the easy cash comes from high-level drug dealing. The judge is probing to see if one of these tykes is maybe a little brother to one of the big guys out there on the streets. Something like that.

The judge is searching with his jovial inquiry. Is there a kid in this row seated before him behind the public defender who is more than he seems? Someone for whom there may be some law enforcement signifi-cance out of the ordinary for these street urchins? Someone who could be persuaded to give up his older brother or father in exchange for leniency? Someone whose own personal interest could be manipulated to get one of the big fish off the street and behind bars?

(Okay, you don't get "fish" off the "street," but you get the picture.)

So, I now need to disabuse the judge of what he's thinking. Last thing I want is for him to think young master Gregory is more than he is. Trust me, kids like that are less than they are. I simply need to convey this to the court.

93

I smile at the judge. Shake my head. Tell him, "No, Your Honor. Though I do wish my young client was a man of means. No luck there, I'm afraid," I add, still returning the judge's friendly smile.

I then point down to Tamara who's sitting beside me. Touch her arm so she knows to rise before the judge.

"Your Honor," I say. "This lady is Ms. Tamara Watson. She's a paralegal in our office. [Yeah, I know. I'm pushing the job description here a bit.] Gregory Watson . . ." Here I point the judge to the kid in the wheelchair. "Young Mr. Watson is this lady's nephew. Afraid I'm here as an act of charity, Your Honor," I tell him.

(I can feel Tamara stiffen just a bit at my use of the word "charity.")

"Pity," the judge says, now teasing me. "Thought maybe the law managed to snag someone with a line to the top for a change."

" 'Fraid not, Your Honor."

I gently indicate to Tamara she should retake her seat.

"Come on up and join us," the judge tells me.

So I walk to the rail, hold aside the thigh-high swinging door, walk into the well of the court, and sit next to the assistant public defender. He nods to me. There's enough dandruff on his shoulder to make a snow-ball.

"How you doin'," I whisper to him.

"Okay, back to business," the judge says. Then to the ADA, "Have we got a prepack-aged disposition here?"

Meaning has she already worked out some kind of plea agreement for these kids? Maybe a deferred guilty plea with each youngster spending some quality time at the adolescent cesspool called Junior Village, which is Camden's municipal answer to sleepaway boot camp for underaged thugs. It's common knowledge that over the years Junior Village has graduated some of New Jersey's most violent future adult offenders. (I think even Slippery Williams may have spent some juvie time there.)

The ADA looks over to the public de-fender. He rises.

"Nothing yet, Your Honor," he tells the court. "We're still working on it."

"Ah, a work in progress," the judge says, eyeing the two young combatants now lean-ing forward in their chairs since their hands are cuffed behind their backs.

Neither kid is paying attention to anything other than his sincere desire to have at the other kid. A chance they will likely soon get when this proceeding ends and the bunch of them are back in lockup.

"Counsel," the judge tells the ADA and public defender. "I do not want to have a full proceeding and bring those charter school kids in to this courthouse as witnesses. You're not gonna make me do that, are you?"

Both shrug, signaling they will try. But who knows?

"Mr. Salerno," the judge says. I rise.

"Your Honor?" I say.

"Perhaps you can be of some assistance here?"

I smile at both the ADA and the public defender. Then back to the judge.

"I'll do my best, Your Honor." I retake my seat.

The judge sighs. He's got to move this show along; else he won't make his way through his day's docket.

"What's the story on prehearing release for these gentlemen?" he asks the ADA. "Anyone here to take release responsibility for them?"

I stand.

The judge adds, "Other than Mr. Salerno and Miss . . ."

"Watson," I say.

"Miss Watson, right." Then to the ADA, "Any objection in releasing young Mr.

Watson here (the judge pointing to Gregory, who's eyeballing the two cuffed kids, hoping for some more action between them before they are all sent back to lockup) to the custody of his aunt?"

"No objection," the ADA tells the judge.

"So ordered," the judge says. Meaning Gregory will be processed, then released into Tamara's custody pending a final outcome of this case.

The judge searches the courtroom.

"Anyone else here for any of these kids?" he asks.

None of the grandmothers are. No one else either. Except the doped-up woman from the earlier outburst.

The judge looks back to her. She's out cold, having nodded off after her outburst. Took too much of her failing energy, I guess. The judge leaves her be. Even if she was awake and on her feet, no way is this judge going to release whichever kid is hers to the custody of an addict.

And whichever kid it is, doesn't let on that's his mama. No way is he going to do that.

"All right, then," the judge says, nodding to the jailers. "Head 'em up and move 'em out," he tells them in his best cowboy accent.

The jailers do their job. The ADA rises to call the next case. I get up to leave.

"Nice to see you again, Mr. Salerno," the judge tells me, smiling.

"Likewise, Your Honor," I tell him as I start to move back to where Tamara's sitting so I can lead her from the courtroom and explain out in the hall just what taking custody of Gregory's going to mean for her.

Is she doing the right thing? Will Tamara have the strength of her convictions to right this wrongheaded kid, already a casualty of the thug street life?

Gregory. Bad as bad can be.

Tamara will try. A for effort.

But that Gregory.

Just wait. You'll see.

CHAPTER 11
SAMI GETS
A TASTE OF BIG LAW

The pretty secretary, all smiles, exquisitely dressed, walks into the ornate reception area where me, Mickie, Sami, and Rafat have been cooling our heels for about twenty minutes now.

Compared to Arty's place . . . What am I saying? There is no comparison between the reception area of the white-shoe, silk-stocking, fancy-schmancy Philadelphia law office where Gerald Rubino holds forth as a senior litigation partner, and Arty's bucket shop.

This reception is filled with taste. Nice furniture you'd expect to see in a bank president's office. Classy art on the walls. Nothing too showy, mind you. Just muted, stylistic oils of some nineteenth-century tiny jockeys posed atop the most beautiful, gigantic thoroughbreds ever galloped the earth. Stuff like that.

The receptionist behind the counter when

me and Mickie walked in direct from the elevators (Sami and Rafat were already there) could as easily have been a *Vogue* fashion model. A young twenty-something, thin, all smiles like the secretary now standing before us. This receptionist has a stylish, short hairdo, just the right amount of makeup. Directing her immediate attention to us. Cheerfully telling us, Good morning, how may I help you? Letting the phones ring for the five seconds or so it took to welcome us to this heaven-on-earth law firm.

"I'm so very sorry," the secretary standing in front of us is saying, outfitted in a dress costs more than a secretary's salary should afford. She's speaking more to Sami and Rafat than me and Mickie. She knows Sami's the one footing the bill for this firm's work on their behalf.

"But Mr. Rubino has been unexpectedly held up on a conference call on another matter."

Sami nods. No smiles though. He doesn't give a shit what Jerry Rubino's doing. Though he's impatient to get this show on the road. Meters are running. And he's the paymaster here. He doesn't say anything though. This place has got him intimidated, like it's supposed to.

"Can I offer you some coffee, tea?" she asks us all.

We decline. Then still all smiles she turns and walks back to the inner sanctum of the firm. I see Mickie conspicuously clocking her swiveling rear. Geeez. Can't take him anywhere.

So we wait. Rafat's glancing at one of the financial magazines that grace the lacquered coffee table in front of the sofa he and his dad are sitting on.

A couple of lawyers from some other firm walk into the reception area from the elevators. They are business-suited and necktied, sort of like me and Mickie, but you can see these two guys are uptowners. They tell the receptionist which lawyer they're here for. The receptionist places the call to let the lawyer's secretary know her guests have arrived. The two guys take a seat.

We get a quick-glance assessment from them.

They've got it. They make Sami and Rafat for the clients they are. Both wearing casual clothes, Saturday-morning-at-the-country-club stuff. Open-necked shirts, dress slacks.

And me and Mickie for the downtown lawyers we are.

Can see it on their faces.

Mickie does too.

"Hey, how you guys doin'?" he says to them in his best Camdenese, as they settle into their seats.

One guy ignores Mickie, picks up a magazine. The other one says only, "Hi."

"Lawyers, huh?" Mickie says to them.

What the fuck is he doing this for? I'm thinking.

So, okay, these two guys are from the big leagues. BFD. And their silent, flashpoint dismissal of us? Who gives a shit.

Mickie does. I can see it in his eyes.

But before he can get started, out comes the lawyer they have come here to see. She's got the look of a midlevel partner. Tall, not too attractive, and clearly all business.

We watch as she greets the now standing guys with a firm handshake. Thanks them for coming and then, without more, leads them from the reception area back to the working halls of the firm.

Mickie watches them go. He would have liked to tangle with them just a bit. All because of the look they gave us. That look saying, Inferior lawyers. Plain as day.

So we wait. Then Gerald Rubino himself comes out. His pace is just a touch quickened. You know, like the moment he got off the phone he dashed out here to meet his clients and us.

Somehow, I'm thinking, this is an act. Like he got off the phone, read the e-mails came in while he was on, brought in his secretary, and went over the rest of the day's calendar. Only then, when he had everything else in order, he comes out here, making it look like he hustled his ass fast as he could.

"Mr. Khan," he says, grinning familiarly to the now standing Sami, like they're old friends, vigorously shaking hands with him. (I'm wondering does Rubino feel the same total lack of grip I did when I shook with Sami? If he does, he doesn't let on. He shoots a glance at that lopsided hairline though.) Then Rubino turns to Rafat and shakes with him. So far, Rubino has not even thrown a glance in my or Mickie's direction.

"I'm so sorry to have kept you waiting," Rubino tells Sami. Shrugging, letting him know, something completely unexpected and important. Otherwise he would have been out here long before now.

Sami doesn't respond. At least not verbally. But his face, body language's telling Rubino, Not a problem. Maybe he's intimidated by his surroundings, like I said he's supposed to be.

Then, finally, Rubino turns his attention to me and Mickie.

He shakes with Mickie first.

"Jerry Rubino," is all he says. Then not even waiting for Mickie to say his own name, or hi even, he disengages and does the same thing with me.

"Jerry Rubino," he tells me as we shake. Like maybe I didn't catch his name.

Then Jerry bids us all to follow him to the conference room he's reserved for our meeting.

We silently follow Jerry down one carpeted hallway, then another, Jerry greeting lawyers by name out of their offices as they hurry by us, and also some of the secretaries sitting behind their workstations as we pass.

We get to the conference room and Jerry motions us in ahead of him. Once inside we see there are three other lawyers in there, clearly waiting for us.

Sami takes this in. Here are now six lawyers, including me and Mickie. All with meters running.

He shoots Jerry a look. Jerry ignores it. Still graciously smiling at his new best friend, Jerry shuts the conference room door.

Jerry directs each of us to where we are to sit. He puts his lawyers on one side of the table. Me and Mickie on the other, each of us bookending Sami and Rafat. The seat directly opposite Sami he leaves vacant for himself. He takes it.

"Okay," he says. "Let's get started."

Just then there's a knock on the conference room door. A waiter in a white waist jacket, white shirt, and black bow tie enters the room. He's Hispanic, somehow older looking and more sun worn than he should be for this job. The man's completely silent, like the firm's administrative staff has instructed him. He's a nonperson in here. He's to (a) set up the refreshments, (b) not utter a single word, and (c) not look anywhere near the table where we are all now seated.

Jerry points to the waiter and his cart as the guy starts laying out coffee dispensers, small silver containers of milk, sugar and Sweet 'N Low, a plate of Danish pastries, bagels. Even a platter of lox.

"Gentlemen, there's coffee," Jerry tells us with casual understatement, pointing to the horns of plenty being laid out on the counter. "Help yourselves."

I take a sideways peek at Sami.

Now, you know this law firm hasn't decided to feed us out of simple courtesy and good manners. Every packet of Sweet 'N Low, every fucking bagel and slice of lox will find its way onto Sami's bill. With a markup on cost, no doubt embedded in the "expenses incurred on behalf of client" portion. The item will probably read, "Meeting refreshments." You know, like the way the FBI does with its inventory of items seized during their searches ("Misc. papers").

Sami's not liking this. Not the cornucopia of delicacies quickly turning to room temperature over on the counter. Not the three lawyers beside Jerry, pens at the ready, waiting for the big man to get this show on the road.

Me and Mickie don't learn until much later that when Sami came here for his first meeting with Jerry Rubino, to formally hire him, the only people in this very same conference room were Sami, Rafat, and Jerry. Jerry did the initial conference all by his lonesome. No other firm lawyers in the room then. No food and drinks. Jerry lightly mentioning to Sami that he and perhaps some of his "colleagues from time to time" would be in on the case.

The other thing we later learned is that when Sami agreed to hire Jerry, impressed, thinking this guy's the real deal — the kind of big-shot lawyer who might actually extricate him and his son from the shit storm of trouble they're in — well, he agreed to pay Jerry a retainer of $500,000.

That's right. $500,000. (And I thought Mickie was high at $50,000.)

Jerry told Sami that a third was due within ten days of the initial meeting. A third ten days later. And the final third ten days after that. Jerry explained that charges would be by the hour, deducted against the retainer as they're logged. Assuring Sami that any of the retainer not eaten up by hourly rates and costs would be refunded by the firm at the end of the case. But telling Sami, This is quite a serious case. It's gonna take some serious work to get the right result.

Translation? Don't be looking for some fat payback of any portion of your retainer when this is all over. Sure as day follows night, the balance on your retainer at the end of the case will be zero. If anything, you're gonna owe more before this thing ends. You're gonna need to supplement the retainer with more money if you want me to continue as your lawyer to the end.

Jerry claimed he wished his firm's hourly rates for its lawyers and paralegals weren't so awfully high. Shrugging his shoulders. Letting Sami and Rafat know, it was up to him alone? He'd be more than happy to charge less. Just to be able to render assistance to these two fellow travelers stuck in the emergency lane of the world's highway of distress. But, hey, what can you do? Business is business. Meaning, you want the best? Then you gotta pay through the nose for it.

Sami's no dummy. He knows he and his son are neck deep in shark-infested waters. But $500,000?

He tried haggling with Jerry, saw Jerry glance at his watch, like maybe he's made a mistake sitting in here all by his lonesome with these two bumpkins. Then quickly Sami tells Jerry, Okay. But can I have twenty days for the first third? No, Jerry tells him. But you can for the second third. Making it clear that Sami doesn't get another minute of Jerry's time until there's some serious cash on the table.

So, Sami's looking over to the counter with the drinks and food. His appetite — not to mention his saliva — gone. He waves refreshments off. Rafat takes his cue from Dad as Jerry's other lawyers make a beeline for the grub. Hey, a free breakfast is a free breakfast.

Me and Mickie decline Jerry's kind offer.

We wait until Jerry's kids are settled. Once seated, he introduces them.

"This is Robin," Jerry tells Sami and Rafat, pointing to the chubby third-year associate who has more bagel in her mouth

than I would have thought she could manage on the first bite. Since her mouth's full
and she can't get even "Hi" out, she simply
wiggles the fingers of her left hand, since
that's currently the one that doesn't have
any food in a death grip.

"Seth," Jerry says, pointing to Seth.

This kid's a bit older than Robin, probably a seventh- or eighth-year associate. The
boy's likely poised for partnership consider-
ation. He looks like death warmed over.
He's Ichabod Crane in a business suit. Eight
years of toiling in the bowels of this law
firm. Hour upon hour upon hour. No sleep
for years. No life. Work, work, work. If
there's any blood left in his veins, it's only
trickling through his corpse-white skin. This
guy's so pale he's virtually translucent.

"And finally Alistair," Jerry says pointing
to the third Mouseketeer.

Alistair's got the look of someone who's
not only already made junior partner, but
made it in record time. Because this good-
looking kid is just so very smart. Always has
been. Best schools. Played Rugby. Tennis.
You can see just by the way this kid is sitting here, nibbling some of the fruit which
was also on the waiter's cart, that he sees
himself as the next Jerry Rubino.

And of course, there's Jerry Rubino. Who

has done a first-rate job of completely ignoring me and Mickie. We're the two elephants in the room. A couple of street crime, small-time lawyers Sami's brought in on Slippery Williams's strong recommendation. Jerry Rubino and his crew are clearly displaying that we are going to be as useless as tits on a bull.

Me and Mickie don't know Jerry, except by professional reputation. The guy's a star. But our boy's a chameleon.

Here's what we learned.

Born Brooklyn, New York, to parents off the boat from Italy just like me and Mickie's. Born Giovanni Rubino. Yeah, but unlike us he drank the WASP Kool-Aid in one big gulp. At Princeton he legally changes his name to Gerald. Keeps Rubino though. His transformation takes a little more time to be completed. So, over time this guy dumps any mannerisms, cultural ties, what have you to anything even remotely Pisan. Like he's embarrassed, maybe even disdainful of where he comes from.

Jerry's about our age. Better tailored, better all-around appearance. Average height. Prematurely gray hair in an understated haircut costing him $100 every two weeks or my name's not Salvatore. Gym body. His facial features are sharp, nose straight and not the least bit "Roman." Eyes sky blue. So this guy's family hails from somewhere up north, far from Sicily. Jerry doesn't have a hint of the North Africa sometimes creeps into the genes of folks from the lower part of the Italian boot.

He's sporting an expensive watch. Nothing flashy. Some leather-strapped Swiss make that's French unpronounceable. Dark blue suit, crisp white French-cuffed shirt, powder blue solid silk tie. White linen folded square pocket hanky.

Everything about this guy says success, smarts, class.

I can't see them at the moment, since we're all seated at the conference room table, but I later notice that Jerry's sporting the same "Eyetalian" expensive slip-ons Mickie's so fond of. Would seeing this now change my opinion that this guy has bid his heritage goodbye like an unmoored dinghy slowly drifting off to the open sea?

Nope.

"Okay," Jerry says again, rubbing his hands together like he simply can't wait to get his teeth into the fascinating legal problem our boys Sami and Rafat have brought him.

He smiles at Sami, real personal, like the two of them are the top dogs in this room, a couple of bonding buddies. (Truth is, Sami wasn't a big, fee-paying client? Jerry wouldn't piss on him if he was on fire.)

"Now, we have given some considerable thought to this case," he tells Sami, with a nice full glance at Rafat. To me and Mickie, nothing. We are still invisible.

Jerry nods meaningfully to the young lawyers on his side of the table. Robin and Seth are finishing up their chow. They know enough not to have their mouths full, chewing away when Jerry Rubino starts pontificating, like he's about to do. Alistair's been in the game all along, quietly watching, no doubt making mental notes how Jerry Rubino does what he does. For when it's his turn to be running the lawyer-client dog and pony show.

Then Jerry lays it out for Sami and Rafat.

CHAPTER 12
JERRY RUBINO'S BIG PLAN

While Jerry's speaking Rafat remains stone-cold still. He's had the same worried look on his face ever since me and Mickie first met with him. I think I'm getting it. Whatever it is Sami's done, his son may be along for the ride. But I'm guessing it's more from filial loyalty than any kind of desire to actively participate in what Sami's been up to.

Sami's also listening intently as Jerry lays out his plan of attack in the case. It looks to me like he's not really understanding much of anything of what Jerry's saying. The details of this legal game plan are completely lost on him. What Sami is picking up though is the tone of confidence cut into Jerry's words like an expert diamond engraver's chisel into a precious stone.

Out of the corner of my eye I'm watching Sami, reading his mind off his eyes. Okay, he's telling himself, this lawyer is costing me a fucking arm and a leg. Yeah, sure I can make it up if he can work the miracle I need. But the guy has a gun to my head. Emptying my pockets. What can I do?

And what is Jerry doing? What exactly is he telling his two clients, each sitting across from him, each in their own world, as they quietly listen?

Mickie gets it. Me too.

What we all are listening to is Big Law 101.

Here's Jerry's plan in a nutshell.

First, he and his team will comb every facet of the case. Both legally and factually. Find any conceivable discrepancy that might even arguably exist between what the prosecutors will want to allege and what actually happened. It will be noted.

For the legal stuff, a list of issues will be created that can be researched by a team of lawyers. (There are no doubt several other junior lawyers stuck in the library at this very moment in time, hitting the books, reading their laptop screens tuned in to the legal research sites. Sami and Rafat won't ever meet them. Won't even see them. They will just be more names on the bill with a listing of hours logged next to them.)

Legal memos by the score will be written. Then passed from junior lawyers to midlevel lawyers to more senior lawyers for rewrites, then back again to the juniors for further input.

Senior lawyers with different specialties, like obscure tax issues, will be consulted, seeking their off-the-cuff opinions of this or that. Fifteen-minute conversations will be logged as "Conference — one hour."

Jerry and his boys and girls will amass these reams of legal issues and factual quibbles. No stone will be left unturned. Every conceivable legal challenge, no matter how iffy, will be researched and written up. Wherever any part of the fact pattern surrounding the operation of Sami's business and internal bookkeeping practices can be interpreted more than one way, no matter how stretched that other way, it too will be analyzed and written up.

When all that's well under way, Jerry will set a meeting with the federal prosecutors. He will purposely attend without his clients, but with an eye-popping show of firm power strength by having a too-large number of his junior lawyers assigned to the case in attendance. Not only Robin, Seth, and Alistair, but a selection of those down in the firm's dungeon they call the law library where they day and night slave away.

He will so crowd the small, government-issue, modestly furnished conference room in the federal building, that some of his young lawyers will need to sit at the same side of the table as the one or two prosecutors in attendance. And the one FBI agent, there for moral support.

And then Jerry will hold court. He will tell the prosecutors (ignoring the FBI agent like he's doing me and Mickie) that his clients are the victims of some gross misunderstanding. They are, in fact, pure as the driven snow. Vestal white as the angels of the Good Book.

Everyone in the room will know that Jerry's windup is pure, unadulterated horseshit.

Ah, but the punch line is on its way.

Jerry will then spend way too long, maybe more than thirty minutes, without permitting any interruption from the other side. (Big dogs like Jerry can command that kind of begrudging respect — even in the prosecutors' offices.)

He will then catalogue every factual dispute his juniors have come up with so far. List every legal issue; every even arguable infirmity that he will tell the two young assistant United States attorneys will be the ruin, the absolute death knell of their case.

And his point? What all this means?

Jerry is signaling the Feds that if they really want his clients' scalps, well, he and his team will lay a fucking mountain of legal paper on them. Then will make them slog through tropical jungles of work thick with the foliage of factual disputes and legal motions requiring hours of toil. These young federal prosecutors might as well give whatever other cases they're handling to others in their office. Tell their spouses and little kids not to expect them home for dinner. Not even for that good night kiss.

But, if they want out of this nuclear wasteland Jerry's predicting, all they've got to do is offer up some lesser charge plea bargain. Something that gets Jerry's clients off the hook. Maybe a guilty plea to some minor tax offense. Some misdemeanor. With a modest fine and probation.

The prosecutors will need to turn a blind eye to the mountain of merchandise sold but never reported for sales tax purposes, the seriously underreported income Sami and Rafat have listed on their own tax returns. Instead, the prosecutors will let each plead guilty to the income tax version of spitting on the sidewalk. Permit Sami and Rafat to fess up to some minor clerical error on their returns. Something they can later claim their careless accountant did, but for which they will take the blame (if you can call it that) simply to get these misdirected prosecutors off their back. That way they can resume what they do best: provide New Jersey's wonderful residents with the lowest possible prices for the highest-quality electronic products. Case closed.

Or possibly — just possibly — Jerry will signal, he might consider a four to six month prison sentence served in some low-risk facility. A place without cells. A dormitory facility with badminton and a driving range. ("Club Fed," those places are called.)

This is Big Law 101. And know what?

It works.

Not all the time. But what does work all the time?

Jerry Rubino does not as a rule actually try cases. He pleads them out. Can he try a case to a jury if he has to? Yeah, though by now he's probably a little rusty since he stays away from the courtroom as much as he can.

Jerry knows full well that the economics of Big Law make actually going to court unprofitable. Takes up way too much of his time. Day in and day out in court. He can't be schmoozing up new clients. Will actually have to work day and night like he did when he was a young associate or junior partner, slugging his way up the law firm ladder.

Nope. The real money's in the prep work. Laid off on his team of junior lawyers clocking billable hours like a high-speed Lamborghini roaring down the open road.

And nine times out of ten, if not ten out of ten, the clients who come to him are guilty. So, he goes to court. Tries to scrape enough rust off himself to connect (reconnect?) with the judge and jury. At the end of the case, the jurors hand his client a guilty verdict. The judge sends the defendant away to prison forever and a day. That gets in the papers. Then guess who stops getting the big case referrals? The big army of lawyers working — and billing — day and night? The big dog, big firm partner's income?

Nope, for guys like Jerry, actually going to court, taking a shot with the jury for an acquittal? For him it's a sucker's game.

Instead, Jerry has his lawyers scorch the earth. He signals the prosecutors: life as they know it will be over for a good chunk of their young lives should they choose to actually go forward with this case.

And sometimes lawyers like Jerry will so spook the prosecutors that they will start to cut corners, do things under pressure they need to make their case, things a private attorney would get disbarred for. Then Jerry's got them another way. He catches them red-handed. Maybe holding back a document they are required to produce to the defense that might support Jerry's case. Or pressuring a witness into making his story sound better than it really is.

If that happens, the facts of the case disappear behind a curtain. Center stage is Jerry's motion to dismiss all charges because of prosecutorial misconduct. Case goes away. It happens. Trust me, it does.

Jerry's winding down. A self-satisfied look on his face. Letting Sami know, everything's under control. Your money's being well spent.

I see Jerry peek at his beautiful watch. Time's up. He's got some other unfortunate soul or corporation on the brink of ruin that needs some hand-holding.

"Okay, then," Jerry says to Sami.

The junior lawyers start making leaving noises. Snapping pens shut. Flipping notepads closed.

Mickie gives me a look down the side of the table.

This sure isn't how me and him do this.

No army of young lawyers for us. Just me and him.

Yeah, we file motions. Stuff like that. But that's not where our action's at. Me and Mickie are go-to-court lawyers. We are in one courtroom or another most days of each week.

If a prosecution witness has a weakness, then chances are either me or Mickie are going to see it during our cross-examination of him or her. We will bring it out clear as crystal for the jury. If the prosecution has fucked up in some other way, we will sooner or later see it during the trial. Then we will hammer it home. Make sure the jurors get it.

You hire us, you don't get hour upon hour of research and beautifully written briefs. Chances are you don't get a plea bargain. At least not one based on megahours of make-work designed to so overburden the other side they say uncle. For us you don't pay the really big bucks.

But know what? Even if you're guilty as original sin, if there's a way of creating reasonable doubt in the minds of the jury, you got a real good shot at getting acquitted using us.

So, Mickie's giving me that look. Letting me know, ain't this something.

It's just not our way. Not our thing. We're in it for the hard acquittal.

Everyone's up on their feet now. Jerry's come around the other side of the table. He's got his arm around Sami. (I see Jerry take a quick glance at Sami's lopsided toupee.) He's letting Sami know, it's all in good hands here. Try and relax (and keep paying).

We are being herded out of the conference room. Jerry shoots me and Mickie only a brief nod. Not even a handshake goodbye this time.

Sami, Rafat, me, and Mickie are now in the elevator, heading back down to the lobby. Sami keeps his own counsel. There isn't going to be any, What do you guys think? Nope, Sami's withdrawn deep into Sami. Rafat's almost too worried-looking for words.

So we all ride down in silence.

So, which way is better? Big Law 101? Or me and Mickie giving it our best experienced shot in court?

Jerry's good, no doubt about it. But so are we. Okay, without the polish. But trust me, we are.

Good question.

Guys like Slippery choose us. Guys like Sami could go either way.

Oh, and by the way. I forgot to tell you. Those two jewel thieves? The ones being tried for murder? The one Mickie was appointed to defend? Acquitted. So was the other one. Jury was out less than two hours.

There you go.

CHAPTER 13
ARTY GOES BYE-BYE

Mickie and me no sooner get back from Jerry Rubino's law offices, we walk into the Bernstein, Smulkin, reception area, the chubby girl behind the desk is off the phone for a change, urgently trying to tell us something.

Saying to us, "Arty, Arty." Pointing at the hallway. Jabbing her finger, that way. That way.

As me and Mickie turn the corner leads to where our offices are at, we hear Arty.

He's not happy, screaming at someone, "Get your fucking hands off me."

Down the far end of the hallway we see Arty struggling with two guys in bad suits. They have just handcuffed him, arms forced behind his back. Arty's resisting.

Me and Mickie watch. We make the two guys pretty easily. FBI agents. If they're doing what they're doing then there's an arrest warrant tucked into one of those suit jackets.

Arty's struggling, making a bad situation only worse. His hairdo's quickly losing its sculpted shape as he futilely tries to pull himself free from these guys. One of his scales of justice braces is coming undone, slipping down his shoulder. He's having a fit.

Arty is too occupied to see Mickie and me.

"I'm gonna fucking sue you both for every fucking penny you're fucking worth," Arty screams at the agents, his face turning candy apple red, as he throws his shoulders first this way then that. (Like Chink did. Remember?) Both agents firmly gripping Arty's arms.

That's good, Arty, I'm thinking. Threaten the FBI. Good thinking.

Then Arty looks down the hallway. Sees us.

Me and Mickie notice Tamara poking her head out from her cubby office, watching all this. She sees me and Mickie. Rolls her eyes. She too sees that what Arty's up to is stupid as hell.

Arty shouts to me and Mickie, "Get these motherfuckers off me." Then he turns to the agents.

"Those are my lawyers," Arty screams at

the agents, spraying saliva in their faces. "Now you gonna be in for some deep shit tsoris [Yiddish for "trouble," rhymes with "Horace"]. You fucking assholes."

We see the agents look down the hallway at us. Mickie and me don't move. The agents have really been agitated by Arty. They're riled. If they have a warrant for Arty there's nothing much we can do to help him until he's in court for an initial appearance.

Still, idiot that Arty is, he is still our client. Mickie tries to calm things down.

He takes a step toward them, starts to tell the agents that maybe if they let us speak to Arty, we can settle him down. But it's too late for that. These two guys are way too pissed off at having to keep a firm hold on cuffed, struggling Arty, all the while he keeps hurling nasty insults and threats at them.

"Step back, sir," the agent holding on to Arty's left arm tells him.

These guys are cops. Federal cops, but cops. They know that things can quickly turn dangerous for them in situations like this when the arrestee is out of control. Mickie and me have been there, back when we wore blue.

"I said step back, sir," the agent tells Mickie again.

"Sure, okay," Mickie tells the agent. "But listen," he tries to say, holding up palms, placating.

But Arty isn't going to leave it alone.

"These guys," he says, shoving his head in our direction. "They will fuck you six ways to Sunday when they're through with you," he tells the agents.

Good move.

We watch as the agent on Arty's left draws his service pistol. He doesn't point it at us. It's down at his side, but the message delivered is clear as can be.

Mickie and me back out to the reception area. (Tamara ducks her head back in her office and shuts the door.)

We watch as Arty is led kicking and screaming past us. The one agent keeps his eye on us, but can now see we won't be any trouble.

Doesn't take the agents long to lead the still struggling Arty through the reception area and out to where the elevators are past Arty's full-to-capacity waiting room. His bandaged, slung, and crutched clients watching in amazement as their lawyer is dragged away in cuffs.

Me and Mickie watch as they force Arty into the emergency stairwell so they can get him out of the building, into the waiting car, and then to a cell.

As the stairway door bangs shut behind them and Arty's screams and threats fade with each flight down, things begin to settle back to normal.

So, why was Arty arrested?

What a fucking dodo he is.

Despite what we told Arty when he tried to inveigle us into his scheme to illegally wiretap the lawyers working for him — when Mickie kept telling Arty no fucking way — well, our boy went ahead and did it anyway.

Brought in some private investigator. Some sleazeball used to be an Atlantic City cop. The guy did electronic surveillance for the force. Phones and home bugs both. Then the guy starts doing his own thing. In the nicer hotels on the Boardwalk. In cahoots with a hooker. She gets the johns in the room. He films and records them. Then together he and his hooker girlfriend blackmail them.

He gets kicked from the force. Gets indicted. Does time.

Now he's out and on his own. For hire. For guys like Arty.

So Arty pays the guy (after haggling down the price) to tap the phones of the lawyers working for him he suspects of having cut deals with the Feds. Not only their phones. Has their offices bugged too. All, like I said, illegal.

Turns out Arty was right about at least two of those lawyers. They had cut deals. Had agreed to cooperate and testify while they continued working there at the firm. So, the Feds — just like Arty feared — had a couple of insiders helping them. In order to help their own selves out. Since they were in on Arty's fraud, doing the same things he did. Bribing insurance adjusters and what-not.

So, Arty was right.

The thing is, these other shyster lawyers had already told the Feds enough about Arty's operations to provide them with sufficient probable cause to convince a judge to issue an order permitting a wiretap on Arty's phone.

And of course, it was that wiretap which resulted in their hearing Arty, on his phone, talking to his guy about his illegal wiretaps.

So, now Arty can be indicted for illegal electronic surveillance and obstructing justice, along with the underlying fraud charges he's being investigated for.

And when sentencing judges have defendants before them convicted of bad things like wiretapping and obstructing justice, they throw the book at them.

Especially if those defendants are lawyers. Like I said, Arty's a dodo.

CHAPTER 14
THE DA HUFFS AND PUFFS

Another conference room. This time it's in the Camden DA's beat-up municipal offices. Me and Mickie. Also Dumpy. The three of us were summoned here. The DA's secretary calling, saying, The DA wants you in his offices tomorrow at ten A.M. Can I tell him you'll be there?

Now, you'll remember when we were in state court and Judge Thurgood Rufus Brown ordered Slippery released on bail. Remember how the DA, all pissed off, stormed out of the courtroom?

Well, we're about to learn his mood hasn't improved any since then. And he's still yet to make a decision what to do about Slippery's retrial.

So, the DA calls. We come.

Out in the waiting area, Mickie and me are sitting there. The secretary ignores our "Good morning," telling us the DA's not ready yet. Dumpy walks in.

131

Off the bat, we can see Dumpy's in a foul mood. To me, I get, How you doin', Junne? For Mickie, he's got only a nod. He's too pissed off to toy with Mickie. Try and bait him like he does. He takes one of the two remaining seats.

The secretary tells him the DA's not ready yet. He ignores her. Man, is Dumpy in a funk.

Me and Mickie don't learn this until later, but yesterday, Dumpy made one more pitch to Slippery for him to replace us as lead lawyer. He was at Slippery's house.

Slippery put the wood to his ass.

"Listen, I got this, Slip," Dumpy's telling him. "You don't be needin' no others. Know what I'm sayin'?"

Slippery sitting in his Barcalounger, got it pushed all the way back. Slippery's bare feet, his electronic ankle bracelet just about in Dumpy's face, who's sitting in the chair from the dining alcove he pulled up. Dumpy in his lawyer suit, all fancied up like usual. Slippery in a terry cloth bathrobe, like he just got out of the shower. Only a pair of light blue bikini underpants. How Slippery dresses around the house these days.

"Yeah, Dump," Slippery tells him. "Yeah, I know what you sayin'."

Dumpy's no longer playing the race card

on us. Knows that won't work with Slippery. Not when it comes to me and Mickie, anyway. Now he's just hammering away at it. Telling Slippery how he's got his back, representing Slippery's lieutenants were indicted along with him.

Like I said earlier, Dumpy filed a motion for their release on bail after we sprung Slippery, Judge Brown giving Dumpy's clients tit for tat. Slippery's out on bail. He lets them out too. For them, doesn't even require electronic ankle bracelets, the judge telling the DA in court, This what you get until you make up your mind what you're gonna do with this case.

Dumpy showing his loyalty to Slippery. Carrying messages, doing Slippery's bidding for the kinds of things Slippery knows Mickie and me won't do. Telling Slippery you don't be needin' them two. You got me.

Yeah, but what Dumpy's missing is that, while Slippery will continue to use Dumpy like he does, he knows full well no lawyer should be doing shit like that. So, he doesn't respect Dumpy. And if he doesn't respect Dumpy, then Slippery won't completely trust him either. Slippery's got Dumpy on "need to know." No further.

"Okay, then," Dumpy's telling Slippery, trying not to show that the odor from

Slippery's bare feet is starting to get to him. (Slippery sticking his feet in Dumpy's face on purpose.)

"Okay, then, what?" Slippery says to Dumpy.

Dumpy's not sure where this is going. Not too sure what he should say next.

Slippery pushes on the arms of the Bar-calounger and snaps his body forward into the chair's sitting position.

He leans in close to Dumpy. His terry cloth robe open, Slippery's bony chest showing, his blue bikini shorts, his crotch bulge.

Tells him, "Now listen, motherfucker. I'm tired of this shit from you." He waits a beat, then adds, "You hear me on this?"

Dumpy's about to protest. He's leaning forward in the chair, his gut pressing against his two fastened suit buttons. It's hot in here. Dumpy's starting to sweat. The top of his squiggly-haired head's starting to gleam.

"Now, Slip—," is all he manages to get out when Slippery erupts.

"Don't be 'now, Slippin' ' me, mother-fucker. You do like I say you do. I don't wanna be hearin' no more shit about them two white boys. You be in the case what I say you be. You don't like that, well, we can deal with that."

Now Dumpy's scared. He's pushed it too far. Slippery Williams is not someone to trifle with.

So Dumpy starts shucking and jiving with Slippery. Saying things like, "Yeah, okay. I got you good, Slip. You the boss man, boss man." Holding his arms up in surrender. Trying his best to make a joke out of it. Slippery still staring at him. No ambiguity where he's at on this thing.

So, smiling and jiving Dumpy beats a retreat from Slippery's house. Soon as he's back out on the street his mood turns dark as night.

And now he's sitting here glumly along with me and Mickie. Waiting for DA Cahill. Dumpy's eyes mostly on Mickie. (The phrase here is, if looks could kill . . .)

The two ADAs were in court when we were in front of Judge Brown enter the DA's waiting room. They nod hello to us.

The secretary, seeing them, picks up the phone. Tells her boss, They're all here now.

So, it's them two we've been waiting on.

"You can go in now," she tells us all, cradling the phone, returning her attention to her keyboard and big-screen computer.

Once in, we take opposite sides of the conference table the DA has fitted in perpendicular to his desk. That way he can stay seated behind his desk and at the same time be at the head of the conference table.

No cordialities from the DA. He hates lawyers like us. We try and spring the bad guys. This DA can't separate the lawyering from the criminaling.

The DA's in shirtsleeves, tie down. The two assistants dressed like they're appearing in court.

The two ADAs wait, like we do. One is an Asian woman. Korean-American, I'm thinking. Very serious attitude. Straight, bobbed hairdo. No smiles from her. She's the junior of the two, so she didn't handle much at the trial. So I'm really not too sure how good she is. The other ADA is a young white guy. Good looking kid. He handled most of the trial. Did a shitty job.

"Okay, here's the deal," the DA tells us.

Me, Mickie, and Dumpy all exchange glances.

Deal?

But we don't say anything. We wait.

The DA points an accusing finger at me and Mickie.

"Your client," he says, "will plead guilty to two felony counts of possession with intent to distribute. The state will agree to recommend to the court that he gets credit for time served and does an additional five years."

Then the DA turns to Dumpy.

"For your scumbags," he says to Dumpy. "The deal of the century. If Slippery Williams takes the deal I'm giving him, then I will let your boys off with a plea to one felony count of conspiracy to distribute. I will recommend not more than two years' confinement for each."

Then the DA gets this weird little shit-eating grin on his face. Tells Dumpy, "If Mr. Williams decides not to take his deal, then here's what I'll do for your dickhead clients."

Now we see the DA grinning at his two assistants. Like he's telling them, Watch this. See how fucking clever your boss is. The DA loosens his tie another half inch. He's showing us he's got this covered. We're in for it now.

"What I'll do is this," he tells Dumpy.

"They agree to testify against Slippery Williams. Appear as prosecution witnesses at the retrial. They plead guilty to one count of possession. I will recommend no more than one year in the slammer. Then they're out. Back on the street. And with Slippery by then convicted by the jury with their help. And how long you think he's gonna be

137

locked up? Doing the hardest of hard time. Oh, let's see," he says, leaning back in his seat.

We wait. The DA is having too good a time with this. Like he's the cat finally got the fucking mouse.

"Let's see," the DA says, rubbing his chin like he's struggling to come up with a number. "Life," he then says, leaning forward, elbows on the desk, now pointing again at me and Mickie. You know, like we're the ones gonna do the time. "Life with no possibility of parole."

So, the DA's game? Me and Mickie have no trouble seeing it. My guess is Dumpy does too.

The DA's laying some weight on Slippery.

He pleads guilty, does five years. Well, then his boys get off way lighter than they will if Slippery forces the case, and them, to retrial and they all get convicted. Then Slippery probably does get enough time for all intents and purposes to amount to a life sentence. Like maybe twenty-five years without the possibility of parole. Maybe even more. And of course, Dumpy's clients will do some major time in the slammer themselves.

So, if Slippery nixes the deal? Well, the DA's probably thinking, Dumpy's clients will get all pissed off on account of they're now looking at some heavy time they wouldn't have to do if Slippery were to look out for his boys and cop to the five for himself.

Ah, but there's more. The DA's handing Dumpy Brown just what he needs, though the DA doesn't know it.

If Slippery turns down the deal and Dumpy gets his clients to agree to testify against Slippery? Well then, they not only get off real light, Dumpy will ensure Slippery's conviction and see to it that he's put away for so long he's out of the game. Then maybe one of Dumpy's clients steps up to the plate. Or some other enterprising street guy takes over Slippery's corners, his distribution network. All of it.

Dumpy's the man did the deal. The street will have spoken. He's likely to wind up top-dog lawyer. And Dumpy gets some nice payback on Slippery. Disrespecting him as he did.

This is manna from heaven for Dumpy. Just what the doctor ordered.

And the DA gets his conviction, without the risk of another hung jury, or an acquittal after a retrial.

Yeah, but.

Neither me, Mickie, nor Dumpy have lost

sight of the fact that the DA still hasn't said he will actually retry the case if he has to. That's still out there, like a whispered secret.

The DA's pushing hard here for a plea bargain. We take it? Case goes away. He offers us a deal, puts some weight on Slippery. Offers Slippery's clients a sweeter deal if Slippery makes them face another jury.

The DA's dealt us our cards.

He's waiting on us. The room is tight with the tension of whether we'll fold or not. He's eyeing first me and Mickie. Then Dumpy. He's given Dumpy the ace in the hole.

Dumpy may have been chastised by Slippery. And I'm certain Dumpy understands full well how pretty he could be sitting here if he takes the DA's deal.

Say what you will about Dumpy. The way he feels about me and Mickie. Mostly Mickie. And the way Slippery treated him. Still, Dumpy is a lawyer. Like me and Mickie are lawyers. Dumpy will play his cards like the professional he is. Nothing will get in the way of that.

The DA's bluffing. He hasn't contacted Judge Brown's chambers, scheduled the case for retrial. Got a firm date for jury selection.

He offers a deal after that? Could be a

different situation. Still, Dumpy's not so easily going to sell Slippery down the river. A move like that's bad for your health. My guess is that Slippery's boys, charged along with him in the case, probably share that sentiment.

Dumpy sucks his teeth. Rubs his hand over his face like he's truly considering how many chips to throw into the pot. Then he gets his own shit-eating grin on. Turns to the DA waiting behind his big fat desk.

"Here's the thing," he tells the DA. "The gentlemen I represent. Well, they just don't know nothin' 'bout no drug dealing. Know what I'm sayin'?" Turning to the DA's two assistants, who are watching this, stiff as cigar store Indians. Telling them, then the DA, "I mean, they just ain't got nothin' to help y'all with."

Dumpy sniffs the air. Like he's detected something foul in here. Keeps grinning at the DA, shaking his head. Letting the DA know, sure like to help. Wish I could.

The DA is seething, his usually sallow, grim face reddening. He keeps shooting looks, back and forth, back and forth, to his cigar store assistants, to me and Mickie, to Dumpy, who's still smiling up a storm. Happy as a pig in shit to be here. And just sorry as sorry can be he can't help the DA.

This meeting has come to an end. Watching the DA, I'm thinking what he'd like to do right now is scream at us. Order us the fuck out of his office.

"Is there anything else we can do for you?" Dumpy asks the DA with a tone of solicitousness about as sincere as the Hertz counterman after you complain about the compact he gives when you ordered mid-sized.

The DA simply shakes his head no.

In the ensuing silence, me, Mickie, and Dumpy get up and leave.

Once out in the hall, Dumpy turns to the two of us.

"Motherfuckers," he says, his pronouncement on the DA and his assistants. Then he simply abandons us. Turns and walks toward the elevator.

Still, got to hand it to Dumpy. He steps up when he needs to. That's what lawyering's about.

At least our kind.

I can see Mickie shares that sentiment.

After a while we too head down the hall to the elevators.

CHAPTER 15
MONEY IS MONEY

Sami Khan stands by and observes. Like he has always done.

His son is here too. Rafat prefers to stay away. Really doesn't want to see it. Doesn't want to think about it.

But he's here today. Sami can see how unhappy he is. How worried. He knows Rafat is an obedient son. It is the tradition of their culture. Whether in India or here. It doesn't matter. Rafat will do as he is told.

They are in a smallish warehouse down the block from the main Sami's Electronics distribution center. In an industrial park off the interstate. There is no sign outside. The rent is paid through a straw corporation. Neither Sami's nor anyone else's name close to him appears on the papers.

Slippery's boys have delivered this week's cash. They don't stay. Don't watch as the money is counted out, verified. Their instructions from Slippery are clear. Deliver the cash. Leave. No need to stay. No one is going to short Slippery.

Sami personally takes receipt. He knows the lieutenants who come here. Though he never really exchanges pleasantries with them. The talk is only of business. To him they are darkie thugs. Like the Untouchables from the streets of New Delhi. He takes delivery. Hears what they've got. Hears how much they think they will bring next time. Nods okay. Stands by as they leave.

Then he watches, as his few trusted employees do what they do.

Ever since Slippery Williams made his way to the top of the heap, ever since the cash coming in from his operations grew to the hefty amounts come in day in day out. Year in year out. Ever since then, Slippery has had the need to turn the tens, twenties, fifties and so on from drug sales, dirty money, into usable funds.

His old friend and partner Sami has provided one of the principal outlets for laundering Slippery's drug profits. (Me and Mickie are clueless about this until way later.)

Years ago, Slippery had come to see Sami. They had sat in Sami's office, Slippery congratulating Sami on his success. Rafat was in that day, but Sami had told him no need for him to join the meeting. Sami telling his son, no worries, boy, I know you are busy with other things.

Slippery didn't take long to get to the point. He explained how his business enterprise had also grown to a very substantial level. Had explained how cash from drug sales had come in at unprecedented levels, small bills upon small bills — had joked how it was a pity he too couldn't effectuate credit card sales like Sami did with much of his merchandise. Sami nodding understanding to Slippery, his nimble mind already racing toward what Slippery was about to propose. Slippery saying, if Sami could assist on a regular basis in absorbing some of this cash, clean it up by converting it into a form of usable value, well, it would be a win-win situation for them both. Slippery letting Sami know, he would happily pay a handsome fee for the service. Sami still nodding, then assuring Slippery he knew just the way.

It's been an amazingly simple and effective operation. One that cleans up Slippery's money into something noncash. Legitimate appearing. And it's done the same for the money Sami has been skimming from his business in the form of cash sales never

145

reported for tax purposes. Though Sami's sums are far smaller than Slippery's.

Still, money is money.

Sami has been running what his records show to be a charitable enterprise. He takes appliances either outdated by newer models or slightly defective. Appliances which could rightfully be returned to the various manufacturers Sami buys from. Instead, he keeps them, getting certain merchandise credits for future orders from these oh-so-grateful companies.

Then Sami sends these appliances, as well as others that perhaps don't move on the floors of his various stores throughout the state, sends them via cargo ship consignment to India. Sometimes for sale at bargain basement prices in areas where appliances such as these are simply hard to come by. Making sure that they will work on the different 240-volt AC electric current by providing cheap power adapters. Most he "donates" as a charitable act for those unfortunate enough not to have had the opportunity as he has to walk America's paved-with-gold streets.

Sami even takes a sizable charitable deduction for this pretend act of social conscience.

When the appliances arrive at the New

Delhi distribution center, after customs and other regulatory matters have been dealt with — usually with cash payments in plain white envelopes delivered to the most "helpful" officials — when night has fallen, then the machines are systematically taken apart so the cash bills secreted in them can be removed. Then they are reassembled and next day sent to their various destinations.

The money is then transported to a local bank that is all too happy to receive and deposit this cash — for a considerable fee — and see to it that the funds involved are then wire-transferred to one of several Cayman Islands banks and bank accounts.

Sami takes a fee from Slippery's cash, adds that to his own hoard of unreported cash sales and all that gets hidden in the appliance, along with Slippery's drug money, for the long ocean voyage.

Sami has stopped taking in unrecorded cash and credit card sales from all his outlets. Knows he needs to do that under the present circumstances. But this operation for Slippery will continue unabated. No one knows about it. Sami thinks his "charitable" acts will show him in a good light. Portray him as a good naturalized American citizen.

And the profit margin in untaxed cash fees

Slippery Williams pays for this laundering operation is simply too good to let go.

Sami takes his share of the money from the Cayman bank accounts in the form of bearer bonds. They are held offshore. Slippery's funds are fed into various offshore, interlocking straw corporations that invest in all kinds of businesses. Apartment complexes, commercial real estate ventures. Even the U.S. stock market. These investments throw off what appear to be honest profits. Slippery has little need for these funds today. They are mostly for tomorrow.

Sami will stay here until all of the cash from this delivery is packed away in the appliances that will make up the next India shipment.

Rafat can't take it anymore. He knows he must not ask his father for permission to go. Should stand here with him. Show himself to be strong, a worthy son for the task.

He stays as long as he can. Then turns and leaves.

Sami silently watches as Rafat goes. Then he turns his attention back to his few trusted employees and their task.

He knows he need not worry about Rafat. He is, after all, a loyal son. In America, yes.

But of a different culture. An obedient culture. ture.

So he doesn't worry.

CHAPTER 16
SLIPPERY'S HOUSE PARTY

Two days ago the DA dismissed all charges against Slippery and his crew. No press release. Just a dismissal filed with the court. (Like I said, for the DA that was the better play. Shitcan a losing case. Wait for a better one. That is, if he can catch Slippery. Still, the DA must be as unhappy as a blind man at a peep show.)

Same day as the dismissal was filed, two Camden County sheriff's deputies came by Slippery's house. Removed the electronic ankle bracelet. Told Slippery, far as they were concerned, he was still a scumbag. That they'd be keeping an eye on him. Get him yet.

Slippery thanked them for coming by. Wished them a nice day.

So, here Mickie and me are, at Slippery's house. For his get-out-of-jail-free celebration.

Got to hand it to Slippery. He knows how

to throw a party.

Me and Mickie aren't going to stay long. This is very definitely not our scene. Still, we are here.

Slippery could easily afford to have this soireé in any of the hotels or banquet halls in Camden, not to mention across the river in Philly. Like for instance the ballroom of the Four Seasons Hotel. But he has it at his house.

Much smarter. This way he can control who is here, also who is serving the drinks and whatnot. Keep out the undercover cops.

Slippery knows what kind of a scene it would be for the regular patrons of the Four Seasons seeing these pimped-up dudes and their whorey-looking babes coming in through the hotel's tasteful, ornate lobby. How the regular patrons and hotel guests would react once the drinking started in earnest, once the DJ cranked up his sound system to high frequency distortion levels. And of course, some of those observing there or near there snapping pictures. For the press. Also for the DA.

Slippery's dressed in something other than his terry cloth bathrobe for once. As he walks over to the foyer where me and Mickie are standing, having just arrived, he's smiling.

Slippery's such a slight man. He can't weigh more than 130 pounds. When he dresses, he dresses quietly, like his nature. Unlike many of those here, invited to celebrate because they're in the game, either working for Slippery's operation or in some noncompeting drug-related sideline. Outfitted to the nines in gaudy finery. Most of the men big guys, bruisers. The women endowed, all tits and asses. The place looking like a hip-hop video. Instead, Slippery's got on an expensive open-necked dark brown Italian designer shirt, lighter brown, perfectly creased slacks, and even lighter brown slip-ons.

"Yo," he says to me and Mickie, giving each of us the right-hand-to-left, upside-down clasping handshake, then quick one-armed hug, most people in his world give to friends.

"Yeah." He's smiling. Chuckling. Letting us know, me and Mickie did good. Played it right.

"How ya doin', Junne?" Slippery says.

I run my eyes past him to the crowd, all in the early stages of fueling up.

"Nice party," I say, as some buxom black babe in a skintight cocktail dress walks over, puts her arm around Mickie.

" 'Member me?" she asks Mickie.

He doesn't, but he's not about to say so.

The girl looks to Slippery, seeing is it all right if she's here with us. Slippery's in a good mood. He doesn't care.

"Come on, baby," she tells Mickie. "You ain't forgot me already, have you?"

Mickie just can't place her. She kisses him on the cheek, winks at Slippery, then leaves to rejoin the party in the living room.

Mickie smiles apologetically at Slippery. Shrugs, Hey, what can you do?

I'm wondering when she and Mickie did it. Because that's what it's got to be. How else would he and she come together?

"Come on in," Slippery tells us, motioning to one of his boys to lead us to the bar set up at the far end of the living room.

As the guy makes way for us through the crowd, me and Mickie get respectful nods of recognition from the gangsters here, friendly smiles from the women at their sides. But no one approaches us.

Me and Mickie are the lawyers. Slippery's lawyers. For that we get recognition. A certain kind of respect. It's got nothing to do with the fact that we are the only two white people in the room.

No, from these life-of-crime hard-edged men, we get a certain recognition. But we are not one of them. Our presence here is a testament to who and what Slippery is. Anyone we talk to will respond. It's just that none of these party guests will approach us, initiate a conversation.

Me and Mickie are on a different footing in the pecking order that regulates the drug-and-gangster set. We're going to make our appearance here, put down a few drinks, and leave before the party really starts, before this place erupts in booze, loud music, and generated heat.

Believe me, you don't want to be here when the real party starts.

So we get our drinks. No sooner do we have the first slug of scotch down, here's that voice.

"Well lookie here. If it ain't the White Shadow."

Me and Mickie turn to say hello to Dumpy Brown, standing before us, dressed to the nines himself. And, as Mickie and me have no trouble seeing, already sloshed.

Dumpy's also got a glass of whiskey in his hand. He takes a long pull, then holds out the glass as the woman beside him, also drunk, refills it from the bottle of Johnnie Walker Blue Label she's holding by the neck.

"Thank you, baby," Dumpy tells her, stumbling left, then right.

She smiles coyly at him, then us.

"Baby," Dumpy tells her. "Let me present my colleagues . . . my white motherfucking colleagues at the bar."

Dumpy's slurring his words. I can see he's got that look in his eyes. Dumpy's smiling; the booze he's already consumed has loosened him. Whatever inhibited rage he walked in here with has been drowned in 80 proof whiskey. Gone for the moment is that sour demeanor he gave me and Mickie when we were at the DA's office. After Slippery let him know what's what. And who's who.

"You boys be feelin' pretty damned good, huh?" he says.

"Yeah, sure, Dump," Mickie says, not wanting to get into it with him here at Slippery's house party.

Dumpy turns to the babe still at his side, who's also smiling up a storm but without a clue to what's been simmering between Dumpy and us.

"The White Shadow here," he tells her, off balance again, bumping into her hip, then regaining at least some footing. "And his boy, Snowflake," he says pointing to me. "They here prancing like their ofay shit don't smell. Know who it was in that DA office made this case go away?"

155

"No, who, baby?" she says.

I can't tell if she has any notion of what Dumpy's talking about. This girl is as fucking gone at the moment as Dumpy is.

"Weren't no motherfuckin' pale-faced whatchamacallits. Unh-uh," he says, shaking his head no. Pounding his chest with his left fist, the Johnnie Walker he's holding in the glass in his right splashing onto Slippery's expensive wall-to-wall.

"Who the lawyer called it?" he says to Mickie.

"You, Dump," Mickie says. "You the man."

Dumpy looks into Mickie's eyes. Trying to see if Mickie said that to him mockingly, or straight up. I can see Dumpy can't hold a focus. Anything could happen right about now.

Just then, Slippery comes over. He's giving Dumpy that look. The state Dumpy's in, it's anyone's guess if he's catching this or not. But whatever state he's in, he knows enough not to take on Slippery.

"My man," Dumpy clumsily says to Slippery, holding his hand up for the ritual shake and hug.

Slippery takes his hand, smiles at Dumpy. But no hug.

"How you doin', counselor?" he says to

Dumpy.

"Yeah, yeah. Good, Slip," Dumpy says, still weaving.

We are all standing there awkwardly. The girl's still grinning. Having the time of her life, completely oblivious to the undercurrent of tension we've got going here.

Then one of the bruisers brings over two more whiskeys for me and Mickie. Takes away our empty glasses.

"Yo, Mr. Dumpy Brown?" one of the other gangsters standing not far from us in his own small group says to Dumpy. "Y'all got a minute? We be needin' to axe you somethin'."

I look over to this small group of men and their women. I'm thinking Slippery has arranged this. Like to get Dumpy away from me and Mickie. Cool this down.

You see, although he too is a lawyer, Dumpy is approachable here. It's not because he's black. Nope. The reason is because Dumpy has allowed himself to be in the game. Taking messages back and forth between Slippery and his crew when Slippery was in jail. And then under house arrest. Probably doing other things too. Things no lawyer should do. No matter how careful or smart he is.

That puts him in the game. Makes him

approachable by these guys.

Dumpy stumbles over to where the guy and his pals are standing, the girl in tow.

Slippery smiles at us, tells us to have fun. Then leaves us alone.

Me and Mickie down our second scotches.

The guy must be on duty, watching us, because no sooner are our glasses drained, another two are placed in our hands.

So, me and Mickie stand around for a while longer, the whiskey taking effect. We see the groups standing here and there, some sitting around Slippery's furniture. Dumpy's now locked in conversation over to the side. Yukking it up. Me and Mickie forgotten at the moment.

The music's getting just a little louder, on its incremental way to blast off.

I notice Mickie looking at the woman came up to him in the entrance hall. He's trying, but he just can't place her. She's no longer interested in him, standing with some guy looks like an Afro Arnold Schwarzenegger, big face, chin and all, his muscle-bound arm around her, whispering something into her ear she's smiling about. But shaking her head no, uhn-uh. Letting the guy know, whatever he's suggesting's not going to happen tonight.

And then we leave. We thank Slippery for

the invite. Tell him we're off to something else. He doesn't expect us to stay. Tells us he'll be in touch. Then me and Mickie are outside in front of the house.

"I'm meeting Carla for dinner," Mickie tells me. "Wanna come?"

I don't. First of all, Mickie's already starting to bitch about her. She snores. She gives him shit about making his dinner, saying, I'm not your wife. (Italian men like Mickie have certain requirements. Cooking for your man is certainly one of them.)

Second, I really don't want to be the third in a twosome. Know what I mean? The odd man. The useless appendage?

"Naa," I tell Mickie. "I'm beat. Think I'll head on home."

"You sure?" Mickie says. He really will not mind if I accompany them to dinner. In some ways, I think he'd actually prefer me there with them.

"Yeah," I say.

So we part. Mickie goes to his car. Me to mine.

I remain at the curb for a minute as Mickie drives off.

Here I am alone. Again. The booze is affecting me. Easing my inhibitions.

At least that's my excuse. For doing what

I shouldn't be doing.

I pull from the curb and head for Philly.

CHAPTER 17
WHAT WAS I THINKING?

I shouldn't be here. I'm not doing this in Camden. Still. Philadelphia is close enough. I have spent most of my adult life avoiding this. At least around here.

I've taken a seat at the bar. Walked in and found the first free stool my eyes lit on. I haven't looked right nor left. Ordered a scotch on the rocks when the barman came over. Now I'm sitting here. My drink in front of me. Thinking, What the fuck am I thinking?

The place is called Bump. It's on Locust Street. At the corner of 13th. It's all modern, sort of blond-wood Danish looking.

And it's a gay bar.

Jesus H. Christ, I'm thinking. This is a bad idea. I shake my head.

"Don't need a penny for your thoughts," I hear a voice next to me say. I look up to the glass panel behind the bottles stacked on shelves at the rear of the bar. I see the face of the guy next to me reflected in the mirror. He's young-looking. Blond. Smiling at me. I turn toward him.

To say what? Leave me the fuck alone? You pervert?

I'm in a gay bar.

Earth to Junnie? Hello?

I let out some air. Shake my head again. This time to this guy.

"And?" I say.

"And you are most definitely not comfortable in here," he says.

Just then two Hispanic guys walk in. They see a friend, who's got the seat on the opposite side of the blond-haired guy. Another Hispanic guy. The three of them look like construction workers. They're wearing jeans and tight-fitting T-shirts. It's no longer warm enough these nights to go without a jacket. But they do. Makes them look more buff, I guess.

One of the guys who came in greets the guy sitting at the bar with a quick kiss on the mouth. I watch. The blond-haired guy is watching me watching them.

"Hola," the guy sitting at the bar says, smiling sweetly at the other two.

"Hola," the kisser says back.

"Salud," the other singsongs.

Then the three of them are off in some

conversation. Spanish words and sentences flying between them like twittering piano notes. Voices lisped. Eyebrows raised in mock delight. Eyes rolled. Can you believe it, they're saying to one another about whatever it is — more likely, I'm guessing, *whoever* it is — these guys are gossiping about.

If they notice me and Blondie watching it's of no concern to them.

I see one of the standing guys fold his arms over his chest. (And by the way, these three guys are really built. They're muscular. They have great chests. You know, in a gym guy, weight lifter's way. That's all I'm saying. Okay?)

Just what am I saying?

Oh boy.

Anyway, me and Blondie see the standing guy with folded arms look up to the heavens. He then says something that takes a lot of Spanish words. But he's making a point.

"Claro," the seated guy says, nodding in clear agreement.

"Magnifico," the other one says.

Now they are all giggling, touching one another's arms in gentle emphasis.

These three guys are having a good time. They're obviously friends. Are they really construction workers? I'm thinking. Yeah, and if so? What?

I decide to return to my scotch. Which I take down in one big gulp. I hold the empty glass toward the barman, signaling, Another over here, please.

"You should leave. Go home," I hear Blondie tell me.

Again I turn to him as another scotch is placed before me.

"What?" I say. Although I heard him.

"You should leave," the guy says. "You aren't ready for this."

Blondie is late thirties, maybe early forties. He's good looking. I'll give him that. His hair is longish. And straight, covering the sides of his face. From time to time his right hand flicks hair back from his forehead. When I watch him do this I don't consider it an affectation. Although he's seated he looks about my height. The guy's wearing jeans and a long-sleeved collarless sport jersey. He's pushed the sleeves up to just below his elbows. I can't help noticing the guy's strong forearms, matted with blond hair. I watch his hands. One cups his drink glass, the other lies comfortably beside it, palm down on the bar.

I am intrigued with this guy's arms and hands. Especially his hands. They're in-control hands. Self-assured hands. Really

164

nice hands.

Blondie sees me staring. I look up into his face. He's grinning. But in a quiet, non-mocking way. He's wearing a two-day stubble, which I can see is intentional, since he's taken care to shave the edges. It's a fashion statement.

He's got green eyes, a nose that doesn't overshadow his high cheekbones, or that smile he's giving me.

It's my turn to say something.

I can't think of anything.

I look into my drink. This time I gulp only half of it down.

The guy watches me a while longer.

"I mean," he says, "why torture yourself?"

There's no mystery to what he's telling me. I get it. I look at him. But I still can't seem to find any words to say.

I feel like a fucking idiot.

Is this guy reading my mind? He's nodding, letting me know, yeah, I know you do. But don't worry about it. Let it take its time. Run its course.

So I say it.

"I feel like an idiot."

He reaches across to shake hands. I grab his hand. His shake is firm. Manly.

"Jason," he says.

"Junne," I say. He raises his eyes. June?

he's thinking, Like the girl's name?

"It's a long story," I tell him, starting to calm down a bit now that we're (I'm?) actually speaking words out loud. "Real name's Salvatore, but I was a Junior. Morphed into Junne." Holding up the two fingers of my left hand, like in the victory sign. "With two 'n's," I say.

He nods, Okay, got it. Releases my hand. Nothing slow or suggestive. Just the end of a friendly handshake. I'm starting to like this guy. Feel comfortable with him when he repeats.

"Go home, Junne. This ain't for you."

He's right. But I don't move. The Spanish guys are still yukking it up. They've been served drinks. These guys are in for the long haul tonight, I can see that.

And in some way I can't quite say, I'm momentarily jealous of them. Of their friendship. Swishy and off-putting to me as it is, it's clearly genuine.

"What do you think you're looking for?" Jason says to me after I don't answer him. "A quick blow job in the men's room?"

I shoot him a look. Is this guy asking me to do that? With him? Have I so misjudged him?

"You see? You should see your face," he says, as I instinctively turn to my reflection in the mirror behind the bar. I'm still searching for my face when Jason says, "See what I mean, Junne? This is just not your scene. Go home."

And I do.

I slide off the bar. Then realize I have forgotten to pay for my drinks. Still standing, I try and signal the barman who's down at the other end. He's talking to a couple of other guys seated there.

"I got it," Jason says to me.

I look at him in protest, about to tell him there's no need for him, a complete stranger, to pay my bar tab.

But the way he looks at me. Letting me know, hey, it's okay. Go home.

So I do.

CHAPTER 18
SAY WHAT?

"Arty?"

I try again. "Arty, get up and come over here."

Me and Mickie are in the federal courthouse. We are scheduled to appear at a bail hearing in the case of *United States v. Arthur David Bernstein,* which is what Arty's case is called now that an arrest warrant has been issued and served on him.

Mickie's out in the courtroom asking the judge's bailiff if he could move Arty's case up on the docket. It's listed last for the afternoon session. And the docket is heavy today. I'm back here where the lockup is. Adjacent to the courtroom. Trying to get Arty's attention. Trying to tell him to get up off the bench where he's sitting, at the far wall, in the one large holding cell.

I can easily see him through the cell bars. Arty's maybe twenty feet away so he's not having any trouble hearing me. But he's not moving.

"Arty, get up. Come over here," I call out.

One of the other inmates, probably one of the guys been tormenting Arty ever since he was arrested and put in the slammer, thinks this is funny.

"Yo, counselor," he calls over to me. "That man don't need no lawyer. You lookin' for a client? I be your client."

He says this last bit turning his face to the others in the cell with him and Arty. Like he's the class clown. The others mostly ignore this moron. I see one standing guy smiling, shaking his head.

After Arty was dragged from the office by those two FBI agents, he was placed in the federal section of the Camden County Jail. The jail is a New Jersey state facility, not a federal one. Some time ago the Feds rented a wing because of overcrowding in the nearby federal prison. The Camden jail is much worse than the federal facility. That's why the Feds like to stick some of their inmates in there. To soften them up.

The U.S. Attorney's Office is the federal version of the Camden, New Jersey, state DA. The young prosecutors who work there usually come from better law schools than their Camden counterparts. Otherwise they are mostly the same. Some lawyers underestimate the state prosecutors and overestimate the federal ones. That's mostly law school driven. Not me and Mickie. The courtroom can be unforgiving. Where you went to school maybe gets you in one door or another. After that, it's how you do.

The federal prosecutors have been playing hardball with Arty. When he was arrested, Mickie called their office. Guys like Arty aren't flight risks. They can easily make bail. In fact, mostly the judges let guys like that out within hours. On what's called their own recognizance. Meaning they promise the judge they will show up in court when needed. No actual bail bond money has to be posted.

But not with Arty.

Mickie calls after Arty's carted off. The assistant United States attorney handling the case is relatively new, neither me nor Arty know her.

She tells Mickie, "Sorry, Mr. Mezzonatti, my schedule simply won't permit a bail hearing today or tomorrow. And with the weekend coming. Well, how's Monday afternoon? Tuesday maybe?'

"What?" Mickie shouts through the phone. "You gotta be fucking kidding me!"

"Excuse me?" she says, her voice making no effort to hide her anger.

"My client is not going to sit in a fucking jail cell in the Camden County Jail until Monday. Or Tuesday. Or any other fucking day next week," Mickie tells her.

The next sound Mickie hears is a click, as she hangs up on him.

This forces him to call her back, tell her they must have been disconnected.

"No," she tells him. "I hung up on you."

Then she does it again.

Mickie then calls the judge's chambers. Speaks to the law clerk since one lawyer can't communicate directly with a judge. The other side needs to be present.

No luck there either.

Somehow, the prosecutor seems to have already gotten a message to the judge. Probably through this same law clerk, asking the clerk to clue the judge in on how the Feds want to put some pressure on this guy. This dirty lawyer, menace to the bar. Who needs a taste of what the inside of a jail cell will be like for him. We'll stick him in the federal section of the Camden County Jail. Over the weekend. That'll get his attention. Guys like this defendant tend to fold like a collapsing chair.

So the judge won't schedule an early bail hearing for Arty, sets the court date for Monday afternoon. Arty will be forced to endure a weekend in the Camden County Jail.

Arty's case being last on Monday's docket, once he's bused over from the jail with the other prisoners who've got court dates, he gets to sit in the courthouse lockup while every other inmate has his case heard. That's no accident either.

"Arty," I call out again.

This time he looks over at me. Not sure he actually recognizes me.

He looks awful. Arty's orange prison attire makes an interesting color complement to his green-to-the-gills complexion. His hair is stuck out all over the place. Like he purposefully jammed his finger in an electric socket. (The inmate sitting behind him on the prison bus over here from the jail kept trying to light Arty's hair on fire with a book of matches he somehow got.) Arty's got three days of gray stubble. And not the fashion statement kind.

Arty finally walks over to me. Before his hands can even grab the cell bars I get a whiff of him. I try not to grimace. As many times as I've smelled that jailhouse stink, I just can't get used to it.

Arty's got it in spades.

"Arty," I say to him. "Look at me."

He does. We are now eye to eye. Arty's

telling me something. I know this because I can see his lips moving. Problem is the sound's turned off.

"What?" I say to him.

His lips keep moving. Arty's eyeballing me. Letting me know that what he's saying is important. Very important.

Behind him the other inmates are in various stages of actually speaking out loud (one guy I'm pretty sure to himself). Two prisoners are exchanging insults. The usual worn-out diatribe of motherfuck this and that, "bitch" and "punk-ass" insults, predictions of death and dismemberment. The two of them standing too close to each other, almost nose to nose. Each aggressively tilting his head this way, then that way. Like two boxers before the bell for round one. The others all ignoring them, bored with yet another jailhouse war of words.

"Arty," I tell him. "You gotta speak up."

This has an effect. Just not the one I'm after. Arty steps up the pace of his silent words. His lips are moving a mile a minute. Like he's some religious Jewish guy at the Wailing Wall.

"What?" I'm saying to him. But you see, to Arty he *is* speaking to me. Telling me lots of things he wants me to know. Important things.

Arty's lips are soundlessly speed-speaking. He's now furtively glancing from side to side. Whatever he's saying he doesn't want the others in here to know.

I move my head in close, turn so my ear is just about touching the cell bar. Arty's stench makes my eyes water. But I'm now as close as the bars will allow.

Nothing.

Okay, plan B. I move my head back. Nod to Arty. Okay, I'm letting him know. Got it. Not to worry. I'm on it.

This seems to settle him some. He shoots a glance at the guys behind him. His lips at it again. Soundlessly telling me what I should know but they can't.

I nod at him sagely. Will do, I'm letting him know. Then I leave Arty and go out to the courtroom.

CHAPTER 19
ARTY'S DAY IN COURT

Mickie had no luck with the bailiff. The judge takes the bench and me and Mickie sit and wait while all the other cases are called.

The judge gets to Arty three hours (and two short recesses) later.

The case is called. The marshals bring Arty out, cuffed wrist and ankle. They undo him and place him in one of the seats at defense counsel table.

I make Mickie sit next to him, just about shoving him there. Mickie's head shoots back soon as he gets a whiff of Arty's vile odor.

The AUSA who hung up on Mickie enters the courtroom and calmly walks over to the prosecution's table.

She's a tall, thin woman, all sharp angles. Premature-gray hair cut short for efficiency's sake. She's pale, maybe forty. No wedding ring. Stick legs.

175

The judge is tired. He's had a long day. Other bail hearings. Guilty pleas. Arguments on defense motions challenging this and that. I can see he wants out of here. Maybe he's thinking about that first martini soon as he gets home, or to his country club where he'll meet the Mrs. for dinner.

Mickie and me don't know this judge well. Most of our work is in the state court system. He's late sixties, thin as the AUSA, sallow, high cheekbones, washed-out blue eyes.

He's not a holy terror. Just another by-the-numbers federal judge. And like many of them, he's got a soft spot in his heart for the prosecution. After all, they're more like him than anyone else in this courtroom.

The AUSA is on her feet, making her case why Arty should be held without bail. Telling the judge how this lawyer perverted justice. How he bribed insurance adjusters and thereby defrauded the insurance companies to pay out large sums of money in settlement as damages for nonexistent injuries in trumped-up accident cases. How he also engaged in illegal wiretapping. Finally, to ice the cake, she insinuates (nonexistent) "possible" threats to witnesses.

She does all this to poison the atmosphere

of Arty's case. She knows full well that Arty will make bail. No way is this judge going to hold Arty in the slammer until his trial. Like I said, he's not a flight risk.

You see, this is part of the program. The plan to show Arty, no matter how many lawyers he's got here with him — it could be Clarence fucking Darrow, doesn't matter — the United States attorney is out for blood. Arty will catch no breaks from them. He's a dirty lawyer. They want him to cut a fast deal, a down-and-dirty plea bargain with a guilty plea to some serious multiple counts of criminal wrongdoing. He goes to trial instead? Makes the prosecution take the time and trouble to convict him before a jury. He'll be disbarred. And he'll also get twenty years or more in prison. And not at some country club half jail either. He'll be doing hard time. So much hard time that by the time he gets out of jail he'll be too old for Medicare.

The AUSA is finished with her presentation. She takes her seat.

"Counsel," the judge says over to us. Mickie rises. Given the way the prosecutor behaved to him on the phone he wants to be the one handling this today.

Mickie introduces himself, and me, for the record. He's no sooner three words into his presentation, when the judge interrupts.

"Counsel," he says to Mickie. "The court will allow bail. But I think it needs to be a substantial amount given the gravity of the offense."

The judge then looks past Mickie to Arty, sitting passively in his seat. I take a quick glance at Arty. His lips are still moving. Ever so slightly, but there's definitely a little motion there. I'm thinking, from where he's sitting up there on the bench, the judge isn't seeing this.

"The defendant will rise," the judge orders Arty.

I'm relieved when Arty gets to his feet. That means he's home. Heard the judge. Did what he was told to do.

Mickie's standing close enough to see Arty's moving lips. He shoots me a look. I shrug, but light and quick so only Mickie sees.

"The defendant will approach the court," the judge tells Arty.

And he does. With two deputy U.S. marshals standing behind him.

From where I'm sitting I think I see a quick look pass between the seated prosecutor and the judge. It was as quick as the one Mickie shot me just now.

"Now, Mr. Bernstein," the judge says to

Arty. But the judge hasn't yet really looked at Arty. His head is down as he fumbles with his papers before him on the bench, shuffling them, looking for the one probably has his little prepared remarks on it.

Arty's still speaking soundlessly. Only this time up to the judge.

His eyes still down at his papers, the judge starts telling Arty how serious the offenses he's been arrested on are. Then asks Arty, does he understand?

Arty's speaking to the judge. This is like a silent movie, I'm thinking. Like the next thing we all will see is the black screen with the white lettering on it. Telling us what Arty's saying.

I see the court stenographer on his little stool under the bench looking at Arty. Then he looks up to the judge who's still head down, fumbling with his papers.

The stenographer shoots a look to the prosecutor. She too now is all eyes on Arty, who's Buster Keaton without the silly flat-topped hat.

Finally the judge realizes it's too quiet in here. He looks up to Arty. Sees Arty's lips are moving. But no sound's coming out. I half expect the judge to reach up to his ear to see if his hearing aid battery's dead.

But of course, the judge is not deaf. There

179

is no hearing aid.

"What?" the judge says to Arty.

Arty is probably repeating for the judge what he's been saying.

The judge looks over to the still standing Mickie. If he's expecting an explanation he's not getting it from him. All Mickie does is shrug a "Beats me" to the judge.

Okay, he's the judge. He's in control here. So the judge addresses Arty.

"Mr. Bernstein," he says to Arty. "You will have to speak up."

Now we're back to the Wailing Wall. Arty's lips in furious motion.

The judge is exasperated. He grabs his gavel. Gives it one loud rap on the bench. That does it. Volume miraculously restored.

Problem is Arty goes from mute button to sports arena announcer.

"That fucking schvartze," Arty top-of-his-voice booms at the judge. "Tried to light my fucking hair on fire."

The judge will not have language like this in his courtroom. He bangs his gavel.

But Arty's now simply engaged in a continuation of the monologue he's been at ever since I saw him in the lockup. Only difference is now there's sound.

So as Arty goes on and on in this high-volume soliloquy, cataloguing the long list of indignities he's been made to suffer, the "F" word generously peppered throughout, the judge is now himself shouting at Arty to shut up. And he's hammering away at the bench with his gavel. The two U.S. marshals standing there, not sure what to do. Exchanging covert glances.

Arty's shouting. The judge is shouting and gaveling away at the bench like a crazed auctioneer.

"Quiet, quiet. I order quiet," the judge shouts down at Arty.

"Can you fucking believe it? Can you fucking believe it?" Arty shouts up to the judge.

Finally, he orders the marshals to get this guy out of here.

As the marshals are dragging still shouting Arty back to the lockup, I look over and see the lady prosecutor. She's sitting at counsel table.

Smiling.

Mission accomplished.

CHAPTER 20
THAT GREGORY

Arty was bailed the next day. Somehow, finding his voice settled him down. Helped him recapture his sanity.

After he was forcibly evicted from the courtroom, the marshals returned him to the lockup. Then, with the other inmates he was bused back to the Camden County Jail.

By the time he was back in the federal wing he had the presence of mind to use the pay phone on the wall to call me and Mickie.

While Arty was on the bus ride back to the jail, the judge issued an order for a psychiatric evaluation. That would have resulted in his remaining in confinement for another week at least, possibly even two.

Mickie called the law clerk, pleaded with him to ask the judge to rescind the order and instead reschedule another bail hearing for the following day. Ultimately, the judge did. Not out of any sense of pity for Arty.

Only because the judge was worried me and Mickie would take an immediate appeal, asserting that Arty was in effect being held unlawfully without an actual judicial determination on bail. Remember, all the judge did was order the marshals to get him out of the courtroom and back to lockup.

Probably the fact that he issued the evaluation order in writing after Arty's outburst would have resulted in his actions being affirmed on appeal. (Although the judge issued that order too quickly. Was too pissed to take the time to have it properly worded. There was no actual mention in the order itself of why it was being issued. He should have calmed down, then written an order that made note of Arty's bizarre behavior, his out-of-control remarks in open court [of all places], and then made a specific finding that, in the court's considered opinion, a psychiatric evaluation of this defendant was necessary to guide the court in determining whether or not he could safely be released back into society. Something like that, anyway.)

So I guess the judge didn't want to take the chance. Risk getting his knuckles rapped by the appeals court for not making any kind of even preliminary finding before having Arty ejected from his courtroom and then ordering the psychiatric evaluation.

The second hearing was short. Arty behaved. The judge set bail at $1 million. Way too high. Still, the bail bondsman would charge a 10 percent premium to put up the bond. Arty can spare the $100,000. He was out by the end of the day.

Me and Mickie haven't seen Arty since. He's stayed away from the office for the rest of the week.

Now it's late Friday afternoon. Just past five P.M.

Mickie left his own office a few minutes ago. He's told Carla he's got to work late, can't pick her up when her shift ends at Our Lady of Lourdes like they agreed. Needs a rain check on the Friday night dinner out he promised her. Telling her he'd likely be burning the midnight oil. Big hearing in a major case on Monday, he's telling her.

"On Monday?" she's saying. "And you're needing to work late on Friday night? What?" She's telling him, "You got the whole weekend ahead of you."

Mickie gives her that shrug of his, only she can't see it since they're on the phone, Mickie in his office. She's standing at the nurse's station, one finger in her ear, all kinds of commotion going on with this nurse, that doc.

184

What Mickie's up to is he's got a date with another woman. A legal secretary he's known for years. She's married, but from time to time she sees Mickie. I know her. Not too classy. Trampy, if you ask me. But hot, I guess. And she likes a little on the side every now and then. Mickie's only too happy to oblige.

Mickie's really tiring of Carla. Only a matter of time he'll call it quits. Or she will.

Mickie says to me, "Hey, Junnie. Cover for me tonight. Can you stay awhile in the office in case Carla calls? You know, to check up on me." Mickie saying, "You got no plans, right?"

I nod, Yeah, that's right. A little hurt at the thought of Mickie using me like this. But the fact is I don't have anything to do. And we do have the big motion hearing in the Sami Khan case first thing Monday morning. Extremely unlikely me and Mickie will open our mouths in court. Jerry Rubino will do it all himself. Still, I want to prepare for the hearing. Never know what can happen in court. And you never want to go unless you're prepared to the hilt to do battle.

So I tell him, "Sure, I'll stay. She calls, I'll tell her you're in with the clients."

"You the man," Mickie says, then heads out.

So, here I am. I've ordered Chinese delivery. Might as well spend Friday night here as home alone.

The halls are empty. The Bernstein, Smulkin lawyers and staff have all by now gone home too.

Arty's firm has been buzzing ever since he was arrested. Interesting though. The remaining Bernstein, Smulkin lawyers are behaving like a herd of nineteenth-century buffalo out on the plains. The buffalo hunters up on the crest of the hill shooting and dropping one after another. The remaining herd simply standing there, too scared to move. Too dumb to get the hell out. Stupidly chewing grass and looking down at the ground as each shot fells another animal. At first we told Arty we'd represent him and them too. But me and Mickie changed our minds. Told Arty it might get tricky. Ethically that is. Since his lawyer employees pretending to be his partners might have different interests in the long run than Arty. Arty didn't give a shit, shrugged. Since he's not going to lay out a penny for these guys' defense either way, he didn't care. Fuck 'em, his shrug told us. They're on their own? Fine. Next subject.

So, that's their problem. Now they're needing to fend for themselves. Get their own lawyers. All of them faking their cases, phonying up the injuries of the clients, bribing the insurance company adjusters. Just like Arty. The two lawyers Arty had wire-tapped, who were cooperating with the prosecution, are gone. Once the silver bracelets were clapped on Arty those two blew out of there quiet as a fart in a windstorm.

The delivery guy with my Chinese food order is here. I walk to the reception area to pick it up and pay him. As I do, I pass the small cubby office me and Mickie gave Tamara. Her door is closed, but I can see a sliver of light under the gap. As I walk by I hear Tamara's voice on the phone. She's saying, "Unh-uh. Unh-uh." Even with the closed door you can tell the edge in her voice.

I'm on my way back with the order. The food's still kind of warm, I can feel that through the bag. And smell the sweet, pungent aroma Chinese delivery seems to always have before you start unwrapping and then nuking it, the whole order melding into one mushy taste.

So, I'm once again passing Tamara's closed door. This time I hear her shouting into the phone. I stop and listen.

Like I said earlier, Tamara has come a long way for me and Mickie in a short time. While I wouldn't call her polished, she's got the hang of what we do. She's there when we need her. (I think the night school courses helped.) More than that you can't ask. She's funny with her jive talk. But there's also someone substantial under all that verbal high jinks she's so good at.

I hear Tamara saying, "Gregory, now you listen to me." Then there's silence.

Then I hear Tamara tell Gregory, "What you thinkin', your Aunt Tamara gonna be there for you, each and every goddamned time you needin' me?"

Again silence as Tamara listens to whatever Gregory's telling her.

I start to head for the kitchen area down the other hallway so I can unwrap the Chinese and nuke it. Tamara's shouting.

"You dumbass little motherfucker."

Then, "Don't you hang up on me." A short pause. Then, "Hello, hello," followed by the unmistakable sound of Tamara slamming the phone back into its cradle.

I wait a beat or two, then knock lightly on her door. Open it and poke my head in.

"Couldn't help but overhear," I say.

Tamara is seated behind her small desk in

the windowless room we have for her. Her arms are crossed against her chest. And she's steaming.

It takes her a moment or two to calm herself down. Then she gets embarrassed.

She starts to get up as she's telling me she's sorry for causing such a ruckus.

I motion her back in her chair.

I sit across from her, the cooling large brown bag of Chinese in my lap. The smells from it drifting into her small, windowless office.

And that's how me, Tamara, and Gregory in his wheelchair end up at dinner an hour later.

CHAPTER 21
TABLE FOR THREE

They say the road to hell is paved with good intentions.

They're right.

After Tamara slams down the receiver — after I stay with her and talk, the Chinese on my lap starting to seep through the bag — Tamara's apologizing, saying me and Mickie been more than good to her.

Apologetically she tells me, "Junne, I ain't about to bother you no more with my own shit, know what I'm sayin'?"

That Gregory. A trial date is still pending, the public defender not yet able to work out some kind of disposition for the other boys charged along with him, and me purposefully waiting, laying back in the case. Letting the DA and the PD first agree on something. Then I'll come in afterward for Gregory, playing Gregory's gunshot physical condition, his having an aunt willing to be responsible for him. Using all that to score a better disposition for Gregory than the other boys will get. I'm thinking they will go off for a year or so to Junior Village. Gregory will get probation.

Well, it seems while his case is pending, Gregory has decided to return to a life of crime. But gone are his days of robbing other kids at the bus stop. Nope. Gregory's moving on up. He's enlisted himself in the drug trade.

Gregory makes the perfect corner boy. He's out there on the street slinging drugs along with all the other half-pint wannabe gangsters. The cops coming in at high speed. Pulling up to the curb, out of their cars, chasing the scattering little tykes as they head for their rat holes. Gregory wheels up to the men and women in blue. He's clean, having dumped whatever inventory he was carrying in his lap. He blocks their passage as they contend with him. Wheelchair-ridden. The other boys gone in a flash.

And from what Tamara is describing to me, it sounds like Gregory's ultimate new employer, up the chain, is Slippery Williams. Gregory's working corners I know Slippery owns. I don't tell this to Tamara though. What's the point?

But I am willing to try and talk this kid

out of this. So, I dump the bag of Chinese in the wastebin out by the kitchen area.

It was my suggestion. Dinner for three. Maybe me and Tamara can talk some sense into Gregory.

I mean it's Friday night. Might as well spend it that way than hanging around here. (The things you'll do when you're lonely.)

"Nawh," is all Gregory will say to the waiter.

The three of us at the table. I've got a glass of red wine in front of me. My second. Tamara says she doesn't drink, so has ordered a ginger ale. Gregory sitting across from me, sulking in his wheelchair. He doesn't want to be here. Doesn't want to talk. Not to me. Not to his Aunt Tamara with whom he's now living. That is, when he actually comes home at night.

And certainly not to this waiter. A guy maybe forty, white, wearing the long white waist apron over black slacks and white shirt like they do at Maggiano's. That's the Italian chain in the Cherry Hill Mall me and Mickie sometimes go to for plastic Italian food.

I thought it would be a good place for the three of us. I drove. Picked up Gregory — believe it or not — on the corner he's working. The other boys working there finding

192

this the funniest damn thing they've ever seen, this white man and Gregory's aunt picking him up for dinner in a restaurant. Right off the corner. They're giving Gregory catcalls. Funning him. Calling things like, Yo, Gregory, you be careful you don't come back no punk-ass white boy. Teasing him as Tamara and me are fitting him in the car, collapsing his wheelchair for the trunk.

Gregory is embarrassed, stone-faced, staring straight ahead. Trying to will himself someplace else.

"Maybe some spaghetti?" the waiter suggests to Gregory, still sulking in his wheelchair. Not even curious to look around the place, even though I'll bet he's never been in a restaurant like this ever once in his life.

"I said I don't want nothin'. Okay?" Gregory growls at the waiter.

The waiter looks over at me. I wave him off, tell him give us five.

I take another sip of wine. Is this what it's like to be a married guy, sitting at the dinner table with your wife and brooding teen-aged son?

Well, yes and no.

There's the race thing. Yeah, but it's not that. That's not what's making this the right and the wrong picture both at the same time.

Well, whatever it is, how the hell do I propose to talk to this kid? This fucked-up, damaged-goods kid, who's not letting the likes of me in, no matter how hard I try.

He's going to break Tamara's heart, I'm thinking. Sure as can be.

The waiter's back. I guess the five minutes are up. He's standing there. No smile anymore. This table's trouble. Still, he needs to watch himself. There's always a manager can be called if this guy allows himself to put his true feelings on display. His irritation at having to pander to this sullen little ass-wipe slouched best he can under the circumstances in his wheelchair.

The waiter's going to give it another try. He does, though I can hear the resignation and vexation seeping out from behind his "waiterly" voice.

"Decided on something?" he asks Gregory.

The waiter's waiting for some kind of response from Gregory. If not from him, then from me. Or Tamara.

Tamara is sitting there, glaring at Gregory. A restaurant like this is no small deal for her. She does not want a bad impression to be made. She remains quiet, but her eyes are boring in on her nephew.

"So?" the waiter tries again. His eyes now

wandering from sulking Gregory to the other tables he's working.

Maggiano's is pretty busy tonight. After all, it is Friday night. The prices here are lower than so-called finer restaurants. So the tables are near full, several families here eating. When the three of us got shown to this table we got some eyes from the other diners. This business-suited middle-aged white guy, this knock-out-body black chick in too-tight clothes. And this wheelchair-ridden kid decked out like some rap artist. The indispensable sideways flat-brimmed baseball hat firmly in place.

Yeah, my family.

"Bring him an order of spaghetti," I tell the waiter, signaling also another red wine for me.

"You'll like it," the waiter tells Gregory. I don't know, maybe he's thinking about his tip. It was me standing there with the long white waist apron, I wouldn't waste another goddamn word on this little shit pulled up to the table with us.

Gregory motions for the waiter to bend down his way. Uh-oh, I'm thinking, but not fast enough to do anything.

As the waiter complies, Gregory reaches up and grabs the waiter by his black bow-tied collar. Pulls him even farther down.

195

The waiter's struggling, surprised, off balance, frantically grabbing for Gregory's wheelchair side arms. Trying to right himself so his face doesn't fall in Gregory's lap (like the charter school bus stop kids).

Gregory's got him down low, face-to-face.

"When I tell you I don't want nothin' you best be listening, motherfucker," Gregory's saying to the waiter, who's not sure what to do, still struggling to stay on his feet. This kid in a wheelchair. Surely the waiter doesn't want to lose his job by flipping over a paraplegic kid. Yeah, but I can see the waiter's starting to get steamed. Can see he's losing control.

Before I have a chance to do something, Tamara is up out of her seat. Of course, by now just about the entire restaurant's eyes are on us. Tamara breaks Gregory's grip on the waiter. She apologizes to him then pulls Gregory's wheelchair from the table and bum-rushes him out of the restaurant.

She then speeds him through the shopping mall, down the escalator you're not supposed to use for wheelchairs. Out the main entrance to the lip of one of the parking lots. She reaches in her pocket, pulls out a twenty. Throws it in his lap.

Tells him, "Call a cab. And your ass better be going to the house and not back out on no street corner, else I will see to it you are in that jail before the sun come up. Hear me?"

Then Tamara leaves Gregory right there, reenters the mall, walks back into Maggiano's. Lots of heads up as she does. She returns to the table. Takes her seat. Doesn't yet say word one to me. When finally the waiter comes back over, she doesn't apologize to him again. But she does ask him politely if he would please bring over a bottle of whatever red wine I have been drinking. And an extra glass.

Tamara then proceeds to drink dinner.

CHAPTER 22
NIGHT MOVES

"Here it is," I tell Tamara, as I flick on the hall light, shut the door to my apartment.

Tamara is drunk. Stumbling. She's holding on to me for balance. But I'm as juiced as she is, weaving and bobbing, like a deckhand in a stormy sea.

At least I had enough sense to leave the car at the mall parking lot. Called a cab. I'll pick up the car tomorrow.

Three sheets to the wind. The both of us. The first bottle of red led to the second bottle of red.

The check was on the table, that waiter not uttering word one about where did the youngster in the wheelchair go. Just relieved he'd gone. I made it up to the guy in the tip.

Tamara at the table, polishing off the rest of her glass. Saying how nice it is to drink wine. Musing how she sure doesn't relish the thought of going home tonight and being with sulking Gregory. Or worse, spending the night wondering what trouble he's getting himself into out on the street after she walks into her empty house.

So I tell her you can come home with me. Sleep on the sofa in the living room.

And that's all I meant. And that's all Tamara meant when she said, "You sure?"

Ah but now.

Tamara's still leaning into me in my apartment's small entrance hall. I look at her. Her eyes are not what I would call focused. She's on automatic pilot. Her body's getting comfortable touching mine. Even with clothes separating skin from skin.

"You nice, Junne," she says to me. Almost whispering.

Her hand comes up and touches my face. She moves in even closer. I can hear her breathing take a slight uptick.

Tamara's waiting. It's my move.

While this is going on Mickie's in the rack with his married-babe friend. Both of them going at it hot and heavy. The airport hotel in Philly has been their destination for these occasional trysts for a couple of years now. The room standard-issue Comfort Inn.

Mickie always tells me about it. He says she likes the room lights off, the bathroom light on with the door partially open.

Throws a relief light onto the bed. She tells Mickie each time how this turns her on, seeing him and her naked in subdued light.

She places the plastic hotel glass with a residue of the Maker's Mark bourbon she likes on the night table. Her eyes locked on his as he sits before her on the edge of the bed. She starts swaying to invisible music, then reaches her arms behind her and releases the snap on her dress. Stands and lets it slide off her, liking the way Mickie watches. His eyes following the dress's slow downward coast to the carpeted floor.

She's kept her figure. Her face may show the lines of age, but her tits, thighs, and so on still do her justice. At least, that's what Mickie says.

Doesn't take long before him and the woman are going at it. The bed's bolting. She's got her legs wrapped tightly around Mickie, her arms locked on his neck, telling him, Yeah, like that, like that.

And while Mickie's feeling the first tingling signs of his approaching orgasm, the phone in our office is ringing. Carla is now in Mickie's empty house, home from her shift, the phone pressed to her ear. Calling for the third time. Getting more ticked off by the second.

And of course, I'm not there to answer

the phone because I'm in a drunken clutch with Tamara, who keeps telling me how nice I am. Keeps stroking my face. Her breathing now heavy.

I break away, tell her I'll go get the extra blanket and pillow for the sofa.

"Be right back," I say, sounding to myself like Martha Stewart telling the at-home audience she'll be right back after these messages with more tips on how to make an apple crisp their man will die for.

I'm in the bedroom, rummaging in the closet for the extra pillow and blanket. Asking myself yet again in my fucked-up life, What was I thinking?

And while I'm doing this something else is going on tonight.

Sami and Rafat are in their secret warehouse out off the highway, late in the evening as it is, taking in yet another cash delivery from Slippery's men. Business has really been good out on the streets. Slippery has too much cash. Needs to get it out of town. He had his man contact Sami. Tell him he needs to make an extra "deposit" this week.

Rafat's standing next to his father, thinking he's going to burst like a ruptured balloon. He has tried talking to his father. Tried telling him this needs to stop. It's much too risky.

"For God's sake," he said earlier this evening, the two of them in Sami's office. The door closed. "Dad, we're in the middle of a criminal investigation. We need to stop doing this."

Sami listening to his son. Not telling him there is no stopping with Slippery. Not telling him stopping with Slippery would lead to a fate far worse than the ongoing criminal investigation.

"Hi," Tamara says to me from the doorway leading into my bedroom.

I turn. Tamara is buck naked. She's got one arm leaning against the doorjamb. This does seem to be steadying her. Her hip is cocked. The lighting is dim. (Is this what Mickie's married friend means about subdued lighting turning her on?)

Tamara is built. I've got to give her that. She's perfect. My eyes run up and down her body. Taking in her big boobs, the dark purple of her wide nipples, the triangle you know where. Tamara's reading me reading her. She's encouraged. Why am I doing this? I'm thinking as I nervously continue doing this.

She enters the room walking slowly toward me. She's not too steady without the door-

202

jamb for support. Still, she's most definitely heading my way. I watch as Tamara momentarily diverts her line of vision to the bed on the other side of the room, no doubt making mental calculations of the trajectory for us from where I'm standing at the closet to over there where she's pretty certain at this point we are going to be doing it. She's humming some old Motown tune under her breath.

Okay, now what? I tell myself as Tamara arrives.

"Hey, I've got an idea," I tell her as she places her arms around my neck, still humming. (It's Stevie Wonder's "Signed, Sealed, Delivered I'm Yours.")

I don't think Tamara's listening. Yup, not listening. I can tell this for certain because Tamara now has her lips pressed against mine. Her mouth is definitely opening. Her salty-tasting tongue is paying me a courtesy call. If you thought she was breathing heavy out in the living room, you should hear her now.

I manage to unlip us, though we're still seriously face-to-face. Tamara's eyelids are at half-mast. She's looking at me dreamily. Still telling me I'm nice. Her arms still around my neck.

Oops. We're in motion. Definitely moving.

Me backward. Her forward. Tamara's the Little Engine That Could. Her dreamy face looking up to mine. She's humming again as she pushes me toward the bed.

"Hey," I try again. "How about some coffee?" I say as Tamara's arms are guiding me toward our landing pad.

"Later," is all she says in a hoarse voice as we move closer to my bed.

"You sure?" I stupidly ask her.

Tamara throws her gears into park. We're standing face-to-face at the side of the bed. We're still too close for comfort. (Mine, anyway.) Tamara removes her arms from my neck. She's no longer humming. Next thing I know her hands are trying their best to unbutton my shirt.

She gets a button undone, I redo it. Undone. Redo. Tamara at first, in her state, seems confused by this. I mean she is unfastening the buttons. Why, her alcohol-laden brain must be asking itself, has she not gotten the shirt completely undone? And off?

No matter. With one quick move she rips my shirt wide open. Slowly rubs her hands over my bare chest.

The one night I don't wear an undershirt. (This? This is what I'm thinking? Now? At a time like this?) She's now unfastening my belt buckle.

This just does not seem like the best time to stop Tamara. Tell her, Hey, got a minute? Need to tell you something. You know, about me? You know, like where we're heading?

If I was going to do that, I should have already. Probably around the time Tamara started telling me I'm nice. Maybe even at the table at Maggiano's. Somewhere in between bottles one and two.

Tamara has the belt buckle undone. Next she turns her attention to my zipper.

So, in about eleven seconds from now, when Tamara has the zipper all the way down, my pants and boxers no doubt by then bunched around my ankles — (like Mickie's babe's dress?) — Tamara is going to see that my Mr. Happy is not in a state of elation. (Rhymes with "elongation." "Ejaculation." None of which is in the cards here.)

She will no doubt find this perplexing. And probably more than a little disappointing.

She is, after all, to her way of thinking, more than halfway to the goal line.

And I am now as sober as a minister at a Methodist service.

"Be right back," I tell Tamara, who is still

intent on maneuvering my zipper southward. Lips now pursed, eyes screwed tight, she is in undeniable deep concentration.

I signal to Tamara that I'll just mosey over to the bathroom where I keep my condoms. I do this in sign language trying my best to pantomime the slipping of the plastic, membranous sheath over the proverbial flagpole. (Unfortunately, what we're dealing here with is a limp wiener.)

Tamara gets it. Signals okay, but hurry back.

Now I'm in the bathroom. I'm leaning on the sink, searching my face in the medicine cabinet mirror. For a game plan.

I do in fact have condoms in the medicine cabinet. And if they don't come with a sell-by date, given the near utter lack of usage they get, I will at least have that base covered.

And in keeping with the overusage of sports metaphors I have peppered throughout this episode, let me just say that I am also searching my mirrored reflection to try and see if I can get my game face on. Go out there and rise to the occasion. So to speak.

Instead, I ask myself, Who am I kidding? Then I resolve. Go out there and tell her why you can't do what she's expecting.

For Christ sake, I tell myself.

Be a man.

Okay, well. You know what I mean.

So, with the past-sell-by-date condoms still safely tucked away on the upper medicine cabinet shelf, I open the bathroom door. Fully prepared to march right over to my bed, on which no doubt Tamara is now lying, poised for intercourse. I take no more than two steps into the bedroom when I hear the unmistakable sound of Tamara's snoring.

So, I tiptoe the rest of the way over. Yup, she's out like a light. Naked on the bed. On her back, her legs splayed like a giant pair of ebony scissors.

I stand there a moment longer listening to her gentle snoring. Then I flip the cover from the far side of the bed over her. Gently adjust her head on the pillow.

Then I go get the extra blanket and pillow from my closet and head for the living room couch.

So, in the morning I'll tell Tamara what? I'm asking myself as I arrange my makeshift bedding.

I'll deal with that tomorrow, I conclude. Fatigued like a battle-weary soldier stumbling back into base camp.

I'm out like a light soon as my head hits

the pillow.

Soon there are two of us sawing wood in here.

CHAPTER 23
AFTER YOU.
NO, PLEASE, AFTER YOU.

"That's quite an interesting point," Jerry Rubino says, as he removes his reading glasses and places them on the courtroom lectern. He smiles at the judge. "Frankly, Your Honor, I hadn't thought of that."

Jerry Rubino is well into his oral argument on the motion he and his small army of young lawyers have filed on behalf of Sami and Rafat Khan. It's a pre-indictment motion. No formal charges have as yet been filed. The case is still at the grand jury investigative stage.

This motion, the extensive briefing by both sides, the preparation for and attendance at this lengthy hearing are all part of the Rubino strategy. Make life for the prosecutors hard and unrelenting. Unless, of course, they cut a favorable plea bargain for Sami and Rafat. Cut them loose with a lesser offense. Before the grand jury hands down a major indictment. Maybe with a hard slap on the wrist. Or just a teensy-weensy bit of jail time in a minimum security facility, some honor system place with dormitory beds and no bars.

This motion is his first in-court salvo, the first cannon shot across their bow.

The motion asks the court to quash the search warrant that was executed on their business offices. To quash the warrant for lack of probable cause. Asserting that when the federal magistrate signed the warrant, approving the search and seizure of all those incriminating records, he made a mistake. The prosecutors did not provide the magistrate with sufficient supporting facts and legal grounds for him to have made the determination that there was in fact probable cause that a crime had actually been committed, justifying the warrant and therefore the search.

And if the search is bad, the seizure is bad. All those incriminating documents would then be returned to Sami. More importantly, the prosecution would never be able to use anything they saw in those documents against Sami and his son. And even more importantly, the prosecution would never be able to use against them any "leads" to other evidence they followed based on what they read in those improperly seized, and now tainted, papers.

If the judge grants the motion? Case over. Before it even begins. The evidence is tainted. The prosecution is hog-tied, like a farm animal prepared for slaughter. No evidence. No proof. No case.

Sounds pretty good, huh? Yeah, but the motion is bullshit. The chances that the federal prosecutors did not carefully gather sufficient probable cause before presenting their warrant to the magistrate for his approval are one in a thousand.

You ask me? This is a motion that should be made post-indictment, after actual charges have been filed. Once the prosecution's case has seen the light of day. When all sorts of other legal motions attacking their case are typically filed. When the defense can read in the actual indictment exactly what's been charged and how. And what's not been charged. Where the prosecution's strengths are. And their weaknesses.

"May I address the point you've made, Your Honor?" Jerry asks the judge.

"Yes, of course you may," says the judge.

Mickie elbows me. I give him a quick glance. He rolls his eyes.

This polite little minuet Jerry Rubino and this overly deferential judge are dancing.

211

The two of them bantering. You go first. No, you. No, please, you.

What me and Mickie are witnessing is some kind of Kabuki theater. Jerry Rubino, the big-firm lawyer of stature, is giving his best law school argument of why this motion should be granted. Both he and the judge knowing goddamn well it won't.

But first the two of them will engage in this polite legal bantering. Each deferring to the other. Each making clever points.

Me and Mickie are seated inside the well of the court, not even at defense counsel's table. Behind it, in a row of chairs alongside Sami and Rafat. We're spectators. Bumps on a log. Still getting the silent treatment from Rubino. Me and Mickie tolerated, but ignored. The defense table is filled with Rubino's boy and girl lawyers. The prosecutors have filled the seats at their table: three of them, all baby faced, and one FBI agent, older. There only for appearance's sake. All listening to Rubino's argument to the court.

The prosecutors too are a part of this mock law school debate masquerading as a serious legal argument. They are intently listening. Jotting notes. Waiting for their turn to take the lectern in rebuttal. Show off what they learned at Harvard Law.

"Bear with me, Judge," Rubino tells the

court. He replaces his reading glasses, reads aloud a paragraph or two verbatim from xeroxed sheets of one of the law cases cited in his brief. Then removes the glasses. Returns them carefully to the lectern. Sighs dramatically.

"I'm not sure I follow your point, Mr. Rubino," the judge says, smiling at Jerry. Letting him know, Go ahead, enlighten me.

I'm staring at Rubino, then the judge, then Rubino. Back and forth, back and forth. All of a sudden my bored-out-of-its-skull brain is melding the two. Fusing them. I'm seeing the same guy at the lectern as the one up on the bench in the black robes.

And they're both Rubino. He's debating with himself.

I shake my head to get the real picture back in view. I hear Mickie under his breath murmur, "Give me a fucking break."

So, Rubino goes on. And on and on.

This isn't how me and Mickie would do this. You know, if we were anything but wallpaper here.

We'd play the game differently.

Charges are coming. You can make book on it. Me and Mickie would wait. Take a look at the prosecutors' cards before making our bets. Before throwing our clients' chips onto the table.

"All right, Mr. Rubino," the judge says. "The court has gotten your position. Shall we hear from the government?"

"Yes, by all means," Rubino tells the judge. Graciously extending his hand in the direction where the young federal prosecutors are seated. Inviting them, as much as colleagues at the bar as adversaries, to please come up to the lectern. Make their own brilliant arguments.

One of the prosecutors rises from the table, makes his way to the lectern Jerry Rubino is now relinquishing. Jerry has turned and is walking back to his own table. He's smiling at Sami and Rafat, letting them know how pleased he is with his performance on their behalf.

Just then Mickie burps. Not sure if the sound made its way to the bench. But Rubino's heard it. His eyes dart to Mickie. Then just as quickly away. Thinking, no doubt, What a bozo.

I watch as Mickie reaches in his suit pocket for a Rolaids.

Jerry Rubino's now seated. His back to us, he leans into the kid lawyer to his left, whispers something that causes the kid to glance at Mickie.

Mickie's steaming. Say what you will about him. He's lawyer enough to feel the

214

frustration of sitting here mute. A benched player.

Sami hired us. On Slippery's recommendation. We're being handsomely paid to cool our heels in this courtroom.

Still. This is hard to do.

To watch helplessly as Jerry Rubino does an expert job of taking his own clients down.

I know I'm being hard on Rubino. He's doing a good job of setting this case up for a plea bargain. Telegraphing the young prosecutors that this is just the beginning of the day-and-night workfest he will be subjecting them to. Forcing them to put their other cases aside, telling their spouses over and over how they'll be working late, won't be home before bedtime. Rubino signaling them, Is this really worth it? Why not cut your future losses? Let's allow my clients to plead to some minor, lesser offense. You can end this now. With honor. What do you say?

And like I've been saying, Jerry Rubino is an accomplished lawyer. He's pushing the prosecutors. His shoulder's pressed hard against their half-bolted door. Straining at the chain, letting them know he's about to break into their space. And if he manages to catch the prosecutors doing something they shouldn't, he'll crucify them.

Okay. But what Sami and Rafat don't have

is a lead lawyer who will be their champion. Someone who will actually fight for their acquittal in this complicated set of facts the prosecution needs to prove. You know. Innocent until proven guilty.

That's the system. That's a defense lawyer's role. His or her job. Plenty of time for a plea bargain if things don't go well at trial.

Maybe the deal wouldn't be as sweet. Still, this case is not a whodunit. It's a *how* done it. Did Sami and Rafat violate the law with their way of doing business? Did they cheat? Take in cash sales and not report them? Did they hide credit card sales? Intentionally misfile them in their business records, so the taxman wouldn't know?

Will a jury see it? Buy it? Or will they find doubt? Enough reasonable doubt to acquit on all charges.

And also none of us — not me, not Mickie — no one, knows anything yet about how Sami and son are laundering Slippery's drug money receipts. Helping out Slippery and earning plentiful cash fees from Slippery by transporting his small-bill loot to India for cleansing. And that, of course, is worse than anything else they've done. What if that comes to light while they're all working out the details of a pre-indictment plea agreement? What if it comes out after Sami and Rafat enter guilty pleas? Then the two of them, now convicted of crimes, will be sitting ducks for new, even worse charges.

So, call me and Mickie old school. But this is just not our way. We'd take this baby to the courtroom. For a trial. Before a jury. We'd make the trial of this case so goddamned complicated the jurors would well be within their rights to find reasonable doubt. And acquit.

Yeah well. No one here's listening to us.

Me and Mickie are the pit in the cherries. Spit out when everyone's done eating the good parts.

CHAPTER 24
THE BIG PLEA BARGAIN PITCH

Mickie snaps his cell shut. He and the rest of the "defense team," along with Sami and Rafat, are crowded in the small room next to the courtroom we were all just in. The jury uses this room when there is an actual trial. The judge told Jerry Rubino he and the rest of us could make use of it after the hearing ended.

After the prosecutors made their points at the hearing — and after Rubino once again took the lectern in rebuttal — well, then the judge pulls out his prepared remarks and reads his ruling into the record. Denying the motion.

What a surprise.

Soon as we walked in here, Mickie pulls out his cell, steps to the corner of the room, calls Carla. Whispers to her for a while. Listens. Then whispers some more. Then snaps it off.

Carla's still living in Mickie's house. He

convinced her the night he came home late from the Comfort Inn, smelling of soap after the shower he took to wash off the sex scent. Convinced her he in fact had been in the office. Heard the phone, but was so wrapped up with the clients. Telling her, Remember the guy on the TV with the bad wig? The guy selling appliances and shit? Well, he's the client and I just couldn't get to the phone, baby. I swear on my mother's grave.

Does Carla believe him? Hard to tell. But Mickie does manage to sweet-talk her out of packing up that night and leaving him. So, now he's doing his penance (like the good Catholic he never was), calling her throughout the day. Letting her know how sorry he is, how much he cares for her.

Why Mickie's doing this, I don't know. It's the way he is with women. Wants them, doesn't want them. Wants them, but wants to supplement the batting order once in a while with a pinch hitter. It's why he's single, why his relationships don't tend to last.

Jerry Rubino takes a seat at the table. Motions for Sami and Rafat to sit opposite him. The rest of the seats are taken by Jerry's kid lawyers. Me and Mickie stand against the wall, Rubino's back to us.

"Well," Jerry says, smiling at Sami. "I think the judge really liked our arguments. I think we gave him something to think about."

I can read Mickie's mind. Liked our arguments? he's thinking, mimicking Jerry's lofty speech pattern. The son-of-a-bitch judge *denied* "our" argument, is racing through Mickie's head like an ambulance, siren blaring, speeding a dead patient to the emergency room.

Sami doesn't react. He's been mute throughout the morning. He simply stares at Rubino.

Sami and Rafat are wearing go-to-court suits. Like the rest of us.

Rafat looks more or less like he too could be a lawyer. Suited in a dark blue, well-fitting, muted pinstripe. Conservative tie.

Sami's suit is a washed-out gray, the color you see in black-and-white movies. Matching solid tie over a white shirt. Doesn't really work with his Indian skin. Makes his face and hands look like some kid crayoned in their beige red tones. Sami's strong cologne is permeating this small, closed room. His suit's rumpled, like he slept in it. Even from where I'm standing, looking down and across the table, I can see that Sami is one unhappy camper.

And for once his wig is on straight. Does that mean something?

Still, he remains silent. Lets Jerry Rubino continue.

And Rubino does. Telling Sami that they gave it the good fight. Then he sighs.

I'm watching Rafat seated next to his dad, listening intently to all this, fear and worry jockeying for first place position on his face.

"You know," Rubino begins, both hands flat on the table, leaning in just enough to show the point he's about to make is important.

How many times has he done this with other clients? I'm thinking, as I stand there behind him. Looking at that bald spot he's got combed over. The guy must use a hand-held mirror when he works on it. Picturing Jerry Rubino in his underwear in the morning, standing at his bathroom mirror, maneuvering the brush until he's got it just right. The bald spot as camouflaged as he and his expensive hairstylist can get it. Then a quick press of hair spray and he's good to go.

"Sami, we gave it our best shot," he continues. Then sighs once more. Shakes his head in sincere condolence-call fashion. Says to Sami, "I think it's time to take stock. Time to consider our options."

Mickie shifts from foot to foot.

Sami stares at Rubino.

This is how the man does this. I told you that already. The minute Sami and Rafat walked into Rubino's office the case was over.

"Mr. Rubino," Sami says.

"Jerry, please."

Sami ignores this.

"There will be no plea bargain," he tells Rubino. Leaning forward, placing his arms flat on the table. He and Rubino now a matched set facing each other.

"Mr. Khan," Rubino says, dispensing with the faux familiarity ("call me Jerry") he likes to use. Jerry Rubino does not have his clients run his ship. He's the captain here. They are simply passengers.

Sami raises his hand. A traffic cop. Telling Rubino, Hold it right there.

When push comes to shove Sami doesn't give a shit what Jerry Rubino wants, thinks is best. (For Sami. For Jerry?) Because while he isn't showing it, and while me and Mickie don't get it yet, the state Sami's in? Makes Rafat's worry and fear look like child's play.

Like I said, me and Mickie are still unaware that Sami has been laundering Slippery's drug money. Don't yet get that the real reason Slippery told Sami to add me and Mickie to the defense team wasn't so much because of our local legal skills.

Nope. It was so we could be Slippery's eyes and ears. Let him know if Sami should decide to make a deal for himself. Lighten his load by offering up Slippery Williams to the prosecutors. Decide to help them hook Camden's biggest fish. Sell Slippery to the Feds in exchange for leniency for himself and his son.

It's the best he's got to help himself and Rafat, to avoid spending the next five years or more in prison.

Would Sami do something like this? Serve up Slippery Williams to the Feds? Spill the beans on his drug money laundering operation? To save his own skin, and his son's?

The Feds would love this, take one away from Robert Cahill, the local DA, still unsuccessfully trying to catch Slippery. This would give the Feds bragging rights for years to come.

Would you give up Slippery, if you were Sami?

Would I? Or would Mickie? Not so much if we were Sami, not to the Feds. But as Sami's lawyers who learned what he was about to do — would we tell Slippery?

Sami, Rafat, and Slippery are all three our

223

clients. It would be highly unethical for me and Mickie — based on attorney-client protected information we would get from Sami — to whisper in Slippery's ear that Sami was about to rat him out to the Feds. Lawyers can't do that. By law they must maintain each client's confidences.

Client confidences. Ethical considerations. They don't mean shit to Slippery. And he's thinking they won't mean shit to us either. Not this time around. Because we owe Slippery on account of that Rodrigo matter. Slippery saving our asses. Our lives, actually, like he did when he saw to it that Rodrigo was eradicated.

And because whoever either tries to rat out Slippery, or keeps something like that a secret from him, is a dead man.

Sami knows this. So would me and Mickie. Except we're still in the dark here.

A fuse has been lit directly under us, and me and Mickie can neither hear the slow burn nor smell the smoldering sulfur.

Jerry Rubino has been giving Sami his best level-headed, listen-to-me-I'm-the-lawyer-and-I-know-what-I'm-talking-about look. The look telling Sami, You need to cut a deal with the Feds. It's your only viable option.

It might be working on Rafat.

But not on Sami.

Before Rubino gets out another word, Sami rises from his seat.

We all watch as Sami quietly leaves the room.

CHAPTER 25
A (NOT SO) SECRET ADMIRER

"Monsieur Cahill," the headwaiter says, bowing slightly. Smiling. His tuxedo crisp, pleated, turned out like a department store mannequin. "And of course Madame Cahill," he says in his phony French accent (the guy was born in Poland) as he gently touches Robert's wife's elbow and guides her, Robert following in close behind, to their table.

Le Bec-Fin on Walnut Street has been Philadelphia's premier French restaurant forever. Recently remodeled, everything taken down and rebuilt, excepting the huge and sparkling ornate glass chandelier. After all that work, the restaurant's main dining room still resembles a Disney version of an eighteenth-century drawing room.

Even though Robert Cahill is the Camden, New Jersey, DA — its self-proclaimed Eliot Ness — he chooses to live in Philadelphia. He's from a wealthy real estate family. His

DA job is to be his stepping-stone to higher elective office. He's got all the family money he needs. So a city prosecutor's salary is of no import to him. And while he'd much rather be Philadelphia's DA, his relative lack of ability has not made anything like this possible. Camden was the best he could get. Make that the best his family's money and connections could get.

These days he can't wait to get out of the job, and run for office. Maybe mayor next. Would congressman be too early? He knows he needs at least one significant scalp hanging from his DA's belt. Without that, the job will have been one major fucking waste of time. He needs a big conviction to sell to the electorate. In effect telling them, See what I did with that? Elect me.

The finer things in life have never much interested him. It was up to him, he'd be at home this Friday night. A bottle of Booth's gin, a bucket of ice, and the wall-mounted TV all he would need for comfort. But the Mrs.? She's a different story. Unlike Robert's sallow, withdrawn features, Nancy Cahill is a looker. Just tiptoeing into middle age, she's still got it, the kind of looks that turn heads at tables in fancy French restaurants. She sports long red hair running down her back right up to the line where hip meets ass. With her Irish coloring, her comely freckles, her pretty features, she seems to belong with someone other than Robert as she takes the seat the headwaiter is offering her.

Mrs. Cahill does take care of herself. Her fall coat deposited at the door, her dress showing enough upper body to display the results of her long mornings at the fitness center.

Truth be told, their marriage is not a good one. But she is stuck, Irish Catholic girl that she is. Not to mention her husband's considerable family wealth. So she makes the best of it.

The waiter deferentially hands menus to each of them.

"I wish you both a pleasant meal [*a pleas-aunt mell*]," he says in his Inspector Clouseau accent, lingering at Robert's side until dismissed with a nod.

The Cahills don't speak. She studies the menu. He motions the waiter over for a gin martini.

Cahill doesn't look around the room. He has no interest in who else is dining here, his only interest the martini. (He has had a starter at home while waiting for her to come downstairs dressed.)

He's midway through his drink. She's

ordered a white wine. She's still studying the menu, when here comes the headwaiter, a bottle and two fresh glasses in hand as he reapproaches the table.

"Madame," he says as he displays the bottle to her. (It's Louis Roederer Cristal Champagne — Brut limited edition — $500 on the menu.) Places the two glasses on the table.

"How lovely," she says, pleased, but perplexed. Looking across the table at Robert. This is not like him.

And it isn't from him. The headwaiter telling her it's from an admirer who wishes to remain unnamed.

"Shall I open it, madame?" he asks.

"By all means," she says, craning her neck around the dining area, trying to see who's responsible for this lovely act of over-the-top indulgence.

As the waiter pops the cork, causing quick glances from adjoining tables, she tells Robert, her eyes still wandering the room, "I'll bet it's from Jeb Turner. That would be just like him. Do you see him?" she asks Robert.

As the waiter pours Cristal into her glass, then turns to Robert (he declines), the delighted Mrs. Cahill is busy telling her husband it would be just like their friend from the Philadelphia Country Club. Jeb is such a darling. (She is careful not to be too effusive since she has been sleeping with Jeb off and on for the past two years. Jeb is Robert's childhood friend.)

Robert does a perfunctory 360 around the room, missing over in the corner a stylishly dressed African-American couple, he in a beautifully tailored, well-fitted suit, a diamond earring in each ear, and she in a low-cut, skin-tight chiffon dress, hair piled high, dangling hoop earrings twinkling in the glow of the room's massive chandelier.

The man, of course, is Slippery Williams. Two of his crew have been monitoring DA Cahill's moves for the past several weeks. Always from afar. Slippery is interested in any weaknesses Cahill might display. (Except for the drinking, nothing yet.)

Slippery is with a "date," one of the girls who populate the fringes of his inner circle — girls available for his lieutenants. And for him, when he wants one.

When they entered the restaurant, they had briefly turned heads. Not many African-American couples frequent this place. And while he had gone out of his way to tell the girl how to dress for this evening, meaning how *not* to dress, she still looked more whore than French restaurant dinner companion.

Since Slippery could see she tried her best, he let it go. But her behavior at the table is annoying him. Her pushed-up boobs popping over her dress edge. Her processed hair frozen in place. Long, silky fire-engine red fingernails. Cracking gum. Nonstop yakking to him. He lets it go long as he can, then leans in at the table.

"Shut your mouth, girl," he whispers to her.

She does. Pouts, then asks, "Why we here this place, Slip?"

When they arrived, Slippery wanting to get here and be in place before the Cahills' usual eight P.M. arrival time, the headwaiter had tried showing them to a table on the outer banks of the dining room.

Slippery saying to him, "Unh-uh. Not that one." Then pointing him to the table Slippery knows will be just far enough away, but in line of sight of the Cahills' usual Friday-night table.

"That one," he tells the headwaiter.

"Reserved," the headwaiter says, without his usual fawning pretense, or his phony French accent.

Slippery slips the guy a hundred dollar bill.

"Not no more," he tells the headwaiter.

The headwaiter quickly pockets the hundred.

"This way," he says to Slippery and his date, as he leads them to the table Slippery has selected.

They have been seated here ever since. Waiting.

"Why we here, girl, ain't none a your damn business," Slippery tells her, as she pouts across the starched white tablecloth. He watches Mrs. Cahill run her eyes past them, then take in the rest of the room, still searching for her benefactor.

Slippery waits until the waiter has returned to the Cahill table to replenish her glass, and bring Robert another martini, waits until the waiter reappears and takes their dinner order, until the first course has been served.

Then he tells the girl, "Stay put. Don't say nothin' to nobody." He casually walks to the Cahills' table.

Robert notices the skinny black man heading slowly toward them, a big smile on the guy's face. Instinctively, he returns the smile.

As Slippery approaches, coming into the zone close to the table, Mrs. Cahill notices him too. Slippery gives her a nice smile. She returns it.

Robert's trying to place the guy. About to get to his feet. Shake hands.

Then a picture of a black guy in an orange prison jumpsuit flashes into Robert's mind. A smelly, skinny perp, from the lockup, holding out his hands to be uncuffed by the deputy sheriffs before the judge enters the courtroom. How he and this black prisoner exchanged uncomfortable eye contact while Cahill was denouncing him to the court.

Just as Slippery arrives at the table Robert finally makes him.

His mind racing toward what to do next. Does this son of a bitch have a gun? Is he about to pull it? Shoot me? Here? Now? Oh my God.

As Slippery later told me and Mickie, he's standing there, smiling down at the two of them. Mrs. Cahill also smiling, waiting for this man to say something, her eyes darting to her husband, waiting for him to exchange pleasantries, to introduce her to this well-dressed man. She's finding him strangely attractive. His features are unremarkable. Yet, there is something in his eyes, his smile. Those diamond ear piercings. Something bedroom. Dangerous. Exciting.

But Robert Cahill is now glaring at the guy. Still seated. Speechless.

Slippery gives it a beat or two, then says,

"Mr. Cahill. This nice lady must be your wife."

Robert continues to glare, steam building.

When he doesn't respond, Slippery turns to Nancy Cahill, whose smile is still in place but starting to wilt. Her eyes darting between her husband and this friendly, polite man.

"I hope you enjoyin' the champagne, ma'am," Slippery tells her. "The man tell me it be the best they got here."

Nancy Cahill's instinct is to tell him, Yes it's very nice. Thank you. But another glance across the table at her husband tells her something's very wrong here. So she simply nods, that smile still there, but she's not sure how much longer she can keep it pasted to her face.

Slippery doesn't seem perturbed by her speechlessness. He redirects his attention to DA Cahill.

"I just wanted you to know. No hard feelings. You tried. Just didn't work, that's all. I understand. Just be part of the game. Know what I'm sayin'?"

Slippery has come here tonight because he was dissatisfied with the reports his men had been giving him about the DA. They're telling him, "Couldn't find no nothin', Slip. No strange pussy. He ain't fucking no young boys neither. Nothin' go up the man's nose. He clean." Meaning, of course, they found nothing for Slippery to blackmail the DA with to turn a blind eye to Slippery's livelihood activities.

So, plan B. Slippery has decided he'd see for himself what the DA is made of, how he will react to this intrusion. To a visit from him. He wants to show the DA how easy it is — and will be — to get close to him, should Cahill consider yet another try at prosecuting him. Slippery has no intention of overtly threatening the DA with bodily harm. Knows that won't be necessary to make his point.

Slippery knows that what DA Cahill should do is remain seated, calmly tell Slippery that the champagne will need to go back, ask Slippery to return to his own table. He has been a defendant in a criminal case brought by Cahill's office. Whether the case has been dismissed or not, he cannot accept the champagne and they may not speak, at least not without Slippery having a lawyer present. Cahill should then occupy himself with his meal, ignoring Slippery until he leaves them and returns to his own table.

Cahill remains seated. Mute. Not sure what to do.

"Hey, Mr. Cahill," Slippery says, pushing it further. "My girl over there where we seated?" He points the Cahills to his table and the girl there, cracking gum and watching them. Now waving hi, y'all. "She tell me she dyin' to meet you. Okay I axe her to come over?"

Slippery is just turning to signal the girl to come to the table when Robert Cahill loses it.

He jumps to his feet, throws his linen napkin to the table, points an accusing finger at Slippery. Those seated all around them now interrupt their own dinners, their own conversations to see what's going on at this table.

Jabbing his finger at Slippery, Cahill shouts, "You don't belong here and you know it."

Cahill knows what he means. So does Slippery. But the rest of those hearing this can't believe this white man has just shouted this to a well-dressed black man. They are horrified.

"Get up, Nancy," Cahill orders his wife. But she's stuck to her seat. What the hell is Robert doing? she's thinking. The last trace of her smile vaporizing like a splash of water onto a hot skillet.

"I said get up. We're leaving."

Nancy Cahill finally obeys. Cahill grips her elbow, but unlike the headwaiter's deft earlier touch, he drags her from the restaurant, past the headwaiter's station and out to the entranceway.

Slippery watches them go, then returns to his table and finishes his filet mignon.

CHAPTER 26
HE'S BAAACK

Arty Bernstein calls Mickie on Friday afternoon from somewhere outside the office. (He's been keeping himself scarce ever since the arrest and bail hearing.) Arty telling Mickie, "I need to see you guys. Now."

Mickie telling Arty, "Unh-uh, not now."

It's past five. No way is Mickie going to call Carla on another Friday afternoon and tell her he's working late. No fucking way. He's on too tight a leash to do that. He does? He can kiss Carla goodbye. That train would leave the proverbial station. Without Mickie on it.

"Arty, can't see you now," Mickie says over the phone. "I got one foot out the door. It's Friday, man. I got plans tonight. Let's do it first thing Monday morning. That work for you?"

Mickie's holding the receiver away from his ear, expecting the usual diatribe from Arty, him screaming into the phone, telling

Mickie, When I say now, I mean now. Pushing us like he does. Me and Mickie his for free, beck-and-call lawyers.

But instead, Arty says, real quiet, not like him at all, "Okay, see you then. Meet me in the conference room first thing. Junne too. Does that work for you guys?"

"Yeah, sure," Mickie tells him. Starting to think, Uhm. What's up with that?

Then Arty hangs up.

Mickie tells me about Arty's call, the Monday morning meet. To tell you the truth, I don't give it much thought.

The weekend comes and goes. The weather's really changing now. Mornings are getting cold. Those few scrawny downtown trees are showing fall leaf colors. Won't be long and those trees will be bare, skeletal. And here Mickie and me are, Monday morning, walking down the hall. Arty's at the conference room door as we approach. No real hellos. Just muffled grunts — "How you doing"s. Arty directs us in. Then follows us and shuts the door.

Arty's looking different, sitting across from me and Mickie. Not sure at first how. His blow-dried Larry King hairdo's looking more like it did before he got arrested. He's dressed like usual, with his braces and their patterned scales of justice design, his

Windsor-knotted tie.

It's in his eyes. Something is dead in there. Missing is his semi-crazed, I've-got-an-idea-listen-to-this look. And Arty's lost some weight. His custom-tailored shirt collar is hanging on him. His color is bad.

Cancer? I'm thinking. Is Arty about to tell me and Mickie he's got cancer? That's why he looks like he does. Diseased. Is in the early stages of wasting away.

There's a quick knock on the conference room door. Tamara walks in with a tray of coffees from the kitchen. We didn't ask for this. This is Tamara's idea of being helpful, however she can. In fact, throughout this meeting Tamara walks in here: papers for me or Mickie to sign, to tell us we've got this or that call, do we want to take it or call back? Standing there listening as Arty keeps going, paying no attention whatsoever to her.

And this is not like Arty. He's usually got this smarmy come-on for any halfway decent-looking woman who happens to come anywhere near him. Arty blatantly assessing her, eyeing her up and down, making some inane remark he's thinking is clever. But Arty totally ignores Tamara. (Tamara and me are fine. We had a talk the Saturday morning when she woke up in my

240

apartment. Everything's cool. We even hugged each other as she left for her own place.)

Arty's hands are jittery. His weekly manicure appointment, two maybe three weeks missed. His nails unbuffed, uncut.

And what's he telling us?

Cancer?

Nope. He wants to cut a deal. Plead out his case. Arty can't fight this. The prosecutor's treatment of him has done the trick. He wants out.

"So," Arty says, "I'll turn in the whole goddamn bunch works for me. Go tell the Feds I'll give them whatever they need. Testify as a government witness at trial against the lot. I just don't want to go to jail."

Mickie and me know — and so should Arty — that if push comes to shove, he's the major target in the case. The Feds are always after the big fish. They'll trade up to get the big fish. Make plea bargain deals with underlings. Testimony for leniency. Like the two lawyers already cut deals and were still working undercover in Arty's office when he commissioned the illegal phone taps. But prosecutors don't trade down, won't make a sweet deal with the big

241

fish, grant him leniency, to go after the gup-
pies.

"Yeah, okay, Arty," Mickie says. "But you
got nothing to trade. You can plead. But
you're gonna do time."

Arty's in motion. Wanting to interject. But
Mickie continues. And for once Arty waits,
lets Mickie finish.

"You can't walk on this, Arty," Mickie
says. "Your only shot is trial. Plead and
you'll do time."

Maybe if the other junior lawyers who
haven't copped to their own deals are stupid
enough not to plead guilty themselves once
Arty goes down, and insist on their own
trial, Arty might have a shot. If those junior
lawyers are dumb enough to insist on going
to trial, maybe then, if Arty agrees to testify
against them, the Feds might be willing to
reduce his sentence. But only a little. He
will be a witness for the prosecution. One
rotten apple lawyer testifying against other
rotten apple lawyers.

The jury won't like Arty, won't believe
him on the stand if he gets too sweet a deal
for his testimony, too big a reduction in his
sentence. They will think guys like him will
say anything the Feds want him to say, just
to lift his head off the chopping block. So,
yeah, he might get some time off what he's

already serving when — and if — he takes the stand. Just not a lot.

Arty is fucked. His options, me and Mickie are thinking, are near nonexistent.

"Want more coffee, Arty?"

Tamara's come back into the room with a refill pot.

He ignores her. Mickie waves Tamara off.

Arty's staring at me and Mickie. Then he leans forward, elbows on the table. The new Arty, I'm thinking. A defeated Arty. His dead eyes on us.

Mickie starts to tell Arty we'll do the best we can with the Feds, but . . .

"I've got something to trade," Arty almost whispers, cutting off Mickie.

Yeah, right, me and Mickie are thinking. Who bigger than Arty himself can he give up to the Feds?

And then he tells us, says he's got a way bigger fish he can deliver up to the prosecutors. And it's a fucking shark.

"I can give them Slippery Williams," he says. "Head on a plate."

Of course, this makes no sense to us. We're still in the dark.

Arty's nodding, like he's reading our thoughts. Don't believe me, huh? he seems to be thinking.

He shakes his head. "I can," is all he says.

So, we wait.

I hear Tamara quietly close the conference room door behind her.

And then Arty explains how he's been investing Slippery's laundered drug money for him. He met Slippery, he says, years ago, when Slippery was in here seeing us about whatever criminal case was getting near him at the time.

Arty says he's got records; he's kept a second set of books. Just for what he did for Slippery, namely the property investments made by straw corporations secretly owned by Slippery. Didn't share the cut he got from Slippery with his law partners, did what he did all on his own. He tells us how the wired money transfers from overseas banks can be traced.

But Arty holds back, doesn't tell us everything. Keeps to himself that he's figured out, from things Slippery has from time to time said, that Sami Khan is in bed with Slippery. Arty doesn't know the details. But he's figured it out. At least enough to understand that somehow Sami Khan is laundering Slippery's drug money too. Enough to put the Feds on the right trail.

Yeah, he keeps this to himself. He knows we represent Sami and his son in a separate criminal case. (Remember when Sami and his son were first here? In this same conference room? How Arty stuck his head in the door to speak with me and Mickie? How once he saw who was in there with us, he begged off?) And, needless to say, Arty knows we have been Slippery's lawyers.

Yeah, clever Arty decides to keep what he's figured out about Sami from us. For two reasons.

First, he wants to continue using me and Mickie free of charge. Our rent deal. He's figuring we don't technically represent Slippery Williams at present, since state DA Robert Cahill has dismissed all charges against him. And since Arty will be dealing with the Feds, and not Cahill's office, me and Mickie will have to continue representing Arty. No conflict for us, Arty has wrongly concluded.

But with Sami, Arty's thinking there would be a clear conflict, and me and Mickie would certainly need to withdraw from our representation of Arty. And probably of Sami and Rafat too. A lawyer can't at the same time represent a criminal defendant and the witness against that defendant. So, Arty keeps mum on that.

Second reason, Arty wants to hold something up his sleeve. He first wants to see if what he's got on Slippery should prove to be too little for a good deal for him. If it does, then he'll throw Sami and Rafat into the pot. See if that sweetens the deal.

And how would that affect me and Mickie? Arty doesn't give two shits about us. Only what we can do for him.

"Whoa, whoa," Mickie says. "We can't do this."

I'm nodding my head in agreement, telling Arty, "We can't hear this stuff from you. You're gonna need new lawyers. For Christ sake, Arty. You know better than that. Slippery Williams is our client. Doesn't matter whether there's technically a case pending or not. We can't be hearing this shit about him."

"Yeah," Mickie says after me. "Me and Junne. We are fucking out of this."

"Fuck you are," Arty says. "Slippery Williams is not your client. At least not right now. And I am. So you need to do what you need to do. For me. I'm not going out and getting new lawyers. Forget about it. I've got you."

"Arty, that's bullshit," Mickie says.

"Yeah? Think so? How about I tell the Feds you didn't come in with me cause of Williams. Cause you told me not to give him up. Offered to make it worth my while, from your other client. Think maybe the

Feds gonna start looking at you then? For obstructing justice?"

"Get the fuck outta here, Arty," Mickie says.

Arty gets up. "Don't be stupid," he says to us, then turns and leaves.

When that door slams shut it sucks the air out of this room.

That fucking Arty.

Chapter 27
La Famiglia

Me and Mickie sit in that conference room, stunned. Our stomachs tight, shaking our heads.

Yeah, things are looking pretty goddamn grim. We sit there in silence staring at nothing, then each other. That's not doing much good. So after a while we get up and go back to our offices. There's work to do. Not that either of us gets much done.

But then life goes on. At least until it doesn't. And it's the "until it doesn't" part that's got me and Mickie so distraught.

Yeah, life goes on. Me and Mickie sleepwalk through the rest of the week until Thursday. Because Thursday is Thanksgiving. America's great daylong halftime show. Everything stops. Families get together to overeat. And so, bad as things are, me and Mickie act like most everyone else and we each separately do Thanksgiving.

I'm seated at the table at my mother's.

She's directly across from me. Silently weeping. Surrounding the two of us is the rest of the family. My two brothers, their wives and kids. And more food on the table than three families can eat. The turkey. Of course the turkey. But we are Italians, so that poor dead bird is blockaded by plates of sausage, pasta, lobster chunks with more pasta. Get the picture?

My brothers are ignoring my mother. Their wives are used to their mother-in-law. So they too ignore her theatrics and help the kids load their plates while simultaneously scolding them for being so unruly.

As in my brother Tony's wife, Adriana, to their son: "Anthony, you lay one more hand on your sister and I'll smack your head." (Holding a drumstick like a club to make the point.)

Let me just freeze this frame for a minute. I'm sitting here, but my head's filled with all the stuff me and Mickie have learned. I don't know how I'm going to eat, the way my stomach's churning.

Me and Mickie are in one hell of a bind.

You can't divulge client confidences. Lawyers simply can't do that without client consent.

So if we tell Slippery what Arty has in mind, we violate lawyers' ethical rules of conduct, for which we could be disbarred. Even worse: if Slippery learns from us that Arty's about to roll over on him — give him up to the Feds? — what we're doing is setting up Arty. Then me and Mickie become accomplices to murder. Arty's. Because Slippery will see to it that Arty is silenced. Permanently.

And if we don't tell Slippery? When he finds out the hard way, when the FBI arrests him? Then me and Mickie won't have to worry about being accomplices to murder.

We'll be in the same shallow grave as Arty.

But, like I said, it's Thanksgiving. The national time-out day.

Is Dumpy Brown on his feet at his family table, leaning over to carve the turkey, kids and grandkids all around? Is Slippery at his mom's? Or grandma's?

I do know that Mickie's at his cousin's house over in Haddonfield, Carla in tow. Carla who's got one foot out Mickie's door. Sitting at the table. Answering polite questions from the cousins, otherwise grim. Enduring the meal. Unhappiness hanging on her face like one of those dying leaves outside the house on the trees.

Tamara's in her apartment. Gregory's in his wheelchair across the kitchen table as she lowers her head to thank the good Lord for their bounty. Gregory so stoned his eyes are kaleidoscopes. Tamara finishes her prayer, then lifts her eyes to her nephew. Sighing.

And I'm sitting here with my family. And what I'm dealing with at the moment is my tearful mother across the table from me.

So let's push the play button at the Salerno family table.

"Anthony," Tony's wife is screaming. "This is the last time. Leave your sister alone."

"I'm not doin' nothin'," Anthony whines, as he pinches a big chunk of his chubby sister Madonna's leg under the table. Madonna howls like a she-wolf caught in a steel bear trap.

"Ma," I say over the din of the table noise. "What's the matter?"

"Don't worry about it, Salvatore," she says, dabbing at her eyes with a lace hankie. "Just eat, it's okay."

Then, under her breath in Italian, she says, "*Non sposerà mai. Una semenza sterile.* [He'll never marry. What a waste of sperm.]"

My sister-in-law Adriana picks up one of the pasta bowls and offers it to my mother.

"Ma," she says. "Eat." (My brother Gian-

251

carlo [Johnny], his wife, Allegra, my brother
Tony, all solemnly nodding in agreement.)

And my mother looks tenderly at Adriana,
understanding, takes the bowl, and spoons
some more fusilli onto her plate.

In my mother's house — you got a problem? — eat, has always been what you're
told.

"*Grazie, cara* [Thank you, dear]," my
mother says, handing back the serving bowl,
then palms up to the heavens, she moves
her hands in little concentric circles. Letting
me know, you had a woman like Tony's
sweet wife, Adriana, you wouldn't be sitting
here Thanksgiving by yourself, without a
woman to make you whole, what can I say,
I tell the priest at every confession my
Salvatore will be the death of me.

Then she gently pats Adriana's hand,
smiles affectionately, nods approval. Then
another look shoots my way. See? my mother's signaling. If you had one of these. A
saint. I won't die with the heavy heart you
will be the sole cause of.

The doorbell rings. Then it rings again.
Then again and again. Like someone furi-
ously jabbing a finger into the button.

Little Anthony jumps from the table, missing the executioner's swipe of his sister's
arm.

"I'll get it. I'll get it," he shouts as he runs from dining room through living room to the front door.

Everyone at the table waits expectantly as Anthony is heard telling whoever it is that we're having dinner right now.

We hear the front door close. But Anthony seems to have let the caller in. We hear a woman's voice asking something about my brother Tony.

Tony recognizes that voice.

I hear him mumble, "Oh shit!" under his breath.

He says this just as young Anthony turns the corner back into the dining room. He pops back onto his seat and resumes eating as though nothing has just happened.

We all wait expectantly as the woman enters the dining room. I see Tony exchange glances with my brother Johnny. Then he watches Adriana as she looks at the woman who is now standing at the dining room entranceway, searching the table for him.

This woman looks more or less like my two sisters-in-law. Same long nails, same big, dyed, streaked hair. And like them she's dressed in tight jeans (okay, this woman's ass hasn't begun the Italian postmarriage, post-kids spread). She's heavily made up and she's been crying, her thick mascara running down her cheeks. She's got a big silver cross on a chain embedded between her breasts and rings on her thumbs.

She spots Tony, who I can see is looking this way and that. Like for a hole he can dive into.

"I told you, you bastard [*bastad*]," she screams at Tony. "You tell her [*tell ha*] or I do."

Okay, let's hit the pause button again.

Standing here before us is some gal my brother Tony's been screwing. Italian men from our background? Well, they have a reputation for infidelity. What can I say? Is it well earned? Not all Italian men from around here cheat on their wives. Most, okay, but not all.

My dad had a girlfriend. His *goomah*. My mother probably knew. But would this woman come to the house? Never. Never.

Something needs doing here. It's the men versus the women. You know how it goes, when the difference between the sexes comes to the forefront. Like the old joke:

A woman doesn't come home one night. The next morning she tells her husband she slept over at a friend's house. The husband calls his wife's ten best friends. None of them know anything about it.

A man doesn't come home one night. The

next morning he tells his wife he slept over at a friend's house. The woman calls her husband's ten best friends. Eight confirm that he slept over, and two tell her that he's still there.

So let's hit the play button.

My brother Tony's pointing an accusing finger at this woman. Busily jabbing it in her general direction.

He looks at his wife. "She's crazy," he says to her. Then he hunches his shoulders, arms out, palms up, pleadingly. Tony ready to tell Adriana, Who knew? You show a little kindness to the girl works in the front office at the auto body shop. That's all. Swear to God, Ade. It's not how it looks. I was just being nice to the girl. I never touched her.

But me and my brother Johnny are already in action. Both of us telling Adriana more or less the same nonsense. Johnny and me watching each other, trying our best to coordinate as we improvise why our brother Tony's absolutely within his rights to be so indignant. This girl barging in here Thanksgiving. Getting it all wrong. Misunderstanding Tony's kindness at the shop. Tony actually sleeping with her? Never, me and Johnny trying our best to tell Adriana without ever using the "F" word, or anything even remotely like it. We are, after all, at our mother's table.

So me and Johnny are babbling. The girl, stopped in her tracks, looking at us, not understanding what the hell we're going on about. Adriana's ping-ponging between Tony at the table and this hovering, angry, mascara-dripping woman. Tony's shoulders and arms are gyrating as he pantomimes his unspoken litany of excuses.

And then Mom swings into action.

She rises from the table and, with a swooping motion, she grabs on to the carving knife still lying on the plate containing what is now a turkey carcass. With one deft move Mom now has the point of this knife pressed under the girl's jaw. Right at the neck.

The girl is stunned. She didn't see this coming. This five foot one inch little old lady now poised to jam this butcher knife up into her throat.

The girl is trying to look down at my mother, but the point of the knife is making this a hazardous move. So she freezes. She does manage to shoot one quick look around the room.

Not sure if she can tell, but the rest of us in here are frozen as well. All except young Anthony, still eating.

"Cool," he says to no one in particular.

Then my mother starts explaining the facts of life to this now completely terrified girl.

But Mom is doing this in Italian. Assuming, I suppose, that anyone looking like her two daughters-in-law (both of whom are at the moment slack jawed, eyes wide, gawking) is going to understand Italian.

But this gal doesn't. So, although my mother can speak English more or less fluently (she was eleven when she came to this country with her parents), she turns to me and nods for me to translate.

"I think my mother is letting you know that coming here was a bad idea."

The woman wants to nod in agreement. Of course, she can't do that without puncturing the skin of her neck on the point of the knife my mom still has pressed against her flesh. So she blinks a few times. Got that, she's letting me know.

"And," I continue. "She thinks it would be a good idea if you were to leave."

Blink, blink, blink.

My mother stays with Italian. Thinking it helps keep this bimbo terrified. She utters a long paragraph. In it are references to this girl's morals, her private parts, her family, why my mother should shove this knife right up into her, which she is really and truly thinking of doing. It's a long speech.

When Mom finally finishes, the girl's eyes dart to me for translation.

"Mom says better leave."

Blink, blink, blink, blink.

Mom lowers the knife. The girl has now forgotten Tony. She lets out an ear-piercing wail and runs for the front door.

Young Anthony takes his fork and stabs at the plate containing one of the two remaining sausages, kicking his feet under the table as he resumes eating. Mom points a come-with-me finger at Tony, who dutifully gets up and follows his mother into the kitchen.

The rest of us remain at the table while, kitchen door closed, Mom screams at Tony. She's mixing Italian and English in the same sentences. Telling him he ought to be ashamed of himself. How he's brought shame and dishonor to his family.

And not a peep from Tony. He's taking it like a man. Maybe a ten-year-old man, his mother standing there scolding him. But there's no protesting. All we can hear from Tony is the occasional "Yes, Ma," "Okay, Ma."

When she's finished she releases him. As he returns to the dining room and his seat, my mother stands at the kitchen doorway, now beckoning Adriana.

Once Adriana is behind closed doors with my mother she gets the same treatment. Though the speech is different. Telling her she's not giving her man enough attention, else he wouldn't have his wandering eye, out on the street looking for fulfillment from some other woman. This goes on for a while, Adriana dutifully "Yes, Ma"-ing her. Then she's released.

Soon as Adriana's back at the table my mother too comes out. We go back to eating.

Then we clear the table for dessert.

CHAPTER 28
"BUMPED"

The Friday after Thanksgiving, most offices are still closed.

Last night, the bunch of us sat at Mom's table eating dessert. Like nothing happened. (Pass the cannolis. Anthony, you touch Madonna one more time . . . Who wants more rum cake?) Of course, you know my brother Tony caught some serious shit from Adriana once they got home and the kids were asleep. But they'll get over it. Like I said, Tony's dalliance with Ms. Mascara Eyes isn't what you'd call a deal breaker as far as marriages are concerned around here.

As I later learn, Mickie and Carla leave his cousin's house. They both say their thank-yous, it was great, let's do it again next year. In the car on the way back to Mickie's in Cherry Hill, not a word between them. They get home. She lets him have sex with her, then she turns her back and goes to sleep.

Ah, love.

I spend all of Friday in my apartment. Thinking. Yeah sure, about the cases and the bind me and Mickie are in. But mostly about me. About family. About — what can I say? — happiness. Then I decide.

Friday evening, nine-thirty. I walk through the door at Bump, the gay club over in Philly. I stand there and search the crowded place. Not only is it the beginning of the weekend, but a holiday weekend. So, there are a lot of guys in here. The place is in fact packed. I search the bar. Then the rest of the place.

I see him just as he notices me.

I watch as Jason excuses himself from the group of men he's been standing with. He walks toward me. As he passes the bar I see him lay his drink on the counter. He gives me a warm smile.

And here is where I end this chapter. You get the picture. Tonight is my private business. No need to describe anything further for you.

CHAPTER 29
WHAT IS IT
WITH THESE MONDAYS?

The Monday after Thanksgiving I come in late. Overslept. (Let's leave it at that.)

Mickie's already in. As I pass his office, his light is on, his coat thrown over the chair. Then I hear his voice coming from the coffee room down the hall. I walk over and see Mickie at the small table with Tamara. They've both got Styrofoam cups of Arty Bernstein's $1.20 pay-as-you-go coffee. I pour myself a cup. I notice the plastic bucket for the money is empty.

I join them at the table. Both are looking glum. Mickie's got his tie down. His gut's pressing at his shirt. Tamara's in a sweater dress and high boots. The heat's turned up in here. Outside is downright cold, no recovery from last night's temperature dip. Typical Camden, New Jersey, weather, from late summer direct to early winter, autumn nothing more than a whisper on the wind.

"How was your Thanksgiving?" I ask

Tamara, as I take a sip of Arty's coffee, then grimace.

She rolls her eyes. Awful, she's letting me know.

"You?" I ask Mickie.

"Never better," clearly meaning the opposite.

"You?" Mickie asks me.

"Oh, the usual," I say. "My mom almost murdered some woman came to the house because one of my brothers was screwing her."

Tamara's eyes widen. Mickie just nods, okay, got that.

And so we sit there. After a few more sips of Arty's vile, sour coffee, me and Mickie start trying to figure our way through what Arty's done to us. And what he's threatening to do to us if we don't continue to represent him while he rats out Slippery Williams to the Feds. Tamara sits with us for a while, then she excuses herself and goes back to work.

And while we're sitting in the coffee room, across the river in downtown Philly, Rafat Khan is seated in one of Jerry Rubino's conference rooms, a china cup of coffee (the firm provides freshly brewed Starbucks for guests and staff alike) on the table in front of him as he waits for Jerry.

Sami Khan and his wife had spent Thanksgiving alone. Rafat, his wife, and kids had begged off on the usual celebratory dinner at his parents' house. I can just about hear Mrs. Khan asking her husband why her son and his family were not coming. Can see Sami waving her off. Old school Sami. Old country Sami. To him, a man does not need to explain himself, or anything else a wife doesn't need to hear. Mrs. Khan doesn't protest. Doesn't press the question.

And then, yesterday evening, Sunday, the long weekend coming to a close, she answers a knock at the front door. Rafat is standing there. It isn't hard to imagine what happened once Rafat entered his parents' house.

He greets his mother in the traditional way. Asks her only if Papa is in his study. Then he walks to the study, knocks on the closed door, enters, and takes the seat across from his father who is encamped reading the paper in his usual winged easy chair by the unlit fireplace.

Sami's wig is off. He never wears it at home if there are no guests. He looks strangely older without his toupee. Little sparse strands of wispy hair standing on end across his scalp, like a drought-ruined field of wheat. His shawl-collared house sweater is buttoned; tufts of gray chest hair protrude from his open-necked shirt. He lowers the paper to his lap. Doesn't greet his son. Instead, waits for him to speak.

Rafat pleads his case, tells his father what they both need to do.

"Need to do?" Sami says, interrupting him. "Need to do? You are telling me what 'we' need to do?"

I'm seeing Mrs. Khan sitting at the kitchen table, waiting for the study door to open, listening to their raised voices. The shouted words mean nothing to her. She is concerned only that her husband and their son are being cross with each other. A business problem perhaps, she thinks, as she sits there patiently. Maybe she should bring in some tea? she tells herself. But continues waiting instead.

Sami is lecturing his son. Telling him, "What do you know? You think we can go to the authorities? Tell them about this black criminal? This animal?" Sami saying this to Rafat in Hindi. "That will solve things? Let me tell you. You don't know this man. I do." Telling Rafat to leave things alone. He, Sami, will handle this. Saying to his son, "Now go home to your family."

Sami retrieves the paper from his lap and reads it while his son remains seated, staring at his father. Then Rafat leaves the study. Soon as he opens the door his mother is there. She waits. Rafat says nothing, kisses her on the forehead, wishes peace upon her in Hindi, then goes home.

So, while me and Mickie are sitting in the Bernstein, Smulkin coffee room trying without success to figure out what's what, Rafat's cooling his heels waiting for Jerry Rubino.

Jerry eventually gets there. They meet. No sooner does that meeting end when Rafat's on the phone again. This time it's to us, asking . . . well, more like pleading, can he come over, see me and Mickie, right now? It's not a court day for either me or Mickie. So, sure, I tell Rafat, see you when you and your dad get here. No Dad, Rafat tells me.

"Me only," he says. "Me alone."

No trouble hearing the concern in his voice. What now? What else can go wrong?

CHAPTER 30
JESUS H. CHRIST!

Less than an hour after Rafat's call, me and Mickie are sitting with him in the conference room Arty lets us use. No coffee, no preliminaries. Rafat is in a state. He gets right to it. Tells us how he waited in Jerry's conference room longer than he thought he could tolerate without totally losing it. How Jerry Rubino and his small army of young lawyers finally did arrive.

How when Jerry Rubino and his youngsters entered the conference room, he looked around for Sami. He asked if they should wait for Rafat's dad. No need, Rafat told him. Then once all were seated, he explained why he was there, why he had chosen to stay away from the company's offices today, why his father was not there with him, in fact doesn't even know he's there.

Rafat tells me and Mickie how Jerry listened, nodding sympathetically in all the right places, as Rafat shared his dilemma, telling Rubino how he and his wife spent the entire Thanksgiving weekend agonizing what to do. How to deal with what Rafat's father had done. He decided not to mention last night's visit with his dad to Jerry, didn't want to paint Sami as being that intransigent.

Rafat's telling me and Mickie how seemingly attentive Jerry Rubino was when Rafat told him what a nightmare this had become. Then telling Jerry for the first time about Slippery Williams and his father's long-term dealings with him. Laying out the entire money laundering scheme. And, needless to say, this is the first time me and Mickie are hearing this.

Rafat's talking. Me and Mickie are shooting each other glances. Signaling first, What? Then, Oh no. With Slippery? Oh fucking no.

"So I said to Mr. Rubino, help me make my father see the light," Rafat's saying to us, totally unaware of me and Mickie eyeballing each other.

He urged Jerry please to make his father understand that the only realistic chance they both had of getting through this horrible situation was to cut a deal with the Feds. A plea bargain.

"We have something the prosecution wants, don't we?" he asked Jerry. "This Slippery Williams? We can agree to testify against this drug dealer. Help put him behind bars. Won't that help us? Get us a reduced sentence? Something we can begin serving now, and then we can get on with our lives."

Rafat didn't say more. He had said what he needed to say. He truly believed Jerry was as good as they got. He'd fix this problem.

Jerry at first said nothing. His boys and girls, of course, remained quiet. Apprentice priests, waiting for the oracle to speak.

I see Mickie reach into his pocket and pop a couple of Rolaids. At this point we are bombarding each other with a barrage of oh-shit looks. Rafat is too disconcerted to notice.

As Rafat tells it, that's when Jerry decided. He's done here. Time to bow out. Move on to other cases. Other well-heeled clients. Let some other lawyer sort out this mess. And financially speaking, Jerry no doubt concluded, this case is now in diminishing returns for him. The heavy lifting is coming to an end. All the legal research, the memo writing, is about done. Time to move on.

Mickie and me have no trouble understanding that a big-time lawyer like Jerry Rubino would not like this business about a drug dealer. (Large law firms don't as a rule represent, or have anything to do with, drug dealers, who are left to lawyers like me and Mickie.) And particularly this one. Jerry has surely heard of Slippery Williams. Still, Jerry would quickly appreciate the strategic value of Sami Khan's illicit relationship with Slippery Williams, would easily see that it gave the Khans something to trade for a better deal for themselves. (And Jerry Rubino has never represented Slippery Williams, doesn't have the problem me and Mickie now realize we've got.) On the other hand, the old man won't agree to a plea bargain, making his son into a potential witness against his father. (Under a relatively new federal statute governing the parent-child testimonial privilege, there is no prohibition on a son voluntarily testifying against his father.) But as I've already told you, the same lawyer cannot ethically represent both a defendant and a witness against that defendant.

Rafat is sitting in that well-appointed conference room at Jerry's firm. He is frozen, waiting for a response from Jerry. A lifeline. Anything that helps. And after a while Jerry speaks, starts explaining. Rafat is trying to absorb what Rubino is telling him. Rafat's coffee is untouched, his head is throbbing, he's trying to understand just what this lawyer is saying. At first Rafat thinks he's simply misunderstanding Rubino, but ultimately Rafat gets it. Jerry's telling him, with one client as a witness, the other as a defendant, there are ethical considerations. He will need to withdraw as counsel. Rafat is stunned.

"Won't you even talk to my father?" he asks Rubino.

"Not under the circumstances," Jerry tells him. "Too sticky. Too complicated. Of course we will formally write your dad, explain our need to withdraw. We'll mention you have decided to be a potential witness against him. Have to do this. Hope you understand the position we are in."

"Position *you* are in?" Rafat says to Rubino, trying to keep control of himself, to suppress the rising volume of his voice. "I've decided to be a witness against my father? What the hell are you talking about? I haven't decided anything. Mr. Rubino, what are you talking about?"

But Rubino's done. Rafat tells me and Mickie how Rubino stands, reaches across the table to shake Rafat's hand, wishes him and his dad the best of luck. (Says nothing about returning any of the remaining retainer.)

And then, with his team trailing behind him, Rubino exits. It's like they dematerialized. Vanished into thin air. Rafat cannot even hear the patter of Gucci loafers on the thick hallway carpet.

That, of course, is when Rafat called us, used the phone right there in Jerry's conference room.

Me and Mickie wait as Rafat puts his hands to his face, until he composes himself as best he can. He lowers his hands, looks over at us. He needs us to give him something. Anything he can take some solace in. Some hope.

Despite his Indian coloring, this guy is just about white-bedsheet pale, he's got dark circles under his eyes. You can see the sleepless nights, the overstressed days, in his eyes, his drawn face, even in the way he is sitting at this table.

But there is nothing for us to say. Nothing helpful. My stomach's now tight as a drum. Mickie's a statue.

Rafat's staring at us. Me and Mickie are staring back.

We then explain to Rafat that we too must resign as his lawyers. We tell him that we have represented Slippery Williams, but we assure him we will keep client confidences and not disclose to Slippery any of what Rafat has now disclosed to us. Then Mickie gives him the names of some other lawyers he could go to. And we wish him luck. (That's the second time he's heard this from a lawyer today.)

More silence.

After a while Rafat stands, thanks us for our time, and leaves.

Mickie groans as soon as Rafat is out of the room. He looks at me. Can you fucking believe this? he's signaling.

Unlike Jerry Rubino, we would have agreed to meet with Sami. And try and convince him that he's got to do like his son. Got to try and make a deal. Among other things so his own son doesn't take the witness stand at trial against him as a prosecution witness.

But how can we do that? Now that we know both our other clients have been in bed with Slippery. We just can't. No way. The conflicts for us are real, and unresolvable.

And as Rafat walks through the reception area to the elevators, me and Mickie are both wondering if our inability to tell Slippery what's facing him here will result in our deaths.

I mean sooner or later these guys are going to spill the beans to the authorities. Slippery isn't likely to forgive and forget once he learns that the witnesses against him were our clients. That we knew and held that info from him. (That's why he brought us in on Sami and Rafat's case in the first place.)

"Fuck," Mickie says under his breath.

He gets up and goes back to his office. I go to mine.

Fuck.

And while we're doing this, yet another meeting is going on across town. And in that one, missing-in-action Arty Bernstein is sitting across a desk from Dumpy Brown.

CHAPTER 31
BIRDS OF A FEATHER

Arty Bernstein is just incapable of walking a straight line. What he's decided to do is beyond risky. It's potentially suicidal.

Low-rent, scheming Arty. Sitting with Dumpy, knowing Dumpy Brown represented Slippery Williams's lieutenants at his last trial, either unaware or repressing the fact that Dumpy is tight with Slippery himself.

Arty is pissed at me and Mickie, for throwing him out of his own conference room, for refusing to help him roll over on Slippery. So here he sits with Dumpy, in Dumpy's office.

Arty must be semideranged at this point. Even for a guy like him this is scheming at its riskiest. He knows of the bad blood between Dumpy and Mickie. That's what brought him here.

So, these two guys are sitting across from each other. These two middle-aged legal

275

eagles. Two old-school, overdressed, graying peacocks.

Dumpy's behind his desk, in an old chair creaks with the slightest body movement. He's got his suit jacket off, his powder blue vest tightly buttoned over his protruding belly. His stick-pinned, high-collared two-toned shirt clinches his flesh. Folds his turkey neck into a double chin, nudging it over the rim of his tightly knotted iridescent tie. Dumpy's stringy, dyed comb-over, squiggly sparse strands seemingly glued to his shiny, mocha-colored scalp. Double-pinky-ringed Dumpy Brown. Sitting, smiling, waiting to see what the fuck brings this Jew lawyer across town to see someone like him.

Arty's dressed to the nines. Doing his best to act natural. Relaxed. His suit jacket is on, though unbuttoned. He's tailor-made. Glove-fitted. The shoulders of his jacket TV anchorman perfect. Smiling at Dumpy across the desk, like nothing's wrong, his legs folded, knee over knee. Casually picking at a fleck of lint from his slacks. Showing French cuffs, oversized gold cuff links, his Rolex watch.

"So, how you been?" Arty asks, thinking to himself, Do I call this schvartze Dumpy? Or no? Unaware how the moniker was laid on Dumpy. Better safe than sorry, he silently instructs himself. Leave it off.

"Real good, Art," Dumpy says. He wants to cut to the chase here. Later for this buddy-buddy bullshit. So he adds, "What can I do for you, my brother?"

My brother? Arty's thinking. Whatever, he tells himself, seeing Dumpy wants to get down to business.

"I want to retain you," Arty says, almost saying, "Dumpy." Cautioning himself.

Dumpy knows about Arty's troubles, the Feds' grand jury investigation, Arty's arrest. It's no secret in Camden.

But "Uh-huh" is all Dumpy says. Staying noncommittal. He knows with Arty there's an angle here. Something Arty's got up his sleeve. Dumpy knows Arty is small change. But to him he's still a clever Yid. They all are to Dumpy, the way he grew up. What he heard from his construction worker father at the dinner table, Got to watch those Jews, son, he'd tell Dumpy. You let them, they'll suck your blood dry. It's in their natures, know what I'm saying?

Arty waits a beat, trying to see, will Dumpy say more? Ask why Arty wants to hire him?

The two men stare at each other. Too much time passes. Arty decides he's got to speak. Needs to lay it out for Dumpy. Telling himself, Make it appealing. Arty knows Dumpy's a pro. You get down to it, he's a smart guy, Arty tells himself. One of the smart ones.

"Yeah, well. Here's the thing," Arty says. "You know about my case, right?"

Dumpy nods yeah, but remains silent.

Arty waits, seeing is Dumpy going to say more. Then, when he doesn't, "Yeah, so. Mezzonatti and Salerno represent me."

Here Arty shrugs, signaling to Dumpy, Yeah I know, what can you do? I made a mistake.

"You know, they sublet space from me," Arty says, as though that provides an explanation for why he hired us in the first place. (He leaves out the part about the rent being free in exchange for our services.)

Still nothing from Dumpy. He sucks his teeth.

"Look, I know I can beat those bullshit charges the Feds are going for." Arty shrugs again. It's really no big thing, he's trying to display to Dumpy. "But hell, Dumpy . . . ," he says, kicking himself for using the moniker after all, carefully watching Dumpy for a reaction, missing the electric miniflash in Dumpy's eyes. Then quickly adding, "But to be honest with you, the cost is killing me. And those guys. Well, I've got to tell you . . . [Arty silently cautioning himself, For fuck sake, don't call him Dumpy again], those two guys have really disappointed me."

"Uh-huh."

"So, here's what I have in mind." Arty changes knees, crossing then recrossing back to where he was. "Those guys. Their lease is up. Know what I'm saying?"

Dumpy waits.

"I hire you. You take on my case. I shitcan those two 'Eyetalians.' You take over their space. It's nice. I give it to you free of charge. Not a penny so long as you're my lawyer. Sound fair?"

Silence.

"Look, I'll be honest with you," Arty says, missing the irony in his using that particular figure of speech. "I need to make a deal with the Feds. I got to get this case off my back. I need a lawyer like you. Look. I've got something to trade. Something big."

Dumpy's not going to make this easy.

"Uh-huh," is all Dumpy says.

Arty waiting for more. Not getting it. So adding, "What I say stays in here, right? Lawyer-client protected, know what I mean?"

Dumpy gives him one mini-nod yeah, but

otherwise keeps silent.

Arty deciding to make a joke of it, smiling across the desk.

"You know, like they say," he says, snickering. "What happens in Vegas, stays in Vegas."

Dumpy nods. No smile. You wanna talk, his eyes telling Arty, then talk.

Arty is hoping for more, wanting Dumpy to tell him, Don't worry; what you tell me is privileged. Stays in here. But Arty's got to go with what he gets from Dumpy.

"I can give up somebody big to the Feds. Real big," Arty says, looking for at least some reaction from Dumpy.

Dumpy shifts his weight in the chair. It creaks and groans.

Arty uncrosses his legs, leans forward, like he's about to whisper. But he doesn't. This is harder than he thought it would be. He looks around, as though Dumpy's small office is filled with eavesdroppers, leaning in, trying to hear. He gulps some air.

"I've been doing shit for Slippery Williams."

Arty searches for at least some reaction from Dumpy.

Stone-faced Dumpy.

Dumpy's mind's going click, click, click. But all Arty can see is Dumpy waiting.

So Arty lays it out. All of it. The straw

corporations, the dirty money. The real estate investments.

Arty's going on and on. Now that he's into it he can't stop himself. He's rambling his way through all the bad stuff he's done for Slippery Williams.

And Dumpy's sitting in his creaky chair. Quietly listening. But his brain's humming, crossing and crisscrossing scenarios like those old pinball machines Dumpy played when he was a kid, the silver ball shooting here, there, bouncing off posts, hitting the flippers for another go-round.

All Arty sees while he rambles on and on, and on, is the same old Dumpy Brown, deadpan, seated before him. What he can't see is Dumpy now running plays on the blackboard of his mind, trying to figure out what's really going on here.

Okay, Dumpy silently concludes, point one: Bernstein must have disclosed his illicit dealings with Slippery to Mickie and me. Otherwise Arty wouldn't be here with him in the first place. Dumpy realizes we must have done something Bernstein didn't like. But what?

As it turns out, Arty fills in that blank for Dumpy. He fills it in with a lie, but Dumpy buys it. Arty telling Dumpy that Mickie and me went to Slippery, told him what Arty wants to do. Then we told Arty, Slippery would pay him to keep his mouth shut. That Arty told us, No fucking way. He's trading Slippery to the Feds. It's his way or the highway.

We know that never happened. But Dumpy's buying it. Because it's what he would do.

First, no way Dumpy wouldn't himself run to Slippery Williams the minute he learned from Arty that he was intent on rolling over on Slippery, giving him up to the Feds. Dumpy would do that in a heartbeat. Client confidences or no. Easily considering that to be the smart move, he mistakenly concludes me and Mickie would do the same thing.

And second, Dumpy's thinking, it would be just like Slippery to use his lawyers to offer money to Arty to shut him up. Since Dumpy would do it if Slippery asked him, he's guessing me and Mickie would too.

You see, the way Dumpy's seeing this (and I've got to admit, he's not all wrong), on the street, in what these guys call "the game," Arty's a perceived civilian. Not a player. In Slippery's world of drug dealing and whatnot, killing a player's one thing. Part of the game. Killing someone who is seen as a civilian is another. Something like that really brings the heat down on you. Dumpy knows this. Thinking that's what's going on in Slippery's mind. Of course, in every meaningful sense, Arty is indeed a player. But without any of his dealings with Slippery ever known to the public, he would be seen as a civilian.

Don't get me wrong, guys like Slippery will off a nonplayer (like me or Mickie?) when the circumstances warrant it. And me and Mickie still think Slippery would have Arty silenced in the blink of an eye.

Okay, so Dumpy must be telling himself, Arty's here trying to entice him to take over from me and Mickie, Arty wrongly concluding we have already told Slippery what Arty wants to do. So, no point in Dumpy going to see Slippery. To tell him something he already knows.

Dumpy can picture Slippery giving him shit like he does. Telling him, You a day late and a dollar short, motherfucker. My two white boys already been here. Told me that shit already. Know what I'm sayin'? Dumpy, you a chump. Snickering to his boys. Dumpy standing there like a fool. Again.

And that's when Dumpy makes up his mind. He doesn't care why this nutty Jew lawyer's in the chair opposite his desk. What Arty really wants. Why he's here. What exactly his game is.

What Dumpy decides is that this guy, coming here, is a goddamned act of providence. A fortuity, like they say. Bernstein has just unwittingly handed him the keys to the kingdom. Now Dumpy's got a real way to get rid of Slippery. And us. Clear off the whole entire fucking playing field.

Dumpy's been around. He's a man of experience, knows that when Slippery Williams falls, there will be some other mope to take his place — the drug business being what it is. And that's going to be Dumpy's opportunity.

With Arty Bernstein implicating Slippery, and me and Mickie to boot, for offering Arty Slippery's money to keep his mouth shut, this is as clear an obstruction of justice case as you're likely to get.

Yeah, Dumpy concludes, as Arty rattles on across from him. The good Lord has given him a way to knock Slippery out of the picture. Slippery who never has given Dumpy his due. Dumpy is intent on ensuring that the next guy will. And at the same time he gets rid of Mickie and me as well.

All Dumpy's got to do, he's telling himself, is be careful. Watch his own back.

"Yeah, okay, okay. I got it," Dumpy tells Arty, finally shutting him down.

Arty stops midsentence, waits to see where Dumpy is on this thing. He looks expectantly at Dumpy, then concludes that maybe he's been a bit frantic, so he instructs himself to cool down. He air-pats his hairdo, shoots his cuffs, tries for a look of nonchalance. Back to being Mr. Cool.

"Some amazing shit, huh?" he says to Dumpy.

"Yeah, uh-huh," Dumpy says, wanting to get to where he needs to put Arty. Where he's got to place him in the plan he's just put together. But Arty's back to being Arty, so rather than wait for Dumpy, Arty starts telling *him* how it is.

"So, okay," he says to Dumpy. "You take my case. I evict the two Pisans. You move in. Rent free." Then, not able to help himself, adding, "Of course, when the case is over, you and me will need to discuss a new rent. But, hey, no problem on that, know what I mean?"

Dumpy's thinking, Jesus, what an idiot, but he now smiles at Arty.

"Hey, look," he says to Arty. "I don't need your space, man. I'm good here."

Arty immediately concludes Dumpy's not going to help him. He starts to protest. Telling Dumpy how nice the office space is. Says, okay, maybe he'll extend the free rent for a couple of years. Maybe even three.

Dumpy stretches his arms out, double-palms him, signaling, Slow down, slow down.

Dumpy leans forward, the chair holding him groaning like it's about to collapse. He reassuringly nods at Arty, letting him know, you cool. Everything gonna be okay. Then he tells him.

"Look, man. I don't need your rent. Don't need nothin' from you."

Arty's back to protesting. Dumpy's elbows on the blotter, palms up again, letting Arty know, will you hold off? Wait just a god-damned minute?

"Now, Art," he says. "I'm gonna help you. But I ain't gonna charge you nothin'. We colleagues, man. A couple lawyers been around this town forever. Shit. Wouldn't be right, me chargin' you. No, unh-uh. I'm gonna help you, man. But I ain't gonna charge you nothin'."

Music to Arty's ears.

So, Dumpy explains his plan.

He tells Arty, he'll be his lawyer, but behind the scenes only. No one is to know. (This, of course, appeals to Arty's warped sense of how things are done in the real world.) He tells Arty that since he's done some lawyering for Slippery's lieutenants,

286

he can't be up front "in this here thing." But here's the deal, he tells Arty.

"First thing is you go to see Robert Cahill. Understand what I'm sayin'?" he tells Arty.

Arty is to go on his own. No need for him to be there with a lawyer, Dumpy tells him.

"You a lawyer, man," he tells Arty. "You know how to handle yourself. Am I right?"

Arty nodding, Yeah, sure. Arty's so clever, he can handle whatever. But Arty's still in the dark here. Trying his best to digest what exactly Dumpy is saying.

Dumpy's telling Arty, "You tell Cahill you the man got the goods on Slippery Williams." Dumpy sucking his teeth, giving Arty his dazzling smile, gold tooth and all.

"Sheeat," he says. "Cahill gonna get a hard-on so stiff his pecker's gonna elevate his damn desk. Know what I'm sayin'? You tellin' him you can hand him Slippery Williams."

"Yeah, yeah, uh-huh," Arty says, still trying to dope this out. ("Dope" being the operative word here.)

"But here's the thing," Dumpy tells Arty.

The thing? Arty's lost. What thing?

"The thing is, Art," Dumpy says. "You tell Cahill he's first got to go to the Feds. Got to convince them, prosecutor to prosecutor, they got to take that federal monkey off your motherfucking back. Once the Feds make a deal with you — you walk, no jail time, in exchange for Slippery — then you give up Slippery to them both. You telling Cahill what he needs to do is a joint prosecution of Slippery's whole operation. Let the Feds and the state of New Jersey split it up however the hell they want."

Dumpy sees that Arty's still trying to digest this, that he needs a little intellectual assistance here, a lifeline in the water to pull him back to the SS *Dumpy Brown.*

"You see," Dumpy says, leaning back into his rickety chair. "This way you making DA Cahill your lawyer. He be your advocate with the Feds. You give up Slippery and the two lawyers been representing you. Cahill gonna do all the work for you. See what I'm sayin'?"

Finally the lightbulb over Arty's head flicks on. His head starts a slow up-and-down bob, followed by a faster bob.

"Yeah, okay," Arty finally says.

So Arty and Dumpy are sitting there, smiling at each other. Arty thinking, How lucky can you get: Who would have thought? A guy like Dumpy. Yeah, sure, a lawyer, but one of them. "A brother," with all that means to a white guy like Arty. Dumpy Brown figuring out what those two dumb-

288

ass dago putzes never would have come up with. Not in a million fucking years.

And Dumpy Brown, for his part, not letting on, but thinking this idiot better pray Cahill or the Feds know enough to put Bernstein into protective custody, before Slippery gets wind of this and blows his head clean off.

Chapter 32
No Place Like Home?

I'm sitting in my mother's kitchen.

It's a weekday. I should be in my office. Or in court. Instead of here.

In fact, I had a court hearing scheduled for this afternoon. I just couldn't do it. Hard as I try to work on my other cases, my mind snaps to Slippery like a magnet to a refrigerator door. So I called the court clerk. A good guy. Got a continuance. My client's out on bail. So no particular hurry. A hand-to-hand buy. The dummy sold to an undercover was so patently a cop he should have had "Undercover" stenciled on the back of his jacket like the arresting cops had "Police" stenciled on theirs.

It's really cold out. The sun did make a brief, though weak, appearance earlier this morning. Now it's ash gray out there. We're in the run-up to Christmas.

Camden has its holiday decorations, such as they are, wrapped around lampposts, strung over streets. It's pretty dreary stuff. The city's been bankrupt, run-down, for too long. So whatever decorations the city elders have managed to scavenger from some municipal warehouse are sporadically hung here and there. Not much to look at.

In some of the poorest sections, streets where crime remains up, and incomes down, some folks go all out to light up their houses. Strings of brightly colored lights outlining their roofs, big lit Santas, maybe an oversized illuminated nativity scene on the front lawn.

I've always found it kind of strange, what comes over these folks this time of year. On the other hand, maybe this is a way of showing some sort of pride. Some sort of electrically lit message that they're still here. Still struggling maybe. But still here.

Where I live, my building — nothing much, just a Christmas tree in the lobby, some empty, fake gift-wrapped boxes under it.

Mickie's Cherry Hill neighborhood's subdued when it comes to outdoor Christmas decorations. For openers, a lot of Jewish families live there. Mickie's got a tree in the living room, decorated with the stuff he had when he was married. But that's it. Nothing outside his house.

So I'm sitting in my mother's kitchen, middle of the day. Lunchtime, more or less.

Arty Bernstein's still AWOL from the office. (Me and Mickie don't learn about his clandestine sit-down with Dumpy until later.) And not a peep from Sami. Or Rafat. We did get a call from one of the lawyers whose name Mickie gave Rafat. The guy called to thank us for the referral, said Rafat had called to make an appointment with him. That's the last we heard.

I've been spending time with Jason. I like him. He lives over in Philly, works for an insurance company, has some kind of boring job. But the guy's far from boring.

He's got this knack for sculpting. I've watched him soldering various bits and pieces of metal in this small garage space he rents near his apartment. Jason's got these strong arms, his work shirt sleeves rolled up, the knots of muscles beneath blond hair as he connects one abstract piece of something or other to another. Making it seem to fit. I like watching him work.

And he's introduced me to a bunch of his friends. They're not all gay, though most are. I've got to say, these guys — and a few women as well — are a pretty relaxed lot. They're interesting people and I like spending time with them. And with Jason.

It's just not my world, though. Not where I come from. It troubles me when I think about it. It's conflicting.

I want to introduce Jason to Mickie. Would like Mickie to meet him, get to know him. But that's awkward. I don't want to make Mickie uncomfortable. Or Jason for that matter; although, as I think about it, it's going to be Mickie who's likely to be the uncomfortable one. So I've done nothing. Confused.

Nothing confusing about the deep shit me and Mickie are in.

As you can see, being a criminal defense lawyer can be a risky business. You've got all kinds of thugs and psychopaths who are your clients. They get convicted, and then they try and file something against you after they're sentenced and sent away. Telling the judge in their jailhouse handwritten "pleading" that they were unjustly convicted (not innocent, mind you) through the incompetence of their counsel. That their lawyer made all kinds of mistakes at trial, so screwed up their defense that they deserve a new trial. With a new lawyer.

Or you get paid your fee in some drug case, or from someone accused of armed robbery. Then the DA files a motion with the court seeking to have your fee frozen, telling the judge you got paid with dirty money. Fruits of the crime money that you need to disgorge. To the state, of course.

And, of course, there are the clients just dying to kill you. (Have I said that right?)

So, you've got to watch yourself. Criminal defense lawyering can be a nasty business.

Hey, but what can you do? You put one foot in front of the other, best you can. Hope you can stay on your feet. Try to live your life.

Maybe that's why I'm sitting here middle of the day at my mother's kitchen table. I don't know. I just felt the strongest desire to be here, so I called. Asked my mom, Okay if I come over?

Nothing from her over the phone about middle of the day. What about work? You okay, Salvatore? Nope. I called. That's it. I'm coming over, that's all my mother needs to hear. She's happy.

"*Va bene* [Of course]," she tells me. "*Mangiamo. Parliamo.* [We'll eat. We'll talk.]"

"I can't stay long, Ma," I tell her. "Let's skip lunch."

I really don't want to gorge on a big noonday meal. I'm having dinner with Jason tonight. (My last supper?) I want an appetite left. I know my mother's lunches. Like all her meals, lunch for me will be field provisions for an army on the march, with enough leftover food the supply line non-coms would be offering it to the passing villagers.

"Fine," she says in Italian. "I'll eat alone."

It's at this point in phone calls with my mother that my hand starts to grip the receiver harder than is necessary. My body tenses. I start to have second thoughts about coming over. But I really do want to see her. I want a reprieve, a change of scenery, even if it's just for a few hours. And, there's no place like home, right?

So, gripping the phone, thinking, All that's going on? The shit storm me and Mickie are in? Well, I don't know, I really do want to see my mom. But no way am I going to let her browbeat me into some overstuffed lunch. No way. Then I tell her through clenched teeth.

"Okay, sure, Ma. Lunch's fine."

"Good," she tells me, switching to English. "I'll fix you your favorite dishes."

Favorite dishes? As in what? Three? Four?

So, here I am. Pots are simmering on all four stove burners. The kitchen smells like a tomato factory. It's too warm in here. My mother sits, smiling at me benevolently. I'm trying to decide how I am going to manage to eat just enough, but not too much. I'm not. I know that.

"So," is all I say to my mother.

She cocks her head, still smiling. Her Salvatore is here. God is in his heaven and all is right with the world.

"So," I try again.

I decided on the way over. I'm going to tell her. Own up to it. Who and what I am. I'm having all these crazy thoughts. Thinking, are me and Mickie going to be disbarred? Or imprisoned? Or worse, when Slippery ultimately learns Rafat's going to rat him out? I don't know if I'm simply some kind of adolescent grown-up seeking the comfort of his mommy, or I'm trying somehow to epitaph my life? My death? "Here lies Salvatore Salerno, who just before he was gunned down in a hail of bullets told his mother he was gay."

Yes, I have come to a firm decision. I will out myself. Okay, only to my mother. No one else. But it's a start, no? (Given my present life expectancy, it could be an end as well.)

Me and my mom are facing each other. The clock on the kitchen wall is ticking away. To me, given my mental state, it sounds like the amplified thud of a steel hammer rhythmically slamming onto an anvil.

Hours pass. Days, months. With me seated at the kitchen table. Time is dead. There is no air in this kitchen. I take a quick glance at that wall clock. Less than one minute has elapsed since my last "So."

I gird myself. Inhale, then expel a big gulp of air. Through all of this my mother keeps that blissful, smiling countenance of hers, focused bull's-eye on my face.

"Ma, I have something to tell you," I tell her.

Then before I can get on with it she says, "Salvatore, let's speak Italian. It's such a beautiful language."

She's been doing this to me my whole life. To my brothers too. She knows our Italian is only rudimentary. When we were kids, my parents, also my grandparents, would speak to me and my two brothers in Italian. And we would answer. But often in English, sometimes in that half Italian and half English kids like us grew up speaking. American kids in first-generation Italian households.

My mother's nodding at me, Come on, Salvatore, you can do it.

Another big air gulp. Then, my feeble brain trying to manually translate each word I am about to utter, I begin.

"Mamma," I say. *"Devo parlarti* [I have

something to tell you]."

"*Sì, sì?*" my mother says.

"*È importante.*"

"*Sì, sì?*"

This is ridiculous, I'm telling myself, as I desperately search for Italian words. But my mother wants Italian. What can I do?

"*Voglio dirti* [I want you to know]."

"*Sì, sì?*"

"*Sono felice,*" I say. (That's not right, I tell myself as soon as the words are out of my mouth. I just told her I am happy.)

"*Bene. Mangiamo,*" my mother says. (Good. Let's eat.)

It's like a goddamn sauna in here. I want to tell her we need to open a window. Let some air in this room. But instead I wave my hand at her, letting her know, I'm not finished yet. It's not that I'm happy. (Happy? What's happy?) She's got me working so hard here, a line of sweat's dripping inside my shirt.

And she looks cool as a cucumber. She's dressed as usual in a housedress. Her beautiful, thick gray hair is firmly pinned in place. Her sensible shoes are under the table, both feet planted side by side on the tile floor.

I try again.

"*Mamma,*" I say, taking hold of her hands.

I am now worried the shock of this will be too much for her. *"Mamma. Sono una fata principessa."*

In English, my mother says, "You're a fairy princess?"

At this point I actually moan.

"Ohhhhgggg."

Still clasping hands with me, my mother says in English, "I know, dear, you're . . ." Then in Italian she says, like an elementary school teacher telling the class to repeat after her, *"Omosessuale. Finocchio."* (Homosexual. Queer.)

And I repeat it, like I *am* the elementary school class.

"Omosessuale. Finocchio."

My mother then corrects my pronunciation.

"O . . . mus . . . se . . . suale."

I repeat.

"O . . . mus . . . se . . . suale."

Good, she says to me, releasing my hands. "Now we'll eat."

What? I'm telling myself. What just happened here?

As my mother pulls herself up from the table to go tend to her bubbling pots, I am stunned.

But I am a lawyer, trained in the use of words. That is how I make my living. With words. It's what I do. And I am damned good at it. So how do I confront my mother for what just happened? After all these years of her tormenting me, asking me repeatedly have I met a nice girl? When will I ever be married? How do I accomplish this?

Like this.

"Maaaa?"

Little Salvatore Salerno is sitting at the kitchen table. He's ten. His feet don't touch the ground. He swings his legs back and forth, back and forth (like little Tony at Thanksgiving). Whining to his mother.

Her back to me as she stirs this pot, then the next, she shrugs. Says to me in Italian the equivalent of "Forget about it." Then she takes a serving plate and sets it on the counter space near the stove. In English, she says over her shoulder, "Salvatore, you're a good boy."

Yeah, and? I'm thinking.

But that's all I get as my mother returns to the table. A steaming platter of food accompanying her. Then she ladles some linguini with a steamy tomato-pork *ragù* onto my plate.

My mother sits and smiles at me. And, believe it or not, I feel better.

Yeah, I know it won't last.

Hey, in this world? You take what you can get.

CHAPTER 33
SLIPPERY IS SITTING WHERE?

"What?" I say to Mickie, when he sticks his head into my office, tells me Slippery is sitting in the Bernstein, Smulkin seating area, waiting on us. "Sitting where?" I nervously say.

"You heard me," Mickie says. "Come on, let's go."

Like a zombie in some cut-rate horror movie I follow Mickie out to get Slippery.

Usually, when Slippery needs to see us, we go to see him. It's often in the courthouse lockup, or the Camden County Jail. If he's out and about and he wants us, then we go to his part of town. To a luncheonette or a bar. He chooses.

Slippery doesn't trust offices. He has been here once or twice. (That's how he hooked up with Arty.) But as a rule he doesn't like to come to law offices. Not even this shabby one.

But he's out there. Waiting on us.

Slippery travels these days with two of his lieutenants. They're both big guys. I remember them sitting around Slippery's house when me and Mickie went to Slippery's "coming out" (of jail) party a while back. Two African-American mountains. Like those big black scowling guys you see on *Access Hollywood,* or one of the other TV celebrity shows, guarding some little skinny-assed white rock star — male or female — as he/she slithers into some L.A. dance club.

The one to Slippery's right, perusing a magazine from off the chipped coffee table (*Good Housekeeping*), is called Stink. Slippery met him in prison. Years ago. Slippery's doing time in some other case. Long before Slippery put his self-appointed successor Chink out of his misery. This guy was with another gang at the time. I guess he and Slippery just hit it off. The guy was a short-timer, so when he got released he came to see Slippery, also out by then.

As you have guessed, Stink's got his street name for a reason. Stink does. It's like he never managed to wash off that jailhouse smell all prisons have. Like when Arty was in the lockup before he made bail. The "con cologne." And Stink's got it. You'll always be able to tell when Stink's in the house.

Stink's sitting there, that magazine clasped

in his bear paws, reading how to keep the kitchen the family center of your home. I guess Slippery, who is fastidious to a T, puts up with Stink's odorous aromas because the man is as loyal to Slippery as can be. And will do whatever it takes to get a job done, and *has* on each and every occasion Slippery's called on him to do so.

The other giant is called Pee Wee. Who says the street doesn't have a sense of humor? Pee Wee is seated on the opposite side of Slippery, playing an electronic word game on his smartphone.

"What's a nine-letter word for a rodent covered with erectile spines?" he asks Slippery.

"Porcupine," Slippery tells him.

"Right," Pee Wee says as he uses the virtual keypad to enter the word into his smartphone. His thick fingers are surprisingly nimble.

The Bernstein, Smulkin client base has shrunk ever since Arty's arrest and legal troubles. But the few ambulance-chasing lawyers still with the firm (the buffalo) have a smattering of clients sitting out there in the waiting room.

They're the usual lot: bandaged, braced, and bruised. And they are looking on with undisguised concern at this thin, well-dressed black guy, surrounded by these two goliaths in zippered jackets. Maybe they recognize Slippery from the street. Maybe they simply sense that these three guys are thugs. Whatever it is, they're sitting there, pretending to be reading a magazine or a newspaper, but keeping a weary eye on the three, like a firefight is about to erupt at any moment and they will need to dive to the worn carpeted floor to avoid taking a bullet.

So, why is Slippery here, waiting on us? As I follow Mickie down the hall I'm worried sick Rafat has gone to the Feds.

It starts with a meeting Stink had with Slippery about a week ago.

When Slippery has something to say, or something he needs to hear from his crew, these days he's switched to a new method: a meeting in the basement of his house. He goes down there with whoever he needs to speak to. He turns on the washer and dryer, flips on the Bose speaker dock system sitting on the cinder block wall shelf with an iPod slipped into it, plays some moderately loud hip-hop, then he and his guys sit in folding chairs on the cement floor in the center of the room, where the drain is, and they keep their voices down.

While Slippery does have his house regularly swept for bugs, he's realistic enough to appreciate the limits of electronic prevention in a world where the narcs have super-sophisticated equipment. So he does his necessary talking with his men the old-fashioned way. In the center of enough background noise to drown out virtually any electronic eavesdropping.

Stink asked for the meeting. Pee Wee comes too. It's not until later that me and Mickie learned what happened. But here it is.

The appliances in Slippery's basement are whirling and chugging. Slippery pushes the play button on the Bose. Out comes some vintage Busta Rhymes, rapping over the thud and crack of a drum kit, and the scratch of a needle dragged rhythmically back and forth over a vinyl record. The tune's about bitches, shooters, mayhem in the hood.

Slippery returns to his folding chair facing Stink and Pee Wee. He notices Pee Wee shift his weight just slightly away from Stink.

"What up, Stink?" Slippery says.

Something is troubling Stink. He has been in charge of the cash deliveries to the small warehouse, the turnover to Sami and his guys so the money can be secreted in household appliances and then shipped to India.

Stink shakes his head, letting Slippery know something is off here.

"Man, Slip," he says. "You know that sand nigger we dealin' with? Man wit them boxed TVs? Air conditioners and shit?"

Slippery wants to correct Stink. Sami's no Arab.

"Stink," he says. "That man a Indian. He ain't no sand nigger."

"Aight, then," Stink says. "That cab nigger we dealin' with."

All three snicker.

"Uh-huh," Slippery says.

"Somethin' ain't right, Slip," Stink says. "Last few times we there. You know, passin' on what we passin' on? Well, that man's boy ain't there."

"Uh-huh."

"Yeah, so first time, I don't say nothin'. Know what I'm sayin'? Then the boy ain't there again. So I say to the man, where you son at? Where Ray Fat at, man? And you know, the man get all jumpy. Face go pale. He a fuckin' ghost."

"Uh-huh."

"Man say to me, my boy sick. Then when he don't show the next time, I axe him again, where your boy at? He tell me, none a my damn business. He tell me *he* there. He takin' care a business wit us. Tell me

307

ain't no concern a mine who he have there. Long as the job be done."

Slippery shakes his head okay. Letting Stink know, he's got it.

"Boss," Pee Wee says. "You want me and Stink pay the man a visit, where he work? Maybe have a heart-to-heart?"

"Naa," Slippery says. "We good. I'll handle it."

Stink's now caught up in the Busta Rhymes music, his huge body pumping to the music's beat. Stink remembers the lyrics to this song. He starts lip-synching the words, bopping his head and shoulders. Getting into the act. Forgetting himself, carried away.

Slippery politely waits until the song ends before getting up and going over to the Bose to shut it off.

The next day, Slippery calls Sami. (He changes cell phones regularly. Uses only throwaways.) The conversation is terse. Slippery arranges a meet. Tells Sami where. In Atlantic City, about an hour by car from Camden. Slippery not about to see Sami around here.

Afternoon of the next day, as he was instructed, Sami has driven alone to Atlantic City. It's freezing cold out. The sky is steel gray. The wind off the ocean is fierce, piercing. Sami is bundled in his winter coat, collar upturned, scarf tightly wrapped around his neck. He's wearing a seaman's cap holding his toupee in place. Still he keeps one hand on top of his head so the cap and wig don't both blow away.

Sami walks alone, following instructions. Slippery's boys are watching him, trying to see if he's really alone. When they decide he is, Stink and Pee Wee come up to him. Neither wears more than a zippered waist-length jacket. Neither seems particularly cold. Sami's heart skips a beat seeing them here. Are they going to kill me? he thinks. Right here on this nearly deserted boardwalk?

Sami waits, doesn't utter a word. His hand stuck over top his head. Stink tells him to go back to his car and sit in it until they come around in theirs. Then he is to follow them.

Sami does as instructed, waiting in the car, parked at the curb, his heart racing, his lungs short of air. Is this where they kill him? he wonders, when their car turns up.

A Cadillac Escalade SUV, black, windows tinted, pulls up alongside Sami's car. The SUV's rear window slowly slides down. Loud rap music escapes into the frigid air. Sami braces himself, waiting for the arm to be exposed, the gun aimed point-blank at his head.

As the window descends, Sami sees both Stink and Pee Wee in the backseat. Sami wonders, Who's the driver? Could it be Slippery? Wondering all the while how he can be having these thoughts and not others, about his family, whatever, now that he's a split second away from death.

But no weapon appears. Stink motions Sami to start his car, then to follow them. Sami does as he's told, his hands shaking so he's having trouble gripping the steering wheel, turning the ignition over. But he manages to start the car and then he pulls from his space and follows the SUV.

Together the two-car caravan makes one street turn, then another. Stink's window slides down again. Sami watches as Stink's arm extends out and points to the sandwich shop at the corner. Sami flashes his lights okay and takes the nearest curbside parking space. The SUV does the same.

Sami enters the White House Sub Shop, an Atlantic City institution, been at this corner since the 1940s. The interior hardly changed since then. The decrepit older woman, dyed-blond beehive hair, black roots showing, a pencil stuck in her hair-spray-stiff nest, asks him, how many? Sami sees Slippery already in one of the hardwood booths to the side. He motions the woman there, letting her know he's going to sit with that guy. She shrugs, then turns to the couple that walked in just behind him, asking the two, how many?

Sami slides into the booth. Manages to wriggle out of his coat, remove his cap with only minimal damage to his toupee. Although it is now seriously off center.

Slippery doesn't utter a word. Sami's heart is at the races.

A waitress appears. She's in her thirties, hard looking through her half smile. She's wearing a "White House Subs" dark blue T-shirt and very tight jeans. Slippery catches Sami glancing first at her scrawny tits, then down to her protruding ass.

"Take your order?" she says to them in a thick South Jersey accent.

"Steak and cheese. Extra peppers," Slippery says. "Diet Coke." He turns to Sami, who's still studying the waitress's rear end. "Best subs around," he tells Sami.

Sami lifts his eyes. "Hot tea, please, madam," he tells her.

"Nothin' ta eat?"

Sami shakes his head no. The waitress writes in her order pad and leaves for the service bar.

311

Slippery watches Sami. "How you doin'?" he finally says.

Sami shrugs. Letting Slippery know, since he's about to be indicted, how good could he be?

Slippery watches some more. The waitress returns, places a Diet Coke and plastic glass with ice before Slippery. The hot tea in front of Sami and a saucer with sugar packets, Sweet 'N Low. He would like milk, but doesn't ask.

"I got to be worried about anything, Sami?" Slippery says as he pours Diet Coke into the plastic glass, takes a small sip.

"No," is all Sami says.

Slippery takes another sip of Diet Coke. That's a wrong answer, so far as Slippery's concerned. *Like what?* would have been a better answer. Sami's failing the test as he sits there. But Slippery doesn't want to jump to conclusions.

"How your boy doin'?" Slippery says.

"He is well."

"I hear he ain't been at the warehouse with you."

Nothing from Sami. Slippery notices Sami's tea remains untouched.

The waitress is back. "Steak and cheese, extra peppers," she says as she places the paper plate in front of Slippery with the steaming sub, its ends like amputated limbs hanging over the plate's lip.

Slippery takes a big bite of his steak and cheese. Shakes his head at how good this sandwich always is.

"Unbelievable," he tells Sami, offering the sub to him for a bite.

Sami waves it away.

"So, your boy?" Slippery reminds Sami. "Why he don't be comin' to the drop-off no more?"

Sami takes too long to answer. Slippery looks away, down at his sub, and takes another bite, chews, then reaches over to the napkin dispenser, grabs one, and delicately dabs at his mouth. He keeps chewing, once again watching Sami.

"Rafat has been ill," is all Sami says.

Slippery letting it go. *He is well. He has been ill.*

"I hope it ain't nothin' serious," he says instead.

Silence from Sami. Then, a shake of his head no. "He will be fine," Sami adds, his voice too soft.

"Okay, so we good, then?" Slippery says.

"Yes, we are good."

More silence.

"Well, I know you a busy man and be needin' to get back to Camden," Slippery says as he continues eating his sub.

Sami can't wait to get out of there. The conversation has been too short. He knows that. Still, his flight instincts take control. So, instead of taking his time, telling Slippery he will see him soon. Or saying anything at all, he simply slides out from the booth, nods goodbye to Slippery, and leaves.

Slippery watches him go, finishes his sub, and then calls the waitress over. He orders two double steak and cheeses to go for Stink and Pee Wee and a single for the driver sitting outside with them. Then he takes another sip of his Diet Coke.

So, now me and Mickie are standing at the Bernstein, Smulkin seating area. Mickie nods at Slippery. Slippery gets up. Stink and Pee Wee will remain out here while me, Mickie, and Slippery go to the conference room.

I'm the third in line down the hallway. I can see just by the way Mickie's shoulders are arched as he walks that he's tense. My mind is running fast-frame scenes. Me and Mickie are being shot in most of them. The others are worse. So far Slippery hasn't uttered word one.

Once we're in the conference room we sit, Slippery on one side of the table, me and Mickie on the other. Slippery's wearing a suit and tie. Armani, it looks like. Dark suit, dark shirt, dark tie. Me and Mickie are in ties, but we're both in shirtsleeves. Wrinkled shirtsleeves.

I'm telling you, any unanticipated loud noise about now? Me and Mickie'd pop out of our seats like we were spring-loaded.

No sooner are we settled in, Tamara lightly knocks and then enters for drink orders.

She is tightly wrapped and miniskirted. Slippery smiles at her, but doesn't otherwise pay her any mind. He's in our offices; Slippery has a sense of decorum.

"Something to drink, Slip?" Mickie asks (sounds to me like his voice is half an octave higher than it should be), as Tamara stands waiting.

"Yeah," Slippery says. "Coffee be good."

"How you take it?" Tamara asks.

I notice Tamara isn't smiling as she usually does. She is simply standing there. Kind of stiff.

"This is Avon Williams," Mickie says, introducing Slippery to her. "This is Tamara Watson, works for us," Mickie adds.

Slippery smiles benignly. Nods at her.

"Mm-hmm," is all Tamara says. She knows full well who Slippery is.

This is an awkward moment, I'm thinking, when Mickie adds, "Tamara's nephew works for you, I think."

Slippery looks over at her again.

"He do?" is all he says.

Tamara is having none of this.

Mickie sees he shouldn't have said what he said. Wants to get past this.

"He's a young man, rides a wheelchair," Mickie says, looking for closure to this part of the conversation.

Slippery nods.

"Okay," is all he says, still nodding. Slippery has no trouble seeing Tamara's displeasure with her nephew's current place of employment.

"So how you take it?" Tamara asks again, her eyes on Slippery, no trouble reading her mind.

"Black be fine," Slippery says.

Me and Mickie let Tamara know we're good, don't need anything to drink right now. She leaves.

Slippery looks around the room. The pictureless walls, the mismatched chairs surrounding the table. He smiles.

Me and Mickie weakly return the smile. We are on pins and needles, both of us silently concluding, Slippery knows. How? Exactly what? It doesn't matter. If Slippery knows, we are dead men. Maybe not in here, not this very instant. But this will be the last time Slippery sees us alive. He won't be there when the time comes, I'm thinking. That's what those two oversized thugs out there are for. But I'm trying my best to act nonchalant. This is just a regular client-lawyer conference, I'm telling myself. Act like it. My guess, Mickie right now is doing more or less the same.

"How that lawyer you all's landlord doin'?" Slippery says. "That motherfucker listening to you? Got his shit under control?"

Slippery knows of our arrangement with Arty Bernstein. But so far as he knows, me and Mickie are still completely in the dark about Slippery's money laundering activities with Arty. So, while far as Slippery's concerned we are still in the dark, I'm telling myself he knows. Shit. He knows.

What me and Mickie don't know is that Slippery has been calling Arty, not reaching him. Slippery doesn't leave voice mails and his throwaway cell phones won't show caller ID. Still, he has been unable to reach Arty.

"He's in a heap of trouble," Mickie says. "And he's the same crazy bastard he's always been," he adds, shaking his head, trying to act business-as-usual. Trying to show Slippery me and him got Arty's case under control. Trying to stay clear of any

317

discussion is Arty trying to make a deal with the Feds. And if so, on what terms.

"He around?" Slippery asks, adding, "One a my boys had a car accident. He need a lawyer does what Arty do. Know what I'm sayin'?"

Me and Mickie hunch our shoulders, signaling Slippery, could be Arty's in the office, who knows, neither of us wanting to go any further with talk involving Arty.

Then Slippery lets it go, changes the subject. I let out a barely audible sigh of relief. Slippery doesn't appear to notice.

Instead he tells us the story how he and one of his girls were at the restaurant where DA Robert Cahill and his wife go. What happened when he walked over to their table after the champagne he ordered was delivered by the waiter.

We all have a good laugh over that. (I think me and Mickie are laughing harder than we should. Harder than the story deserves. I'm hoping Slippery isn't seeing this.)

Mickie admonishes Slippery he shouldn't be doing things like that.

"What you hear? The DA gonna bring a new case on me, do you think?"

Mickie tells Slippery, Who knows? Probably not or he would have by now. Both me and Mickie thinking, is this why Slippery's here? To see if Cahill intends to reindict him? I don't want to think about why else he's here.

"Uh-huh," Slippery says. "And how them two boys I sent you a while back doin'? That man run the appliance places. And his son."

"Good," Mickie says too fast.

Tamara comes back into the conference room with Slippery's coffee. He smiles and nods thanks to her, takes a quick sip, and grimaces. Places the Styrofoam cup on the table in front of him.

"That's some nasty shit," he says, shaking his head like, How is anyone expected to drink that?

Again me and Mickie laugh too hard at this.

Then Slippery shakes his head again, troubled.

"Must be the weather," he says. "Somethin' in my bones. Know what I'm sayin'? I don't know. Somethin' just don't feel right."

"Yeah, it's fucking cold outside," Mickie lamely says.

"I know that." Slippery's mouth's in a smile. But his eyes aren't.

I know Slippery has a high opinion of me and Mickie. We've always been there for him. Done good when he needed our legal services. He knows who and what we are and has always been all right with that. But today? Slippery sitting here with us? I don't know. The vibes across this big, scarred table, going both ways. They're just not right. Not good. I'm guessing even Tamara's seeing this as Slippery gets up from the table, says goodbye, and walks out of the conference room.

Tamara picks up Slippery's Styrofoam coffee cup to take back to the kitchenette so she can pour its contents down the sink drain. She gives us a look. Then she's gone.

Once again me and Mickie are left in this room feeling like idiots.

What do we do? What can we do?

The explosives placed directly under us are now primed. The illuminated dial on the digital clock attached to the wires is rapidly clicking down to detonation time. There are only seconds remaining. What do we do? Delicately cut the blue wire? Or the red? Which one diffuses the bomb?

Maybe neither, I'm beginning to think. Maybe we are simply out of options.

CHAPTER 34
WHAT'S UP WITH DUMPY?

It's snowing. The TV weather people who have totally missed this are now in an orgy of predictions. Three inches. Five or more. Sleet mixed with snow. Winds. And on and on.

Well, whatever. It's cold, gray, and snowing. That much is undisputed. We'll just have to see how the storm develops. Still, all of Camden's municipal employees are in a dither. Will their benevolent city bosses let them go home early? Work has come to a halt, everyone so focused on will they get to leave before the roads freeze.

And in all this snow Robert Cahill walks down the steps of the federal courthouse. He hasn't been in this building since the days before he was elected as the local DA. When he was in private practice. Handled just a few cases here.

He's smiling. There is a spring in his step, despite the wet snow that settles on his hair, the shoulders of his overcoat.

He's had a good meeting with the Feds. They've told him, Sure, Bobby, we can work something out with you and your office. If Bernstein can deliver Williams like you say. Sure, we'll work something out. Maybe get that scumbag lawyer sentenced on a guilty plea to three years' imprisonment. Then we agree to move the court for a sentence reduction to probation after he testifies as a prosecution witness in the Williams case.

Yeah sure, the Feds tell Cahill. We can do that. But there's a big *if* here, Bobby. Got that?

Bernstein needs to give us an airtight case, they tell him. We will first need to convict Williams. You understand? Right? If he can deliver Slippery Williams in a solid case. No problems. No diverting issues. We'll need a clean kill. Then? Yeah, we can do some sort of "joint investigation."

Needless to say, they tell him, the prosecution and trial will have to take place in federal court. Not in your Camden local system. That's a precondition, they tell him. Not actually saying they worry that Cahill will fuck up the case again, reassuring him at the same time that he will be given press credit. What he wants and needs.

The Feds know the game. State DAs are

322

elected officials, not appointed to their positions like the Feds. They know guys like Cahill see the job as a political stepping-stone. They're after headlines, making a public name for themselves. Crime fighting is the vehicle.

They know Robert Cahill. Got his number.

Skipping down the federal courthouse steps Cahill is thinking, first mayor. Dare he even think of it, eventually governor. Then, who knows? Maybe even U.S. senator?

So Robert Cahill has a spring in his step, on his way back to his office in the Camden County Courthouse. Once there he will call that Arty Bernstein on his cell. Let him know he has a deal.

Cahill doesn't mind the snow, doesn't care if it snows all day and all night. He's got what he wants. He's a happy man. How that Bernstein came to see him, out of the blue, with his proposal. Well, Robert's got to be telling himself, you never know where opportunity will knock.

And as Robert Cahill heads back toward the state courthouse, me and Mickie are leaving one of the larger courtrooms in there. Today is what lawyers call a cattle call.

Most of the state court judges reserve one

day a week when they call in all the lawyers from all the cases on their dockets in which there are small matters open. Maybe a pending motion, or a discovery dispute between the lawyers over a document or a witness. Or maybe simply a need for a status hearing, so the court can determine if the case is ready for trial. Maybe set a trial date while the lawyers are before him.

So the court clerk herds in all these lawyers. Like cattle. And all of us piss away hours sitting in a packed courtroom as the judge calls the sides up, one case after another. Very efficient for the judge. But for the lawyers, who basically can't get a lick of work done while they're sitting in there waiting for their cases to be called, it's the opposite of efficient.

But the judges trump the lawyers. So your case goes on the cattle call docket. You go.

And Mickie and me are sitting in this courtroom, cooling our jets. Finally, our case is called. It's some old-dog criminal conspiracy drug distribution. It's been up and back from the court of appeals twice already.

We have our three-minute session with the judge. Nothing is decided. The judge telling his clerk seated below the bench to re-reschedule the case for another status hearing next month.

"Thank you, counsel," the judge says, ignoring us, his eyes already on the new file on his stack as the bailiff calls the next case. Me and Mickie pass the next group of waiting lawyers as they head to the inner well of the court. We all roll eyes at one another.

We go out in the hall and there we see Dumpy Brown. He's leaning against the wall, chatting with some doper or pimp who's his client.

I hear Dumpy tell the guy, "Look, man. You got to take this deal. You ain't gonna get better. Trust me on this. Else you gonna be one sorry-ass motherfucker sitting up in the state pen till you old and gray."

The client vigorously shaking his head, no way, he's letting Dumpy know. No fucking way is he going to take this deal. Or any other deal involving a plea of guilty.

I can see Dumpy's frustrated with this guy. The client's working up a head of steam. Maybe if this guy wasn't here in a courthouse, with his lawyer all suited up with the high shirt collar, the purple pocket hanky. Well, maybe a guy like this might make his present viewpoint felt with something other than an angry shake of his head. But he's here and his options are narrow.

Then Dumpy sees us. He whispers something to the client and leaves him cold standing there in mid-headshake. Dumpy comes over to us. All smiles.

"Hey," Dumpy says, quickly shaking my hand, then Mickie's. "Wassup, fellas?" he asks, then passes by us and returns to the courtroom, leaving his client behind.

Me and Mickie look at each other. What in hell was that? Dumpy greeting us without the usual passive-aggressive banter? No White Shadow remarks. Nothing aimed at Mickie. Dumpy too friendly. Couldn't get away from us fast enough. Leaving his perplexed client all by his lonesome out here in the hall?

What in the hell was that about?

CHAPTER 35
SNOW DAZE

At around the time that me and Mickie are heading out of the Camden County Courthouse, the cattle call — for us at least — over, Carla is standing at the curb at Mickie's suburban house. She's wearing a yellow, vinyl, knee-length rain slicker, hood up, snowflakes sliding down its smooth surface. Under the slicker is her nurse's uniform, her white-stockinged feet crammed into the undersized rain galoshes. (She found them in the hall closet. An earlier girlfriend's, no doubt.)

She's shoving the last bit of her clothing and other possessions into her VW Beetle. She's had it with Mickie. Moving out. Carla's history.

Across town, at the Sami's Electronics corporate offices, the door to Sami Khan's office is shut. The battery of billing clerks and other assorted help are sitting in the large adjoining workroom. There are no snow days at Sami's Electronics.

Inside Sami's office there have been shouts and screaming for the last forty minutes. No one can hear exactly what Sami and his son are arguing about. But it's bad. The shouting nonstop ever since Rafat walked in and kicked the door shut behind him.

And out on the street, just blocks from the hospital where Carla's now peering through the still partially frosted windshield of her Beetle, looking for a space on the employees-only lot, Gregory sits in his wheelchair. The snow is falling harder. He's got a plastic poncho over his upper body. Cars are slowly drifting up to the curb at the corner. The storm is really getting worse, a gauzy curtain covering the street scene. Gregory watches as the other corner boys go through the same tired ritual.

One kid approaches the car, gets the order. Calls out some stupid nonsense code.

"Red Devil. WMDs. Two up. Two down."

The call gets relayed until one of the other boys comes up to the car. He's hooded and low-slung jeaned like all the rest, snow nesting on the top of his hoodie, his shoulders. He takes the cash from the skinny, strung-out white guy on the passenger side, mo-

328

mentarily enjoys the heat escaping through the open window. Notices the girl driving, takes in her multiple face piercings, her ink jet hair. Checks the back of the car. Looks in deep to make sure no one's crouched down there. Then another signal and the clear plastic vials are delivered. Gregory holds the cash hoard. These days he keeps two Glock nines wedged in at his seat.

Rain or shine. Springtime or blizzard. It doesn't matter. The street drug bazaar is always open for business. No snow days here either.

The car slowly pulls away. Gregory hears some of the other boys griping about the weather.

"Ain't no cause bein' out here in this goddamn storm, uh."

"Yeah, it a bitch, man. But bidness be bidness."

"Uh-huh. Still, nigger, it a motherfucker. Know what I'm sayin'?"

"Uh."

Gregory listens to these boys, standing there, shifting from one foot to the other. Same old jive talk coming from them. Day in, day out. But they're standing there, moving, while Gregory sits imprisoned in his wheelchair. He doesn't think about it all that much. Gregory doesn't do much thinking, period. But at times like this, his body shivering with cold, unable to move his legs, his feet. Trapped, as these boys go about shooting the shit. Fact is, what he'd like to do is pull out one of the pistols lying against his numb, lifeless thighs and bust some caps in these two. He's close enough to get several shots off before any one of the other corner boys can get to him.

The snow falling on his poncho, his hands and face burning from the cold, Gregory slowly reaches down under the ratty blanket covering his lap and legs. He fingers one of the pistols. After a while he thumbs back the safety.

"Nigger," the kid closest to him is telling his pal. "Just too motherfucking cold out's here. Know what I'm sayin'?"

"You right. But what you gonna do? Like I say, it bidness."

"Yeah, but still ain't no need for no full fuckin' crew, all a us out here on this corner. Slingin' dope. In this snow and shit. Should have us one a them skeleton crews. You know? Like them postal workers do."

His pal snickers, says, "Uh-huh."

Gregory wraps his finger around the trigger, slowly eases the gun from under the blanket.

"Tonight," the kid closest to him, his back

now turned to Gregory, is saying. "Man, I'm here to tell you. Me? I'm goin' over to Bernice house. Know who I'm talkin' 'bout?"

"That girl wit that dyed red do? The one wit them big legs? Live over on whatcha-callit?"

"Yeah, that the one. Me? When her grandma go off to work? She on nights, know what I'm sayin'?"

"Uh-huh."

"Well, I'm gonna get me some a that. Be jammin' her. She got them big legs wrapped around my skinny butt in her big-ass bed. Yeah, I'm gonna get me some a that shit. Know what I'm sayin'?"

Both boys are stomping their feet, poking at each other's shoulders, chuckling. Neither seeing Gregory taking aim, beginning to press back on the trigger.

Then Gregory sees the black Escalade roll up. It's collection time. Re-up time. He quietly slips the stone-cold Glock nine back under the blanket. He watches the passenger-side tinted window slide down. The boy in charge of this corner takes the rumpled paper bag containing this morn-ing's receipts from under Gregory's poncho, the Glock nine now back to resting against Gregory's dead thigh. He walks over to make his report. Hand in the cash gotten so far today.

Gregory sees the man in the Escalade they call Stink take the cash, then say something to the boy. The boy's nodding, showing he's got whatever it is Stink's telling him. Will do, the boy's letting Stink know. He sees Stink hand the boy a different brown paper bag. The re-up.

That's when Gregory slides the brake off his wheelchair, starts to roll himself toward the curb and the Escalade. His hands are frozen from the falling snow, the damp.

But he makes his way over to Stink.

He's got something to tell him.

CHAPTER 36
CHRISTMAS PRESENTS

The storm has momentarily abated. But the TV guys are hedging their bets. Telling us, don't release any sighs of relief yet. It may come back. And if it does, then it'll be with a vengeance. Really bad. Maybe. Or maybe not. Their time-lapse screens are stop-motioning a resurrection of the condition now abating, but all the purples and crimsons could be moving anywhere. To us. Farther north. Who knows?

It's just coming on to the dinner hour. The roads have been plowed and de-iced. It's two days before Christmas. The stores are full with last-minute shoppers.

I'm still in the office. Mickie just left. He doesn't know it yet, but he's heading home to an empty house. Carla's goodbye note propped up on the entrance hall table.

At court earlier, during and after the cattle call, and when we got back here, I saw Mickie eating Rolaids like they were breath mints.

"Hey, Mick," I told him. "You need to see a doctor."

"Naa," he said, shrugging. "I'm good. Just a little stomach upset. I'm fine."

I don't really have too much work to keep me here. But I'm waiting for Jason's call. He's got some errands to run, he said. Christmas shopping no doubt. Then when he calls we'll hook up for dinner.

Jason is in the Cherry Hill Mall. Christmas shopping. As he's walking toward Modell's Sporting Goods four or five storefronts away, he passes a young Indian guy. Neither knows the other. They pass as strangers. As Jason goes one way, Rafat Khan goes the other, heading for the exit to the outside parking.

Rafat's got a loaded shopping bag in each hand as he heads for his car. He remembers where he left it. Lot 15. When he gets to his car he places the bags at his feet, making sure there's no residual snow where the lot has been cleared. He reaches under his parka for the electronic car key in his trouser pocket.

First he pushes the automatic trunk opener and waits as the trunk lid on his BMW slowly lifts. Then he retrieves the shopping bags and puts them in the trunk, laying them on their sides so they won't flop around on the way home. He closes the trunk and then clicks open the door locks.

Just as he's doing this another car pulls up behind him. He turns smiling to let the driver know he's leaving the spot, be right out. The car starts to pull up closer to him. That's not right, he's thinking. Probably an old woman, or a kid behind the wheel, Rafat's thinking as he begins to motion the driver, no, go the other way. His outstretched hand pointing in the back direction.

The window rolls down. Rafat's getting just slightly annoyed. More like frustrated. He's still motioning, again telling the driver, no, go back, not forward, when the window completes its retraction. It's a big car. Black. An Escalade. Rafat steps closer to the car so he can speak over the passenger to the driver, and explain how she needs to reverse.

He sees the pistol with the long barrel. Has no idea there is a silencer attached to the barrel. Doesn't even register at first it's a pistol. By the time it does, the first shot is fired. A ping. Direct to his chest. Despite the force he somehow remains on his feet. He feels no pain, only this incredible pressure on his chest. He looks down at himself, but the zippered parka hides the warm, wet blood now spurting from his chest wound.

Rafat looks back up at the passenger. He sees a huge African-American man. He's studying Rafat.

Then another ping. This one throws Rafat back. His knees crumble beneath him.

Rafat is lying on his back. No longer sure where he is. He's looking up at the high-poled parking lot lamp. He hears what could be the opening of a car door. Then the light is blocked by a shadow.

Stink empties the remaining rounds from his silenced Beretta into Rafat as he lies there, his body jerking as it absorbs the shells. Stink looks around to ensure no one has seen this. Then he gets back in the Escalade, shuts the door as Pee Wee slowly drives off for the exit to the highway. Pee Wee cracks his window to let in some fresh air.

I'm reading one of the files for tomorrow when I hear the phone first ring down the hall where the reception desk is. Before she leaves for the night the receptionist switches the phones to night call, so when someone calls, the line rings three times out there. Then a recorded voice provides instructions. If you know your party's extension dial the number now. If you need a directory, dial this number now. I wait to see if the caller is Jason. Sure enough my line rings.

Jason says he's running a little late, that there's been some kind of problem at the mall. The police have blocked the parking exits. The cop he asked wouldn't tell him why but said that traffic would be moving real soon. So Jason says, rather than me waiting for him to swing by here to pick me up, why don't I just go over to Philly and meet him at the restaurant? Sit at the bar and have a drink if he's late.

Jason has never been to the office. I wanted him to see where I work. But, no matter. We can do it another time.

Yeah, sure, I tell him. After the call ends I grab my coat and head for the firm entrance area. I'll call for a cab since I left my car home this morning so Jason could get me from the office tonight.

About an hour later I'm at the bar. Jason calls again; this time gets me on my cell. Says the lots are open again. Should be there in less than thirty minutes. I hang up and signal the bartender for another.

The doorbell at Sami Khan's home chimes. He's in his study as usual. In his wingback chair, his toupee resting on the Styrofoam dummy's head on his bedroom dresser. He's wearing his shawl sweater.

Mrs. Khan is in the kitchen preparing their dinner. The smells of curry and coriander are mixing with the forced-air heating system. To an outsider it might seem too strong, too harsh. But to Sami it's hardly noticeable. And to the extent that these cooking aromas invade his consciousness, they deliver a sense of comfort. Of home. Of India.

No one is expected. Both hear the chime. Sami does not rise to answer the door. That is woman's work. Mrs. Khan knows her duties. She wipes her hands on her apron, lowers the flame on one of the pots, then heads for the entrance hall and the door.

She is secretly hoping the caller will turn out to be their son. She so wants reconciliation between her husband and him. He is a good boy. A loyal boy. As she places her hand on the latch she is already picturing him standing in the doorway.

A big smile on her lips, Mrs. Khan now has the door fully open. She's shot dead on the spot, the large black man standing there, his long-barreled, silenced Beretta held not six inches from her face. He waits for her body to crumble, then steps over her.

Still in his study, finishing an article, Sami thinks he's heard a ping, then the sound of some heavy object hitting the floor. He waits

338

before turning the page, snapping the reopened paper, as is his habit. He hears what sounds like footfalls in the hall, coming this way.

"Vanaja," he calls over his paper. "Who is at the door?"

There is no response, although the footfalls are getting closer. Perhaps his wife has decided to come here regarding whoever is there. He waits as his study door opens.

He recognizes the large black man standing before him, knows him from the warehouse meetings, has exchanged words with him there.

Sami immediately realizes why this guy is standing there. Now understands what the sounds out in the hall mean. He lowers his paper and waits for this man to do what he has come here for. He doesn't continue looking at him. He lowers his gaze. And waits.

CHAPTER 37
OH, THAT ARTY

We've ordered scotches. This will be my
third. Two at the bar waiting for Jason. And
now one at the table.

When he arrived we smiled at each other.
Shook hands. That's all. No hugs, nothing
like that. Jason keeps it just a couple of guys
out together. Knows that's how I want it.

Even where we eat when we go out, nothing frilly. Tonight it's Smith & Wollensky on
Rittenhouse Square, at the Rittenhouse
Hotel. Steaks, whisky, red wine. A couple of
guys out for a steak dinner.

We're doing this at my pace. Jason's cool
with that.

So, we're at the table. We've given the
waiter our order. Caesar salads, bone-in
sirloins (calling Dr. Freud), baked potatoes,
a good California cabernet.

After the waiter leaves, Jason again apologizes for the delay, says he's still not sure
what the problem was at the Cherry Hill

Mall, says it was a madhouse. A zoo. With all the shoppers in the mall, all the backed-up drivers in the lots.

It's starting to snow again. But we're not driving back to Camden after dinner. We're staying at his place.

The waiter brings the wine and displays the label to Jason. Good, he says as the waiter begins to open the bottle.

Just a couple of guys out for dinner.

I think I better let the wine the waiter has poured into my glass sit. I need to slow down the alcohol intake here. Keep my wits about me.

The waiter delivers our salads, asks do we want fresh pepper? Outside it's really coming down.

Slippery Williams gets a call on the cell he's using tonight. He's at his grandmother's. He came over to shovel the small walkway in front of her Camden inner-city row house. He takes the call as he sits at his nana's kitchen table, eating a stew made of ham hocks, bacon, turnips, canned tomatoes. His nana's standing at the sink, washing out the big iron pot she likes to use for her stews.

This is the second call he's gotten here. The first, earlier, while he was outside shoveling, was from Stink. The phone chimed, Slippery flicked it on.

"We good," was all Stink said.

Slippery said only, "Uh-huh," then flicked the phone off.

Now comes the second call. His nana turns as the phone chimes, but then goes back to her pot scrubbing. She knows full well what Slippery does. Who he is. She doesn't care. Nana's not the stereotypical African-American grandma, not just some loving and caring churchgoing woman, sorrowful over her grandchild's evil ways. If anything, she is proud of Slippery. Proud of his having managed to beat the ghetto syndrome of poverty and dead ends.

Slippery has his cell to his ear. He waits. The boy calling sits in a car outside a split-level on a suburban Cherry Hill street. He and the other two young men in the car have been parked here since it turned dark. They've gone easy on the cocaine. There is work to be done tonight. Their guns are ready, fully loaded. Silencers in place.

The house has remained dark. It's now coming on to nine P.M. The snow is heavy. Every few minutes one of them needs to get out of the car in order to clean off the windows. The caller is starting to get nervous. Even though it's dark and snowing, a parked car, motor running, exhaust billowing from the tail pipe. Three young black men waiting inside. In this neighborhood.

"You don't need to be no genius to see how this playin' out here," he tells the others in the car as he flips on his cell to call Slippery.

"Ain't no nothin'," the boy tells Slippery. "House dark."

These young men are parked outside Arty Bernstein's family home. They are waiting for Arty to return for the evening. Whoever happens to be in the house when he gets there is of no concern to these guys. Their instructions are clear. Take out whoever's there. Then leave.

Slippery knows it's got to be tonight, given what's already gone down. On the other hand, he too appreciates the risk being run with his men parked, motor running, outside Arty's suburban home.

What Slippery doesn't know is that Arty is gone. His family is gone.

Wacky as he is, Arty is smart enough to figure out that once he's met with DA Cahill, and once DA Cahill has met with the Feds, it's only a matter of time before what he's offered to do gets out on the street. Doesn't matter how. He knows it simply will. An ounce of precaution is called for. He knows that much.

So Arty has packed off the wife and kids to her parents' house in New York, out in the Long Island suburbs. He's now explained it all to his wife. She turned pale, grim. Didn't ask a thing. In fact, hardly spoke to him. But she did as she was told. Knowing there was no other option.

Slippery Williams takes another forkful of stew. Chews slowly. He hears his grandma humming to herself at the sink. He thinks it through.

"Shut the bitch down," Slippery says into his cell.

"Aight," the kid says as he flips off the phone. "The man say we done," he tells the others in the car. They shrug as the kid puts the car into gear and slowly pulls away from the curb.

As the car leaves the Cherry Hill suburb, there's a knock on the door of Arty's hotel room in South Beach. He's been in Miami for two days now. Earlier this evening, at the bar, he asked the bartender where he could get some action, peeling two twenties off his roll and holding them under his palm by his drink.

The barman shrugs, tells Arty he doesn't know of any action. Arty adds another twenty.

As Arty opens his hotel room door, the

girl smiles sweetly at him. Calls him "Dar-lin'." Asks, "Aren't you gonna invite me in?"

Once inside, she waits for her payment. Arty has put all his valuables in the small closet safe the hotel provides. He's left out the $1,000 for the girl. She takes the money. Asks can she have a drink. Arty kneels down to the minibar. Scotch, she tells him. He removes the small airline bottle from off the door rack. He watches as she undoes the zipper on the back of her dress. Lets her dress fall to the floor. She's completely nude underneath. Arty gets to his feet.

I'm awake early the next morning. The snow finally tapered off in the early-morning hours. The area schools are closed for the Christmas holidays. The courts are open. The streets have been plowed. They don't seem to be in too bad a shape. And anyway, it's a half day today. Christmas Eve. At least there will be a white Christmas.

I had trouble sleeping last night. I tell myself it was all that heavy food, too much, too late.

So much, I suppose, for "he-man" eating. I can hear Jason in the shower. I'm at his kitchen table, still in my underwear. I've sneaked the first cup of coffee from the still brewing pot. The TV's on.

I wait for the *Today* show to cut to the local news. I'm thinking the snowstorm will be the first story. But it isn't.

I sit at the table as both the anchor and the two separately placed on-scene reporters tell of the triple murder of Camden's well-known electronics mogul and his family. One of the reporters, wearing an Elmer Fudd hat, his breath vaporizing from the cold, stands at Lot 15 of the Cherry Hill Mall.

"Ah, fuck," I'm saying to myself, as Jason comes into the kitchen. He's got on a T-shirt and his go-to-work chinos. His hair is still wet. He takes a cup of coffee, looks over at me, trying to tell what's wrong.

It's nothing. I'm waving away at Jason, but it doesn't take me long to understand what's happened. If Slippery has had the Khans murdered, and probably Arty too, I'm thinking, although there's nothing about him in the story, then are his thugs now gunning for me and Mickie? Is Slippery steamed because we held the truth back from him?

I watch as Jason pours himself a cup of coffee. He's looking at me. I try my best to smile.

I can't.

CHAPTER 38
WHO WOULD HAVE THOUGHT?

I'm hurriedly dressing for the office; Jason's in the bathroom blow-drying his hair. I'm bouncing around on one foot as I try and manage the other sock. I've told Jason it's simply some legal case problem. Nothing serious.

Last thing I need to do is get into all this stuff about Slippery Williams and Arty and Sami — all that crap — with him.

Among other things, I don't want to scare him off. Have him think I'm some kind of a liability. But I did use my cell to call Mickie. Asked, did he hear? "Yup," he said, "sure did." We agree to meet at the office soon as we can. Jason will drop me off there on his way to work.

That same morning Arty Bernstein wakes in his South Beach hotel room. The hooker is long gone. He sits at the edge of the bed, thinking about last night, still peeved at himself for coming too soon. Then trying to convince the girl to stick around for another. Sure, she told him, cost you another grand. Arty using his lawyerly skills to convince her a second was included in the original price, said it's implied if you come too fast on the first go-round. Tells her, everybody knows that.

"Nice try," she says, then heads for the door.

Arty's still trying to compose his argument why he's entitled to a free second from her. Shit, he tells himself as he sees the door close behind her. He rushes for the door, opens it, ready to shout to her down the hall, okay, I'll pay, come back. But the hooker's gone, she took the stairwell rather than wait for the elevator.

So, Arty's awake, sitting on the edge of the bed. His gut's hanging over his briefs. Still pissed about last night.

He's got his laptop there beside him. As he's done the other two mornings, he uses the room's wireless Wi-Fi to surf onto the Web sites for the *Philadelphia Inquirer* and South Jersey's *Courier-Post*. Checking in, as it were. Today it's front-page in both papers.

Bingo.

Arty reads both stories, and then flips to one of the travel sites. Books his ticket on-line. The flight's leaving Miami International in three hours. It won't take him long to pack. He opens the wall safe to get his wallet. His remaining cash. (He's got loads of money squirreled away in offshore bank accounts.) His passport.

Arty took the speed-checkout option from the in-room TV system, now he's sitting low in the back of a cab, the Haitian-looking driver blaring some weird music from his off-brand CD deck, sloppy hand drum rhythms all over the place; the singing more like chanting in what could be French. Arty telling the guy, as he checks left and right from the backseat, his nerves on edge, the cab still on the city streets, heading for the interstate and the airport, "Turn that shit down for Christ sake. I can't hear myself think."

As Arty's doing that, I am sitting in Mickie's office.

I haven't been here long. We've been discussing whether to reach out to Slippery. I mean, if we're in his sights, what harm can it do? If he wants us dead? Well, then we're already dead men. Maybe he'll listen to reason, buy how we are bound to silence about client utterances, no matter how that affects Slippery. Our not telling him about Sami and Rafat. About Arty. How they had the goods on Slippery. Could turn him in.

Getting him charged, then convicted with their testimony, then jailed forever and a day. I'm thinking all three now stone-cold dead. But still, we withheld vital information from Slippery. We protected client confidences, like we're supposed to do. And for that he's going to have us killed.

"Great," Mickie says. "Now we're gonna get shot on account of we did our jobs right."

I know what he means. Last time, with Rodrigo, we did our jobs wrong. Looks like we can't win for losing.

I watch Mickie pop open the plastic Rolaids container. He holds it right up to his mouth and just shakes a bunch in. Then starts chewing, his lips getting chalky white.

I'm not sure what to do myself. But calling, or even maybe going to see Slippery in the flesh, might be our only option.

I'm telling this to Mickie when Tamara walks in with two plastic cups of coffee. Starbucks on the labels. Great, at least we will have had a decent cup of coffee under our belt when we get gunned down by some passing car as we leave our offices for the abbreviated court session today.

Mickie throws up his hands. "Okay," he says. "Slippery kills us, he kills us. I'm done worrying about it."

Tamara hands me one of the two coffees, then gives Mickie the other.

"Ain't no one killin' you," she says. "Unh-uh. Ain't gonna happen. You dead? I'm unemployed. Unh-uh," she repeats. "Ain't no one takin' this job away from me. Certainly not no Slippery Williams."

Isn't that sweet, I'm thinking. Poor Tamara, so worried about us.

She cracks a smile.

"You good," she says.

And then she tells us what she means.

Tamara has been in and out of enough meetings with me and Mickie, and our clients, to have figured it out. How we have held client confidences. How Slippery Williams might well react once he learns that we knew all along Rafat and Arty were going to roll over on him.

Tamara could see from when Slippery was in here that he was already deeply suspicious of what was going on. And so, what did Tamara do?

She used Gregory. Decided she might as well get some good out of her wayward gangster nephew. She sat in her kitchen with Gregory, made him stay there as she schooled him, made sure he had it right. Then she told him, the very first chance he got, he needed to arrange to see Slippery,

351

tell him he was there because me and
Mickie couldn't see him directly. Not for
this. We being lawyers and all. But we
wanted Slippery to know, through Gregory,
Tamara's nephew — wanted to get the message to him in a way that would protect us.
Give us deniability — that Slippery's suspi-
cions were well founded.

Or as Gregory said, in his wheelchair, at
tableside in the café where he met Slippery,
Stink and Pee Wee sitting there too, "My
aunt be asked by them lawyers, could I
come see you? Tell you, Slip, what you
needin' to be hearin'."

Then he tells Slippery. Slippery nods.
Turns to Stink and Pee Wee.

"This boy now a corner captain."

Gregory smiles.

Me and Mickie are trying to absorb what
Tamara just told us. We are off the hook.
But what Tamara has done is wrong. She's
our employee. Our surrogate. She has Gregory (another client, I might add) tell Slippery what we as lawyers are ethically bound
to keep private. Totally confidential.

Well, with the best of intentions, Tamara
has, once removed, caused us to violate our
lawyer's oath. Our legal obligations to our
clients.

The right thing to do is go to the authorities. Explain what happened. Tell all. Implicate Tamara. Gregory. Slippery and his assassin henchmen. And, though we didn't do it directly. Not even intentionally. Us, too.

That's the right thing to do.

Are me and Mickie going to do that?

Not on your life.

EPILOGUE
AND GOODWILL TOWARD MEN

The elevator doors open to the third floor of Our Lady of Lourdes Medical Center. Jason, Tamara, and I get off here.

It's Christmas Day. We spent the lunch hour and early afternoon at Mom's. Everyone was there. The whole family. And I brought Jason.

Everyone was nice to him. Very welcoming. My mother did do a short third degree on Jason to see for herself if maybe there might be just a drop of Italian blood somewhere way back in his family history.

When she finally satisfied herself there wasn't she shrugged, then made sure he sat next to her at the dining room table so she could instruct him how to eat like we do. Jason seemed to really be enjoying her.

I also invited Tamara to join my family. Even though her nephew Gregory is now a part of management in Slippery, Inc., Christmas is just another workday for him.

The drug bazaars of Camden being the 24-7, 365-shopping-day ventures that they are.

Tamara had a really good time. I could see that. Families like ours are appealing to her.

And speaking of appealing, you should have seen my two brothers' eyeballs popping out of their heads when they got their first look at Tamara, dressed up for Christmas Day as she was, all sheathed and cleavaged. Both brothers smiling sheepishly at their wives, letting them know, I guess, hey, what are you gonna do? Something like that, anyway.

But now the three of us are coming down the hall to the room they've got Mickie in.

Last night he checked himself into Our Lady of Lourdes. His stomach was killing him, had him doubled over in pain. Looks like he's got a bleeding ulcer. From all the stress, no doubt.

As we turn the corner to the hallway where Mickie's room is at, we can hear the shouting. Mickie's voice clear as a bell.

"Get the fuck outta here," he's telling someone.

Then we hear a calmer voice speaking to Mickie. Followed by Mickie's, "I said. Get the fuck outta here."

As we arrive at his room, I'm thinking maybe this isn't going to be the best time for me to introduce Jason to Mickie. But, too late now, I tell myself as we three stand squeezed in Mickie's doorway.

An orderly, looks like he was cashiered from the Marines about an hour ago, very buff, buzz-cut, bulging, tattooed biceps, is standing at Mickie's bed.

It's enema time here at Our Lady of Lourdes. At least for Mickie.

There's some other patient in the next bed. Some old codger, out like a light. His sallow, unshaven cheeks hardly moving, his open mouth half-snores, half-groans, as he sleeps through all this commotion happening in the room.

Mickie hasn't looked up yet, doesn't know we three are standing in the open doorway to his room. He's sitting up in the bed, his hospital gown has become untied, so he's got this off-the-shoulder look. Mickie's clutching the bedsheet to him like some naked woman, surprised in the shower, wrapping the shower curtain around her to maintain her modesty.

This is not a good way to see Mickie. He seems to be unaware of his damsel-in-distress appearance, he's so intent on ejecting the orderly and the enema device the orderly's trying to maneuver within rectum range.

Just then I hear the soft footsteps of crepe-soled shoes headed this way. Must be the help Mickie has summoned, I conclude as I turn, and who do I see but nurse Carla approaching. She nods hello to me, but pushes past us and enters the room.

Here's help at last, Mickie's thinking as he looks up and sees Carla standing at the foot of the bed. Long-legged, white-uniformed nurse Carla.

Me, Jason, and Tamara are standing directly behind her, now squarely within Mickie's line of vision.

He takes in Carla, who's giving him this it's-gonna-hurt-you-worse-than-it-hurts-me look. Her eyes are actually twinkling. Payback time.

Then Mickie looks from me to Jason. Jason to me. He gets it, and to his credit, he starts to nod how you doin' to Jason. But then Mickie seems to realize how he looks at this moment, his knees curled up, clutching the bedsheet.

For just an idle second or two everything stops. All except the old guy asleep in the next bed. He snorts, gulps air, snores, then lets out a sonic fart.

All the rest of us got our eyes on Mickie.

(I hear Tamara harrumph under her breath. Still protective of us, I guess.)

We watch as Mickie surrenders to the inevitable. He raises his arms in the air like the cops have him surrounded outside the just-robbed bank. The sheet he's been clutching slips away, and he slides back down in the bed.

Carla turns and says we need to wait out in the hall. Better yet, she says, go get a cup of coffee or something since this could take a while.

Mickie hears this.

Now both Mickie and the old sleeping guy are groaning.

As we three are heading for the first-floor cafeteria, Arty Bernstein is heading for the pool-and-cabana area of his São Paulo hotel. He's bought a matching tropical-flower-patterned bathing suit and jacket top from the hotel gift shop. He holds his gut in best he can, keeps the top two buttons of his jacket open to show off his graying chest hair, as he makes his way through the isles of bleach white, canvas-covered sun lounges.

Arty has decided he'll wait until Monday, after the holiday, when everyone's back in the office, and then he'll call Dumpy Brown. And Robert Cahill. No reason why he can't keep his deal alive from here, he tells himself. And if not, well, he's thinking, it's doubtful Slippery can reach him here. Even if his whereabouts become known.

So, he's feeling pretty good as he checks out the female sunbathers, trying to see is there any unoccupied lounge chair here, next to someone worth putting his towel down. He spots a middle-aged woman in a string bikini, her hair dyed silver blond, her skin too deeply tanned, her boobs two rubber balls of silicone. He flashes a smile, heads her way.

Jason, me, and Tamara are in the cafeteria, at a small table, sipping Cokes. Since it's Christmas Day, the hospital is half empty. There is only a smattering of orderlies and other health-care workers sitting at the tables around us. It's unusually quiet in here.

But, I'm feeling pretty good myself.

At least for now.

ACKNOWLEDGMENTS

My first novel was published when I was a puppy lawyer. I didn't continue writing, at least for a while. I had a practice to develop, a young family, and near zero assets. So I spent the following years learning my profession, establishing my practice, and squeezing in as much family time as possible. I have always loved stories. That didn't stop. So my nose would be in novels on those interminable plane rides to distant courthouses as much as in legal briefs.

From the very beginning, a publisher named David Rosenthal kept an eye on me. Checking in from time to time. Encouraging me to write, to find the time. A wonderful mentor, a good friend. On his watch I wrote *Shark Tales — True (& Amazing) Stories from America's Lawyers* and *Death by Rodrigo,* for which this book is a sequel. David has moved on to other green pastures, but the expert care I have received from his successors hasn't skipped a beat.

I think I have one of the best editors working today. Karen Thompson's collaboration was insightful, skilled, masterful. And more fun than anyone deserves. She is truly amazing.

Jonathan Evans's copyediting on this book was every bit as expert as on the last one. I have learned a great deal from him. It's been a pleasure. (Ms. Bloom, my long-deceased tenth grade English teacher, has no doubt now finally been able to breathe a posthumous sigh of relief.) I am also grateful to Iliana Del Riccio for ensuring that when my characters spoke Italian, it was the right Italian.

The marketing and publicity team assigned to me has also been fantastic. Rachelle Andujar's easy attitude and patience actually resulted in my learning how to manipulate Facebook like a pro and to Tweet with the best of Tweeters. Michelle Jasmine's publicity efforts got the word out like the word's supposed to get out.

I have also been fortunate to be the beneficiary of two very capable agents: New York's Leigh Feldman and Los Angeles's Lynn Pleshette. Leigh is also my consigliere and friend. As the old lyrics go, who could ask for anything more?

I have saved the best for last. Simma, Shana, Margot, Michael, and Nate. My family is all. Without any shadow of a doubt. And my love for them transcends all.

ABOUT THE AUTHOR

Ron Liebman was a senior partner in the Washington, D.C. office of one of America's top law firms. He specialized in litigation, both domestic and international. He is the author of the novels, *Death by Rodrigo,* which was optioned by David E. Kelley, and *Grand Jury,* and also the nonfiction *Shark Tales: True (and Amazing) Stories from America's Lawyers*. He is married to the artist Simma Liebman.

SGR 3/14
MT05/14
3L A/14
HAR 11/14
0K 2/15
Blen 7/15
SO 7/15
LEG 8/18
AMR 9/18